Phantasmagoria

She wondered again how far their relationship would have come if Vaughan hadn't been always waiting in the wings. Marriage almost certainly, but would either of them have been content?

She didn't hear Vaughan enter the closet, but she felt his presence like a ripple through the fabric of the small, dark space. It warmed her long before he curved his hand over her bottom.

He didn't speak, just allowed his palm to brand her with his intentions.

His eyes were probably closed, so that their long dark eyelashes dusted his cheeks. His cruel, sensual mouth probably curved into the ghost of a smile. Just the thought of his expression made her writhe harder against Lucerne. There was no denying they both belonged to Vaughan.

And how he enjoyed making them squirm.

By the same author:

A Gentleman's Wager
Dark Designs
Passion of Isis
Possession

Phantasmagoria

Madelynne Ellis

BL

Black Lace books contain sexual fantasies.
In real life, always practise safe sex.

First published in 2008 by
Black Lace
Thames Wharf Studios
Rainville Rd
London W6 9HA

A catalogue record for this book is available from the British Library.

www.black-lace-books.com

Typeset by SetSystems Ltd, Saffron Walden, Essex
Printed and bound in Great Britain by CPI Bookmarque, Croydon, CR0 4TD

Distributed in the USA by Holtzbrinck Publishers, LLC, 175 Fifth Avenue,
New York, NY 10010, USA

ISBN 978 0 352 34168 6

To my family, for their love and support

Prologue

New Year's Eve 1799

The haunting strain of a violin marked his escape onto the moonlit balcony. Vaughan Peredur Forvasham, Marquis of Pennerley, brought his palms down hard against the flat stone balustrade. 'Hell's pits!' he barked. The impact stung but he didn't flinch, just glowered at the black blot on the horizon – the city. He could just make out the dome of St Paul's.

Vaughan pressed his fingers to his temples. His dark ringlets fell forward over his face, concealing his expression. Why was he here? What was he doing? It was New Year's Eve. They were supposed to be enjoying themselves, celebrating. He had been enjoying himself. He'd smacked Lieutenant Wilkes of the 52nd Oxfordshires across the cheek with his glove for his insolent remarks towards Bella. Nobody got to call her a whore, except him. The poor fool hadn't dared call him out. Reputations were wonderful things, although the influence of their host, the Right Honourable Herbert Gillray MP may have played a part too.

Oh, and he'd taught that pompous arse of a Frenchman, the Vicomte de Maresi, just how knowledgeable an Englishman could be about certain *manly* pursuits.

Vaughan ran his tongue over his teeth. The Vicomte was achingly beautiful and had cheeks as sweet as a cherry bun, but he smelled like a perfumery and he had none of Bella's fire or Lucerne's charm.

Hmm! He sniffed hard, suddenly reminded of his feckless lover. Pox on the man! Why did he have to be so bloody gig-happy?

The door behind him swung open, and a spear of light struck the ground beneath him with the radiance of two thousand candles. He didn't turn, just stared resolutely into the darkness. He knew who'd come after him, the only person who truly dared. Well, perhaps there was one other person, but *she* was too busy dancing to bother about him. He dragged a hand through his hair and let it slide slowly through the tangles.

'Vaughan.' Lucerne curved his hand over Vaughan's. 'Are we fine?'

'Yes. We're fine.' Vaughan sniffed again. Liar, he chided himself. Clearly, they were very far from fine.

Too close to be just friendly, Lucerne slyly traced the curve of Vaughan's arse. It was a subtle movement, not without risk. The assembly room behind them was full of their peers. On another occasion, the affectionate gesture might have won him around. Vaughan liked to take risks, but tonight it elicited nothing but a shudder of irritation. 'I'm just brooding, Lucerne. It's New Year. It's what I do.' He painted on a smile, then turned so that he stood inside Lucerne's embrace. 'Go back to the party. I'll follow in a moment when I've conquered my mood.'

'If you're sure.' Lucerne brushed his thumb across Vaughan's cheek.

'I'm sure.'

'Don't get too maudlin out here, will you?' He drew the caress to Vaughan's lips and rubbed over them slowly. 'The night's barely begun. We have to see in the new century yet.' He flashed Vaughan an impudent smile loaded with sweet promises.

'Away with you.' Vaughan watched him rejoin a group of drunken bloods. It was no good. He couldn't pretend he wasn't hurting, that he wasn't revolted by the way Lucerne carried out his affairs.

He paced the length of the balcony to where the ivy hung like mermaids' braids. Quietly, without a scene, without so much as a whisper.

Vaughan claimed a deserted glass from among the foliage and swallowed the rich, syrupy liquid without really tasting it. He held up the dregs to the moon in mock salute, then let the glass drop over the balustrade. It smashed on the paving below, where the shards glinted like angels' tears. Several women shrieked. He didn't look to see who. He didn't care. Let them scream. Let all the bitches scream. Soon, everything was going to shatter.

1

October 1800

'Quick, Lucerne! Hurry up.'

Ignoring the extended hand of the waiting footman, Bella Rushdale leaped from the landau and sprinted up the townhouse steps, the train of her slender empire-line evening dress looped over her arm to prevent her tripping. She reached the door and turned to face the carriage. 'Do you think he'll have noticed we're gone?'

'He notices everything.'

Viscount Lucerne Marlinscar slid his six-foot-two slender frame across the leather seat and stepped carefully from the interior, a silver-topped cane clasped tightly in one hand and a hip flask in the other. He was dressed in a dark-blue evening coat, cut short at the front to show off his black and silver waistcoat. His breeches, cream, cleaved to his thighs like a second skin and were, Bella suspected, at least partially responsible for his slow descent.

'Yes, but will he be on his way yet?'

Lucerne pocketed the silver flask and peered at his fob watch. 'That rather depends on how well Henry Tristan's delaying him.'

'That's who you left him with?'

'Why, yes.'

Bella skipped back down the top three steps and grasped

Lucerne's coat cuff. 'Then he won't be above five minutes. Come on.' She dragged Lucerne through the front door and across the echoing hall. Her first instinct was to squeeze into the broom cupboard below the stairs and get frisky among the mops, but she knew Lucerne would object. Too dusty, and he didn't like spiders. He'd be far too concerned about his clothes and not nearly enough about her pleasure, and that would be no good at all, since Vaughan was probably already turning his black phaeton into the street.

Vaughan. Marquis Pennerley. Of course, if she'd been with him rather than Lucerne, there'd have been no qualms about the cupboard. He might even have led her past the house and into an alleyway. Vaughan had no respect for anything – clothing, furniture. None of it mattered, nothing got in the way of his pleasure. It was how it had been for the last two, almost three years, ever since she'd recklessly climbed into his carriage and waved Yorkshire goodbye.

'This way.'

They ran up the stairs. Lucerne headed for the master bedroom with the enormous canopied bed the three of them shared, but its sumptuous cushioned comfort wasn't what Bella was looking for. Before he dragged her down into its embrace, she swung left and bundled him through the door of the walk-in closet. The sharp smell of mothballs wafted over them, tempered a little by the scent of the lavender bags she'd made in a moment of boredom.

Not that there'd been many such moments. Her time in London had passed in a swirl of evening dresses and sexual excess. Only the fashions of the *beau monde* seemed to mark the seasons. When she'd first arrived, it had been all stays, bums and hoops. Now her waist had risen to somewhere beneath her breasts and diaphanous, Grecian simplicity was all the rage.

Bella liked the freedom of the new costume and the excitement of change, but not all the new fashions were so good. For starters, the men were all cropping their hair. She'd always liked Lucerne's untidy fringe, but she admired Vaughan's sable ringlets more. Thankfully, the marquis showed no signs of giving way to the dictates of fashion and the 'dandies', led by Mr Brummell. He'd sworn that he'd damn well please himself. No penniless army captain was going to tell him how to dress. Besides, she thought, where was the fun if all men dressed alike as blue and cream sheep, and they no longer had the likes of the macaronis or *les incroyables* like Henry Tristan?

Bella grinned. Lucerne was taking advantage of her distraction and exploring the swell of her breasts, while his lips teased the back of her neck. 'Uh-uh!' She swung him around and pushed him into the silken rainbow of hanging coats.

'Uh-uh, yourself.' He slapped away her hands, but Bella pressed in closer. Lucerne peeped coyly at her from beneath his eyelashes. 'Just what sort of tryst is this, Miss Rushdale? It seems a touch indecorous to assault a fellow in a closet.'

Indecorous? Assault? Her fingertips sought passage beneath his tight clothes. Yes, that was about it. She strained on tiptoes to reach his lips, narrowly avoiding the foot-high pile of cravats at her feet. 'Why so many layers?'

'I could ask the same.' Lucerne tugged open the buttons on his waistcoat, then reached for her hem. He slipped his hand up her stocking to the bare flesh of her thigh. 'Except –' he cocked one elegantly arched eyebrow '– you appear to have mislaid a few.'

'Ah . . . Um, yes. I forgot them.'

Her new dress looked better without numerous petticoats beneath it; she had only her knee-length shift on, and she'd dispensed with her stays weeks ago, even though she'd had one of the new types made with a front busk. One or two of her acquaintances had taken to the new red silk drawers that had come over from France, but Bella thought them both hot and inconvenient.

'Strangely enough,' said Lucerne, 'so did I.'

Bella wriggled her hand inside the placket of his breeches. Her fingertips found and traced the slender line of golden hairs down to where they thickened around his loins.

'All that extra fabric ruins the line.'

Bella grinned and traced the column of hot flesh. 'You mean it wasn't just so you're always ready for action.' She slipped the buttons that fastened the flap to his waistband and shimmied down his body so that she was eye level with his revealed glory.

'No-o, I don't think that was it.'

She ran her tongue up the length of his erection. 'Are you sure?'

'Yes. No. All right, maybe a little bit.' He cupped his hand behind her neck. 'Come a little closer, minx. Don't be shy.' With his free hand, he teased his cock closer towards her lips.

Bella kissed the plum tip, then rose to her feet. 'More of that later if you're good, my lord.'

'Aw!' He dipped his head so that she could reach his lips. Bella pressed her hand between their bodies and covered the hot column with her palm. 'Vaughan will be here any minute.' She could almost sense him getting closer, driving the phaeton hell for leather, his sable curls stirring in the breeze, all black silk and fire. 'Let's not waste time.'

She tucked her skirts up around her chest, rudely displaying her naked rear, then clamped Lucerne's wrists against the closet walls. He didn't struggle, just sank back against the coats and watched her with a hungry, fearful sort of longing.

Keeping one wrist pinned, Bella freed the other and wetted her fingers between her thighs, which she then fed to Lucerne to dutifully suck clean. He did so with a kitten-like gentleness, trying to soothe her, but Bella didn't want to be soothed. She didn't want sweet and nice. She wanted rough, sticky and dirty, something Lucerne only seemed capable of with Vaughan. It was always a battle trying to rouse that same response. She smeared saliva across his chin, held his mouth open for her to ravage, while her fingers locked around his wrist and bit into the warm flesh.

Lucerne protested, shaking his arm, but she just squeezed harder and ground her hips against him.

'Bella,' he groaned. His breaths were coming as irregular little puffs of pleasure. 'Can I?'

Helpfully she opened her legs wide, raised one, which he clasped against his thigh, as he slipped inside.

Lucerne's blue eyes glazed. 'You're teasing,' he growled. He clutched at her bare bottom, trying to lift her. She knew what he wanted – to carry her to the bed still impaled upon his cock and tup her across the bedspread, but this wasn't just about him. It was about having him at her mercy.

'Yes,' she hissed into his mouth. 'And there's nothing you can do about it.'

She hooked her raised leg behind his knee and gripped his wrists again, this time adding nail marks to the skin.

His cock didn't protest. If anything, the restraint goaded him to greater effort. His hips bucked as much as their precarious balance would allow, while his bottom clenched in time with the motion.

'Bella, please, don't make it a fight! Be soft for me. I get enough of this spitting and snarling from Vaughan.'

'Yes, and I've seen what it does to you.'

'What *Vaughan* does to *me*,' he corrected, sagging a little. 'And you do something equally precious.'

Reluctantly, she eased her grip. Lucerne slipped the loop of her fingers from his wrists and tangled his hands in the back of her hair. 'Kiss me.'

It was slow and intimate. Understated, but with raging heat. Lucerne wanted her as a woman, not as Vaughan's substitute. She wondered again how far their relationship would have come if Vaughan hadn't been always waiting in the wings. Marriage almost certainly, but would either of them have been content?

She didn't hear Vaughan enter the closet, but she felt his presence like a ripple through the fabric of the small, dark space. It warmed her long before he curved his hand over her bottom.

He didn't speak, just allowed his palm to brand her with his intentions.

His eyes were probably closed, so that their long dark eyelashes dusted his cheeks. His cruel, sensual mouth probably curved into the ghost of a smile. Just the thought of his expression made her writhe harder against Lucerne. There was no denying they both belonged to Vaughan.

And how he enjoyed making them squirm.

It had been four weeks since he'd last touched her. Not the longest Vaughan had ever made her wait, but still a long time to be around him and bereft of his favours. It had been the evening of the Gillrays' late summer ball. The bastard had caught her dampening her petticoats in an attempt to make her new dress cling. He'd blindfolded her, lashed her to the bedpost and then sponge-bathed her, making sure the petticoats were extra wet around her crotch.

Subsequently, she'd spent the whole evening with her fan strategically clamped over the wet patch so that nobody would see her thatch through the delicate muslin gown.

The time before that, he'd painted her nipples with beetroot juice and served her as a side salad to Lucerne and four of his close friends. Vaughan seemed to delight in teasing her. No one had touched her all night, but that had hardly been the point. By the end of the dinner, she'd been desperate to relieve the sensitive ache in her breasts and the fire of arousal in her belly.

Vaughan had ridden her hard that night once the guests had left. She grinned at the memory, even as Lucerne continued to tease her lips. He'd ridden them both hard to be precise. Having strapped Lucerne to a chair, he'd repeatedly brought him to the point of orgasm, only to stop him coming at the last moment, until finally, in the small hours, he'd impaled himself upon Lucerne's weeping cock.

Lucerne's breath whispered across the top of her head. 'I need to move.' He clutched her hips and rocked them forwards, desperate for the friction.

'Tut, tut.' Vaughan curled his fingers into Bella's plump cheek in response: 'Always so hasty, Lucerne.' She squirmed back against him. The best times were always when the two men pressed into her front and back. And now he was here . . .

'You should have waited for me,' Vaughan said. Bella could feel his trapped erection pressing into her arse. 'But I'll forgive you.'

'You can share,' Lucerne blurted.

'Oh, can I now?' Vaughan drawled. He slid his hands around to her stomach, then up to her breasts. 'And what say you, Miss Rushdale? Am I invited to this ... assignation?'

Bella rubbed back against him. 'You were supposed to stay behind. He's mine tonight.'

'Ah, but the distraction was fleeting. You really need to plan more carefully.'

Vaughan sank to his knees behind her, his palms following the line of her silhouette. His lips grazed the delicate crease where her bottom met her thigh. Bella shivered. She was sensitive there. Excruciatingly sensitive.

'Why won't you leave us alone, let us be together?' she gasped.

His tongue trailed lightly over her cheeks, raising hairs and the level of sensitivity to make her squeal. She squirmed against Lucerne, shaking with pleasure.

'Ah, Bella, you know why. You've always known why.'

She did but she liked to deny it. Here in London she was masquerading as Vaughan's cousin, chaperoned by some matron he'd plucked out of obscurity for a yearly wage of twenty guineas. Lucerne was her unofficial intended, but he'd never proposed. Vaughan was adamant that while the three of them were together, there'd be no exclusivity agreements, particularly one that excluded him.

So here they were.

Vaughan's tongue dipped into the channel between her cheeks. He blew whispery kisses and petted her lightly, the licks slowly becoming firmer, more invasive, until he was delving into her hot dark spot and lighting endless sparklers of bliss.

Bella's hips rolled with the motions of the two men. Lucerne was getting close. She could hear it in his breathing.

She hated when Vaughan did this to her. There was something twisted about it. Licking her there always seemed far more taboo than filling her bottom with his prick, and she knew he'd make a point of messily kissing her later. Still, she couldn't tear herself away, even if she hadn't been trapped between two bodies.

'I'm going to tongue-fuck you until you come,' he said, raising hairs all across her skin. 'Then I'm going to molly Lucerne, and if you're good I'll let you watch.'

He would too. Vaughan always kept his promises, and he loved licking and swiving arse almost as much as he loved Lucerne. Sometimes she wished he'd show her the same level of devotion.

Vaughan found her pearl and rubbed. She didn't want to come like this, at his hand, with him sucking greedily at her hole, but her body betrayed her. Her hips moved in time with Lucerne's. She sought his lips, but he was already screaming into the air as she came hard around his cock.

As her orgasm pulsed through her, the two men kissed over her shoulder, ignoring her as they focused on each other. When they showed no signs of parting, Bella sunk to the floor and crawled between Vaughan's legs. So much for Lucerne being hers!

Still, it wasn't all bad. Bella made herself comfortable on the bed and lazily rubbed her clitoris as she watched them petting. Vaughan and Lucerne were sexy as hell, two flipsides of the same coin, and never more so than when they were together performing like this. While it pleased her more to be between them, she'd learned to accept this was part of the relationship, and had no qualms about getting herself off while watching them together.

The two men stumbled out of the closet, limbs still entwined, clawing at each other's clothing. Lucerne's breeches were clinging to his thighs, his pale cheeks scored with the impression of Vaughan's fingernails. True to his word, Vaughan soon bent him over the end of the bed. 'I know what you need,' he hissed into Lucerne's ear. 'Don't even try to deny it. Your cock's never lost its hardness.'

Lucerne gripped the sheets. His feathery blond hair was stuck to his brow with sweat, obscuring his hazy-blue eyes. Lower, the muscles in his neck and those running down his arms were braced for what was coming.

'It's not what I need that you're about. Bella was satisfying me just fine.' Lucerne grinned at her and blew her a kiss.

'So you say.' Vaughan grasped Lucerne's hips and pulled him back against his loins. No matter how many times she saw him do that, it still made her wet. Bella covered her quim with her hand and rubbed her thighs together. There was something incredibly sexy about the way he manipulated Lucerne's body with such ease, and aroused him despite all protestations. 'But you haven't refused me.'

A hot pink glow washed across Lucerne's cheekbones. 'I know better than to try.' Resistance always made Vaughan even more determined. More than once their lovemaking had resembled a brawl, although Vaughan liked to pretend he was above fisticuffs.

Bella kneaded her bud harder. Go on, deny him, she

silently urged Lucerne. Make him work harder. She watched him reach back to lash at Vaughan's arms, but it was already too late. His mouth went wide and he released an urgent gasp. Vaughan was inside him, already moving him to his own special rhythm. There was no resisting left to be done.

Lucerne's eyes rolled upwards. He shamelessly pushed back against the intrusion.

'Nothing makes you feel quite like this, does it, Lucerne?' Vaughan's hands moved in fluttering circles over Lucerne's arse, squeezing, moulding. He reached around, grasped Lucerne's cock and tossed him off in time with their movements. 'Feels good, doesn't it? Ever since the first time, you've never been able to get enough.'

'I'm not so desperate as you think,' Lucerne snarled, his eyelids narrowed to slits. 'I've always been content with a woman.'

'Is that so?' Vaughan milked him harder. 'So slipping a finger alongside my cock won't make you come so hard you'll shoot yourself in the chest?'

'Grrn!'

'Here it comes, Lucerne. Think you can hold out? Of course not. I know you. I know what gets you off.' He nibbled Lucerne's ear. 'If I catch you playing dirty again –'

'You'll what?'

Vaughan went silent. He held himself still, although Lucerne continued to move. 'You'll see. Are you ready?' He wriggled a finger into Lucerne alongside his cock. Immediately, Lucerne held himself rigid. Tense shivers played out across his body. He was breathing hard, trying to control it, panting, determined to deny Vaughan his victory, but in vain. 'You absolute bastard!' he snarled.

Bella watched him sag onto the sheets, where he continued to whimper and jerk for several minutes. When he finally rolled over, his lawn shirt and indeed his torso were sticky with his seed. He pulled the shirt off and mopped his chest.

Vaughan stalked across to the washstand.

There was something going on, Bella was sure of it, and it wasn't the first time the thought had struck her. Vaughan was still erect and untamed, but he seemed content to do nothing about it. Not unusual in itself, but curious.

Lucerne scrambled up the bed towards her. He cocooned himself in her arms. 'You can't change the way I feel about her, Vaughan,' he said.

'No,' Vaughan agreed as he tucked himself back into his pantaloons. 'I don't suppose I can.'

She was definitely missing something, Bella was certain of it as she watched the candlelight glitter like black embers in Vaughan's eyes. But whatever it was, they kept it to themselves.

Vaughan watched the firelight lap at Bella's skin with tongues of gold and orange. Lucerne's head rested in his lap. Idly, he stroked his fingers through the blond strands. It was late, though he had no mind for sleep. His two lovers had both drifted off hours ago, but Lucerne's words still churned in his head.

'You can't change the way I feel about her.'

You can't bully me into loving you, he may as well have said, and it was true. There was no getting around it. He'd been trying long enough.

Of course, the situation was of his devising. Bella had been the compromise he'd made in order to get Lucerne in the first place. The man was too hung up on reputation and respect to risk scandalizing his peers. But neither Bella nor Lucerne were the same people he'd found himself so infatuated with on the wild Yorkshire moors. The city was turning Lucerne into a dissolute fop and Bella into another belle in a chintz frock. She was losing her fire. Oh, she still had a sharp tongue and a wicked sense of fun, but he'd liked her better when she wasn't so vain and the colour in her cheeks wasn't applied with a brush.

He touched the ends of her hair where it lay loose across her back. He wished she'd open her eyes to how things had changed. In the beginning, he'd accepted her as a necessity, convinced that she'd lose interest or patience. No woman wanted to hang on for ever for a proposal. He was surprised she'd stuck it out this long without so much as a whisper of an engagement and, perhaps, slightly pleased.

But Bella wasn't even the real problem. He could handle her. It was the other witch. His lips twisted into a sadistic smile while his fingers tightened around a clump of Lucerne's hair. He tugged in annoyance, inducing a groan of protest. 'Shh, sleep,' he said, gently petting him. 'Don't wake. Don't worry. Enjoy it while it lasts.'

Vaughan sunk his teeth into his bottom lip. It was time. He might not be able to change how Lucerne felt about things, but he could influence the way Bella felt about Lucerne, or at least open her eyes really wide.

Now. Tonight. It was starting . . . Ending . . .

2

Bella woke cold. Lucerne had stolen the covers again. He was turned away, coiled inside the array of sheets and blankets, while the bedspread clung to the bed in just one corner. Vaughan, she guessed, was on the floor beneath it. For all his preening and love of finery, he wasn't afraid of hardship, unlike Lucerne. She'd once found him asleep on a windowsill.

Bella snuggled up to Lucerne and rubbed her nose against the back of his neck, where his hair was shorn close. Last night had been fun, but now she was ready for an energetic wake-up call.

'Still sleeping,' he mumbled. 'Stop jiggling. I need another hour, or three.'

'Fine. You're hopeless.' Bella sat up. 'I'm getting dressed. It's cold in here and you're hogging the blankets again.' She slapped him across the rump, but Lucerne just huddled deeper into the covers and pulled a pillow over his head. It was half past nine. If he surfaced before eleven, it'd be a miracle or a sporting event.

As it turned out, Vaughan wasn't on the floor, nor was there any sign of him downstairs. Bella ate breakfast alone, but as time went on and Vaughan still hadn't appeared, she started to feel something was amiss.

'Has Lord Pennerley gone riding?' she asked William, their first footman.

'Not as I know of, Miss Rushdale, but I've not seen him this morning.'

Bella frowned. Nobody got in or out of the house without William noticing. It wasn't like Vaughan to sleep this late, though, wherever he'd bedded down.

She moved to the parlour, but the constant ticking of the mantel clock only made her more agitated. Tea didn't help either. She wanted some company. Where was he? The house was far too quiet.

Bella paused at the top of the stairs, hand clasped upon the banister. After several moments, she crossed the landing and knocked on his door. When there was no reply, she brazenly marched in. At worst, she'd catch him still abed and he'd throw something at her or, better still, he'd initiate her into some new art of erotic torture.

The bed was unoccupied.

'Damn.'

Bella stared at the inky covers for a moment, imagining his hair like a dark cloud around his sleeping face, before her brow creased in confusion. The curtains were pulled back from the sash window so that the crisp October light streamed in and dappled the bedspread, like the autumn leaves on the pavement outside. There was something odd about the room. She turned her head about but couldn't quite figure it. She didn't come in here very often. There was nothing out of place, not even a discarded cravat or razor littering the surfaces, but Vaughan had always been spartan and neat.

Actually, there was nothing in place, either.

A chill trembled down her spine. Bella shook it off, crossed to the chest of drawers and wrenched open the top drawer. It was empty, as was the second.

'Vaughan!' Her hand came unbidden to her lips. 'Oh, God!' She bit her knuckles. He couldn't be gone. He couldn't be. Why would he go? They were happy. 'Lucerne!' She ran though last night's events in her head. There'd been that weird undercurrent, the strange, guarded conversation she hadn't quite grasped the meaning of. 'Lucerne!'

Panic gripped her. Vaughan couldn't really be gone, not without a goodbye. Her gaze fell upon the smooth bed again. That was it. The locket. The precious keepsake that held a single lock of blond hair and commemorated the first night Vaughan and Lucerne had spent together. If it was still here, that meant he'd be back.

If she couldn't find it . . .

Her fingers closed over nothing more comforting than the cold sheets. In despair, she tore the pillows from the bed, shaking feathers loose in the process. They floated down around her, but there was still no locket. Not ready to give up hope, Bella thrust her hands down between the mattress and the headboard. Still nothing.

'No-ooo!'

Her shriek finally brought Lucerne. He sprinted into the room, half-dressed and trailing his valet, to whom he was attached by a long length of thread.

'Bella!' Lucerne pulled up sharp and looked at her curiously, his eyebrows impressively raised. 'What are you doing? What the blazes were you screaming for?'

She scrambled off the bed into his arms. To hell with decorum; besides, Ivo didn't count and he knew perfectly well what the living arrangements for the household were. 'Vaughan's gone,' she gasped into the open neck of Lucerne's shirt. 'He's left.'

'Don't be ridiculous.' He pushed her to arm's length, allowing Ivo to duck between them and resume sewing him into his skin-tight breeches.

'I'm not. All his things are gone.' She frowned at Ivo, tempted to kick him.

'Leave it,' said Lucerne, tapping Ivo upon the shoulder. 'You can go for now.' He waited until the man had left the room, then took Bella's hand and offered her a humouring smile. 'He wouldn't just walk out, Bella. Think about it for a moment.'

'Look.' She dragged him to the chest and wrenched open the top two drawers again.

'Ah,' he said in response to the absence of linen.

'Now do you believe me?'

Lucerne shook his head. 'It doesn't prove anything.' He paced across to the window. Bella hesitantly followed. Vaughan was not, as she half-hoped, standing on the pavement laughing at them. Judging by his expression, Lucerne had been hoping much the same.

'I expect he's just been invited somewhere for the week and forgot to mention it.' He dragged his hand through the front of his uncombed hair. 'He's been spending a lot of time with the Allenthorpes and their adopted frog recently.'

'Now you're being ridiculous,' Bella chided. 'He says the Vicomte smells like a fermented meadow, and even you don't take your entire wardrobe away with you for a few days.'

'Been through everything, have you?' There was hint of amusement in Lucerne's voice.

Bella glared at him, her temper rising. 'No, I haven't.' She didn't need to. The locket was the only thing of value

Vaughan kept in the room, but she wasn't sure if Lucerne knew about it. She was pretty certain Vaughan didn't know that she knew about it.

Lucerne sat down on the bed, patting the mattress for her to join him. 'Don't fret, Bella. He'll turn up.' He snuggled her to his side, still smiling. 'He always does. Like a bad penny.'

'Maybe.' She allowed herself to be lulled by his embrace. She never doubted that Vaughan would crop up somewhere. But he could be halfway across the Channel by now. Not that France was an ideal destination while they entertained Madame Guillotine.

Had he even slept last night, she wondered. He'd still been staring into the dark when she'd dropped off, which wasn't unusual. There'd been no definite danger signs.

Dammit!

Bella sagged against Lucerne. She was missing something, something obvious. 'Have you argued?' she asked, rising up again so she could look Lucerne in the eye.

He dragged his fingers through the front of his hair again, causing it to flop forwards over his brow. 'You saw us together last night. Did we look as if we'd fallen out?'

Bella sat a little straighter. 'That's just it. How am I supposed to tell when you routinely torture each other as a sign of affection? Even when you had that massive spat last May about the Act of Union, you still fucked like beasts.'

'Bella!' The skin around his eyes crinkled with annoyance. 'Maybe being away from Vaughan will do you good. Leastways, it might improve your language. You never used to be so coarse.'

'Don't start a lecture. He's gone. Can't you see it's a bloody disaster?'

To her annoyance, Lucerne collapsed back onto the bed snorting in amusement. 'Oh, stop it. As if he'd really just leave in the dead of night. He loves what we have here. He's responsible for the arrangement. Remember?' He absently patted her leg. 'Give it a day or two and he'll be back and laughing off the fright he's given us.'

Bella kneaded her temples. She really wanted to believe that but it was difficult. It felt like a chasm was opening inside her chest. Lucerne's hand was warm upon her thigh. His touch slowed to a caress. 'Bella,' he soothed, his voice laced with honey. He brought her fingers to his lips. 'You know how he is. Everything's a game. He's probably just trying to provoke a reaction, and he's succeeding.'

Bella shook her head but allowed Lucerne to cuddle her. He tipped them both over so they sprawled across the soft eiderdown, face to face. 'Don't mope.' His breath was warm against her lips. 'You know how he is. If he was angry with either of us he'd have said something.'

'Yes,' she reluctantly agreed.

Lucerne pressed a kiss to her nose, then another to her cheek. 'Look at me.' His thumb rubbed lightly over her lips.

Bella looked. His smile creased the corners of his eyes, lit up their china-blue depths. 'We've waited for this, Bella. Haven't we? A chance to be alone together.' He kissed her lips. 'We can do whatever we want.'

She felt like sobbing but mustered a smile instead. It was true, they'd had little time to themselves, Vaughan made sure of that. If she could only have been certain he was really coming back, then she'd have no qualms about leaping on Lucerne and having him any way possible. But there was just that niggling doubt.

Maybe he'd moved the locket weeks ago.

Lucerne stretched his arms above his head in an overstated gesture of surrender. 'How about it, Miss Rushdale?' He tugged his shirt from his breeches. 'Shall we rumple the master's bed?'

Some hours later, Bella lay wrapped in Vaughan's bedspread. Lucerne had gone to bathe and dress for his club. They'd spent the whole afternoon together, exploring the contours of each other's skin, taking pleasure in simple contact, enjoying themselves. She sucked on her lip; a bitter taste accompanied her thoughts. Now that she'd salved her lust with Lucerne, Vaughan's absence weighed on her conscience. Had she been responsible for his departure? Despite Lucerne's reassurances, she couldn't believe he'd simply return in a day or two, or even a week. Vaughan might be a creature of passions, but he was also stubborn and he never made any big decisions without thinking them through carefully. The absence of the locket aside, her instincts told her he was gone for good unless they did something to find him. She hadn't the faintest idea where to look, let alone how to win him back. Whenever she'd deliberately tried to seduce him in the past, he'd played her for a fool. She didn't think Lucerne would be any help, either. He was in denial, convinced it was all an elaborate game.

'Oh, Vaughan.' She rose from the bed and pulled the top sheet over her sticky chemise. Outside the sky was grey and already darkening despite the relatively early hour. 'Where are you?' She pressed her cheek to the cold glass. 'Come home.'

3

Bella stared out of the downstairs parlour window at the dreary street. A flock of carriages clattered past, delivering guests to various soirées. Vaughan had been missing twelve days. She hadn't left the house for ten, just in case he came back and she wasn't there. She hadn't spent so much time staring longingly out of windows since she'd left Wyndfell Grange. In London you could go out and find company. In Yorkshire she'd had to content herself with her own. She felt a throb of yearning for her home. She hadn't seen her brother Joshua for months. He'd visited briefly at Easter, but mostly he was maintaining a diplomatic distance. He couldn't be seen to be condoning her behaviour. Lucerne had been particularly sour during the stay, and she suspected Joshua had given him a lecture or two.

Bella rested her chin against the windowsill. She felt so powerless. It was no use talking to Lucerne; he was acting as if nothing was wrong and was relieved to have her to himself for the first time ever. It was working for him, but it felt false and sapless to Bella.

For nearly three years she'd wished Vaughan would leave them alone for just an hour, but now when he was gone she was constructing elaborate fantasies in her head about a sudden reappearance. Yesterday, after rereading *Mysteries of Udolpho* for the eighth time, she'd imagined him as the villainous Count Montoni, come to steal her away from her lover. She'd come twice in quick succession as a result, to Lucerne's astonishment, but she hadn't had the heart to tell him it wasn't his doing. After that, she'd tottered off to bed in her own room.

She wasn't even sure he'd noticed her leave. Too much port at his club had left him blinking sleepily. The sex had just become part of his routine too.

She'd lain awake for a while after that, long enough so that no one was up to see her slip into Vaughan's room where she'd ground herself against his pillows and wet their surface with a thousand hungry kisses.

She hadn't noticed it before but Lucerne was changing, and his total obsession with his appearance was just the tip of it. He was gambling again and his kindness and honour seemed facets he only polished for her. She closed her eyes, recalling the muggy September heat of 1797, the smell of the summer greenery, of parched grass and wildflowers. How she'd wriggled on her stomach beneath the rhododendron bushes at Lauwine to spy on him swimming in the river. She'd wanted to strip and dive in beside him. It'd been like a thread of destiny tugging at her, drawing them together. Lucerne had chased her naked through the grounds. Now he was in her bed, and her dreams were all of Vaughan: the mercurial, beautiful, volatile bastard that had dared to compete with her for Lucerne's heart.

There'd been no word of him about town, although everyone seemed to have heard about his disappearance, encouraging endless speculation. Someone had even suggested he was on a secret mission for Parliament or the King. Bella thought she'd be happy to know he was taking respite in a monastery or a hermit's cave away from the constant strain of their delicately balanced ménage à trois.

At least then she knew he'd be back at some point, his reserves replenished, ready to stage another delicious game.

The parlour door opened to reveal William. 'Mr Henry Tristan,' he announced before bowing out again.

Bella straightened her gown. It was a shabby and out of date one, a dour mid-blue in colour, exactly suited to her mood. 'Mr Tristan,' she said bravely. 'I'm afraid Lord Marlinscar's not at home.'

'Bella.'

She raised her head to find him standing in the doorway, lean and ballsy as an alley cat. He cast his hat onto a side table and slunk towards her, his cane trailing from a loop about his wrist, so that it clattered against the legs of the furniture. He was slovenly dressed in a shocking-blue coat and stockings striped in the same hue, so that the rings wound around his calves like cuffs. His cravat was a hideous contrast, cream with bilious green spots. 'Still pining, I see.' He pressed a powdery kiss to her cheek.

'Henry. And you're not?'

He brushed at the large snuff stain on his oversized lapels. 'M'dear, I've been pining since the day we met, and I realised you were wasting yourself on two consummate rogues.' He pressed another kiss to her fingertips, finally raising a smile from Bella.

She offered him a seat, but he remained standing. 'I do believe that's the first time you've acknowledged that fact, Henry. What's changed? Am I this month's scandal? Are you here to break it to me?'

'No, no.' He scrunched down the front of his ludicrous cravat with his chin. 'Although the *grandes dames* are pressing Lucerne deuced hard about a formal proposal now your cousin's flown.'

Bella shook her head. 'Marquis Pennerley is not my cousin and well you know it.'

Henry turned a pirouette, sending the skirt of his square-cut coat spinning about him like butterfly wings, and finally accepted a chair. 'No news?'

'None of any importance. What about you? Lucerne tells me nothing, but he must hear the talk.' She watched disapprovingly as Henry helped himself to some snuff and sneezed violently.

'My apologies.' He returned his box to his pocket. 'All I've heard is speculation. Of as much validity as Napoleon's claim on Egypt, I'd say.'

Bella returned to the window. She'd hoped he'd bring her better news. 'What am I supposed to do, Henry? I feel like a songbird cooped in a gilt cage, with naught to do but sing for my supper.'

'Which I'm sure you do very nicely.' He joined her by the window, leaning over her to get a view of the street. Bella turned and gave him a hard stare.

'You could take another lover. Luc–' He stopped, licked his lips.

'Henry!' She pushed him away. 'Please. Be serious.'

'I am,' he said, hand on heart.

Bella wrinkled her brows at him. 'It's just not the same since he's gone. I've thought about hiring someone to search for him, but he'll only be found if he wants to be.' She kicked at a chair. 'Damn him, I swear I'll wring his neck for this if he ever does turn up.'

Henry laughed. 'That's the spirit.' He took her hands, turned them in his. 'You know, you're looking awful pale, and dainty doesn't suit you. Ask Lucerne again when he comes home. He may have heard something by then. I'd better go now. I'm expected at the Allenthorpes for dinner, and people will talk.'

Bella watched Henry leave from the landing window. He was as blond as Lucerne, but the complete opposite in every other regard. His coat was ridiculously sloppy and his poor cane was still dangling limply from his wrist. She knew some considered Henry a buffoon for his choice of fashions, but his mind was far too sharp for that and his grip on politics frighteningly exact. His real weakness was that he was hopelessly besotted with Vaughan. Bring them together and Henry would follow Vaughan like a devoted lapdog, the ultimate style-cramping accessory and therefore a target for Vaughan's ruthless sarcasm.

A pity, because, alone, he had an exotic appeal all of his own.

Bella continued up the stairs for no other reason than a chance to walk. She wished Lucerne would come home and keep her company. In Vaughan's room, she curled up on the bed. It no longer smelled of him. She'd muddied his scent with her own, but there was a sense of comfort attached to it.

Soon, surely, she would hear something.

The sound of Lucerne's voice from the hall woke her. The room had grown dark as she'd slept and only a faint glimmer of moonlight penetrated the window. Bella stumbled onto the landing, rubbing the sleep from her eyes. The hall clock was striking eleven. She'd been asleep four hours and managed to miss dinner. She wondered if Lucerne was hungry and would sit down with her now.

Bella padded down the stairs in her soft pumps, hoping he wasn't drunk again. Halfway down the stairs she had a clear view of the hall.

She froze.

He wasn't alone.

Suddenly wide awake, Bella stumbled down the next three steps, hope and fear slicing through her chest. Lucerne was obscuring the second figure as he handed his greatcoat to William. Bella's fingers tightened on the banister, waiting. Her mouth opened on a squeal, which froze in her throat. The dark hair wasn't Vaughan's. Lucerne had come home with a woman.

Horrified, she watched him help her remove her cloak. His fingertips feathered across her bare shoulders, teased a stray curl by her ear. 'It'll be fine,' he murmured.

My God, she thought. What had he brought her here for? He couldn't suppose she was actually going to be fine with this. 'Lucerne?'

He turned towards her growl, giving her a warm smile. 'Bella. Excellent. Come down. Join us.' He rakishly draped an arm around the woman's shoulders.

Bastard, she seethed, a lump of fury forming in her throat. How dare he bring a whore home with him and act as if it were routine? She reached the bottom of the stairs and marched across the hall to meet him. 'What's going on?'

Unruffled, Lucerne pressed his guest forward a little. 'Miss Bella Rushdale. Miss Georgiana St John.'

Georgiana extended a hand which Bella ignored. She didn't care for civil hypocrisy. The woman had to leave immediately. She glared at her to make her hostility obvious. Georgiana took a hesitant step back and peeped nervously up at Lucerne, whose smile never wavered. 'Shall we go through to the parlour?' he said.

He offered them an arm each. Georgiana pliantly accepted, but Bella hung back, seething and grinding her teeth. Lucerne stopped in the doorway. 'Is something the matter, Bella?'

'Don't patronise me,' she hissed. 'What's she doing here?'

He shrugged. 'I think you know perfectly well the answer to that.'

'Well, you can't expect me to accept it.' She planted her hands firmly on her hips, while her mouth twisted into a tight aggressive pout.

'Why ever not?' Lucerne's voice was soft, his tone inflexible.

'You can't just bring any old tart home and expect me to go along with it. Just because I shared with Vaughan doesn't mean I'm prepared to do it with anyone else. Especially,' she clenched her fists, 'another woman.'

'You're prepared to consider another man, then?'

'Damn you – no! This isn't funny. Vaughan's still missing.'

'Yes, I'd noticed it was quiet.' His smile remained fixed but his eyes turned glassy and cold and his body language was rigid, indifferent to her protests. What is going on with you, she wanted to ask. He'd been changing since the moment Vaughan left, transforming into someone she didn't recognise. The scary thing was she didn't know if this was the real Lucerne or just a temporary reaction. She'd met him twice before Vaughan came along and turned their every interaction into an elaborate contest. Once, in Yorkshire, Lucerne had told her London did strange things to people, that he'd almost lost himself there. Bella suspected he was about to lose himself again. Maybe he already had.

'I don't know you,' she said softly, shaking her head.

For just a moment there was a glimmer of something in his eyes. Regret, she thought, perhaps, or sorrow. 'You never wanted to,' he said. 'You were always too obsessed with Vaughan. You're still obsessed with Vaughan.'

They stared at each other, two familiar strangers. It was Lucerne who turned away first.

'You know where he is, don't you?'

Lucerne rubbed his lips.

'Lucerne.' She grabbed his wrist, then slipped in front of him and blocked the parlour door. 'Tell me, where is he?'

'I understand he's gone home.' The admission was barely a whisper. 'Here.' He took a gilt-edged envelope from his inside pocket and handed it to her. 'It's a party invitation. Some sort of phantasmagoria.'

Her fingers would barely work to get it open. The card inside formally invited them both to Pennerley for Hallowe'en. Bella's eyes started to fill up as she read, preventing her from making any sense of the details. She could see Georgiana watching her across the top of her fan, and she wasn't about to cry in front of her. 'Pennerley?' She sniffed.

'Returned to his estate. It's in Shropshire on the Welsh border.'

'When did it come?'

He inhaled slowly through his teeth. 'A while ago.' He crossed to where Georgiana stood before the fire. Bella watched him, mouth open but words failing her. All this time he'd known and said nothing. That hurt more than the damn whore. Hellfire! A scream rose in her throat. She wondered if she should smash something. Instead, she bit down on her rage and retreated to the window. Boiling over wouldn't get her the explanations she needed. More likely, it'd just send him running to the bedroom with Miss St John.

'I don't understand. Why didn't you tell me? Are you trying to end it?'

'I'm not the one who left, Bella.' He sounded weary. 'But you can be certain of one thing, he's not being chaste and virtuous. It's not in his nature.'

'Is that your justification?' She clung to the curtain, frantically blinking back tears that spilled regardless. Everything was going so wrong. She'd never expected it to last for ever; the balance of power had always been too delicate. But she'd hoped for a better ending than this.

In a fit of claustrophobia, she opened the shutters and wrenched up the sash window. The night air was biting. It seeped into her limbs, numbing the pain.

'Bella.' Lucerne's tread sounded on the carpet behind her. He traced a finger down the side of her neck.

Bella shook him off. 'Don't.'

'Please . . .' His arms encircled her, trapping her within his familiar embrace. His heartbeat was strong against her back, his hold a touch possessive. 'Can't you forget him a while? Just tonight even?' He pressed a kiss to the top of her head, among the jumble of carefully constructed curls.

He was just a pale shadow in the dark glass. The ghost of what could have been if that day by the river three years ago had turned out a little differently. They could have been expecting a child by now, like her friend Louisa and her husband. Instead, everything was crumbling into dust.

'I know it's been a little stale between us,' Lucerne whispered against her cheek, 'but it could work again. It just needs something to heat it up. Come and play. Come and laugh with us, Bella.'

She turned her head towards Georgiana, not even slightly tempted.

'I haven't heard you laugh for so long,' Lucerne continued. 'I hardly recognise you. What happened to the woman who filled vases with weeds and never changed out of her riding habit?'

'You brought her to town.' She turned to face him. Looked up into his cornflower-blue eyes, seeking, she didn't know what. Some glimmer of love perhaps, some glint of the old Lucerne. 'If that's the woman you want, take me to the country, don't ask for an awkward night in a shared bed.' She grasped his arms, strained forward on tiptoes. 'Let's do it, Lucerne. Let's go and find Vaughan, and then head north to Lauwine. We could send word ahead to Joshua, he'd see that everything was made ready.'

'No.' Lucerne slipped free of her grip and backed away. 'I can't. Not yet, anyway. Maybe come the New Year.'

'Why?' Her brow crinkled into a frown.

Lucerne hit the back of the settee, but continued to edge away from her. 'Because I need space if it's ever going to be right between us again. I don't miss him, Bella. Not in the way you do, anyway.'

'That's a lie –'

'No.' He cut her off. Bella stared at him, her mouth agape. His words tore at her heart like glass splinters. She turned back to the window. Was it really true that he didn't miss him?

She missed Vaughan with every ounce of her being, longed for him and craved his touch. She'd shared some pleasant moments with Lucerne over the past week, but that's all they'd been. Their lovemaking lacked the edgy intensity she felt when she was with Vaughan. She stared at her dour reflection, barely recognising herself. God's blood! She wished she knew what to do.

Her image blurred as a carriage rumbled past outside. When it solidified again she found herself looking at her lover embracing another.

Lucerne held Georgiana against his body as he slowly explored her lips and throat. It was unbearable. But with sickening morbidity, she couldn't help but watch. How could he believe she was interested in being part of this or that she'd forgive him for his deceptions? He caught her looking. 'Bella,' he mouthed. 'Dear Bella, come to us.'

'I can't,' she mouthed back.

'You'd do it for Vaughan.'

'No!' She snapped from her trance. 'No, I wouldn't.'

She didn't remember leaving, just collapsing, breathless at the top of the stairs, her mind and heart full of poison. How dare he? He was ruining everything.

Once in her room, Bella wrestled a small trunk from the closet. She tipped out the collection of shoes and put back two pairs, practical, and evening slippers. On top of them she packed several dresses, two shifts, an assortment of linen, a muff and a winter cape. Luckily, her gowns took up considerably less space these days since the whalebone paniers had dropped out of style.

Lucerne had driven Vaughan away, and now she was leaving too. The bond they'd all shared was in tatters but she was going north to mend what was left.

She put on her pelisse and hat, and took one final look at her room. She couldn't stay here a moment longer knowing that woman was in the house.

The parlour door was closed when she reached the bottom of the stairs but the pained look on William's face told her all she needed to know. They were probably stripped naked by now, rolling around on the fireside rug.

'Will there be a message, ma'am?' William asked, after he'd reluctantly carried her trunk outside onto the deserted street.

'Tell him I've gone out.'

'And will you be requiring an escort?' He looked hopeful.

Bella smiled at his concern. 'No, William, I'll manage just fine alone.'

He watched her down the steps. Bella waved from the bottom. Then her gaze slipped sideways to the parlour window. The shutters were still open and she could just make out Lucerne's shadow against the wall. 'The answer's no,' she whispered to it. 'It'll always be no. I won't do it for you, and I wouldn't do it for him.'

Yes you would, said a disquieting voice in her head. If Vaughan gave you that choice, you'd do it. You wouldn't be able to help yourself. But Vaughan would never ask. And if he did it would be about her pleasure, not his vanity.

Her temper had both heated and cooled by the time she reached the end of the street. She was going to meet Vaughan, and that made everything simpler. She had an image of him in her head, barefoot, his dark hair knotted with cobwebs and coal dust smeared across his face. It was a treasured memory from last spring, one that made her heart ache for him even more. She knew he'd laugh at her for that and he wouldn't care how much his mocking made her insides knot; how it made her love him that little bit more.

She stopped abruptly and bit down hard upon her lip. How had that slipped out? Love! That had never been what they were about. Yes, that was part of the relationship between her and Lucerne, and Lucerne and Vaughan, but never between them. To Vaughan, she'd always just been a playmate, or perhaps more accurately, an adversary.

When she'd first stepped into the carriage with them after Louisa's wedding, she'd thought everything had been made equal. It hadn't taken long to realise that wasn't the case. The first night, they'd stayed at a coaching inn. Vaughan and Lucerne had shared a room, while she stayed alone in the room next door and listened to them making love though the wattle walls. She'd known then that no matter how raw or intense it got, it would always be about them, never about her.

At dawn, she'd slipped in alongside them. That morning, she'd watched them fuck for the first time. They'd been beautiful together, perfect – the scent of their bodies musky and intoxicating. She remembered Lucerne's fragile blush and the devotion written so plainly in Vaughan's violet eyes.

Ever since, she'd wished he'd look at her like that.

There was a clatter behind her. Bella scampered back from the roadside just in time to avoid the splatter off the carriage wheels as they churned up the waste in the road. Come daylight, she'd book passage to Pennerley, post-haste, but right now she needed a room for the night.

'Bella Rushdale!' The carriage stopped a few yards on and disgorged a man in an enormous square-cut coat. 'What the devil are you doing on the streets at this hour?'

Henry Tristan brushed his hound's-ear locks of hair back

from his face and blocked her path with his cane. He caught sight of her trunk and his easy smile transformed into a look of concern. 'My dear, whatever's happened?'

Bella let go of the heavy trunk. It was not going to be easy to explain. Not even to Henry, who already knew, or at least guessed, so much.

'Wait.' He pressed a woodsy-scented finger to her lips. 'Come on in and tell me.'

She presumed he meant the carriage, but instead he signalled the driver on and had one of his men take her trunk. He led her across the square to his town house. 'Don't be fearful, you're perfectly safe with me.' He smirked. 'Come in, come in. Tell me all.'

The interior was not a bit like she'd imagined. It was scrupulously plain to the point of austerity. Henry stood out amongst all this asceticism like a gaudy moth. 'We'll retire to my private sitting room,' he said, with a faintly insolent twinkle in his eyes.

His sitting room was small and square. It consisted of one oversized fireplace, an array of Turkish pouffes, a small table and two wicker thrones.

'Let's have some light.' He lit some lamps with a taper from the fire as a servant brought in two steaming cups of chocolate, and soon a heavily spiced aroma began to seep through the air. Bella yawned and sagged into a chair. The fragrance seemed to tug at her eyelids. She hadn't realised how exhausted she felt.

'Maybe I should take you to bed.' His voice was low and gravelly. He leaned over her and smoothed a strand of hair from her face.

Bella batted him away. 'Don't. I've had quite enough absurdity for one night.'

'Ah, yes.' He settled in the other chair and handed a cup to her. 'Why were you dragging a trunk along the street?'

Bella stared down into the drink, her thoughts as bitter as the chocolate. Was there an easy way to say her lover had discarded her in favour of another? Well, not even discarded.

'Have you heard from Pennerley?' Henry asked, providing her with a question altogether easier to answer.

'He sent Lucerne an invitation.'

'Yes.' Henry rubbed his nose uncomfortably. 'I wasn't entirely truthful with you earlier. I've had one the same, and so have others. Some of the bloods are already heading north. It should be good. A spectacle in the manner of "Monk" Lewis and Mrs Radcliffe on All Hallows Eve.' He sipped his drink and then licked a smear of foam from his lips. 'I wanted to tell you earlier. Everyone knows how much you like that sort of thing, but it seemed best if I left it to Lucerne. Was I wrong?'

'I don't know.' Bella felt herself flush. 'Damn it, Henry, he brought a woman home. Georgiana St John. He's tupping her on the parlour floor even as we speak.'

'Ah!' He grimaced. 'Particularly unclever, Lucerne.' He got up and rang for a servant. 'Have a bed made up for Miss Rushdale. She'll be staying a while.'

'Just the night,' Bella corrected. 'I'm leaving for Pennerley tomorrow.'

'Tomorrow! Isn't that a little sudden?'

'I've waited long enough, Henry.'

He moved the drinks aside and leaned across the table towards her, so he was looking straight into her eyes. 'Don't you think you should talk to Lucerne again, first?'

'No.' She sat back. 'We've nothing to discuss. And I'm not

prepared to wait until midday for him to get out of bed. I'm catching the first coach.'

Henry rolled his eyes. 'We'll take my carriage. It'll be far more comfortable. Though Lord knows, I expect I'll regret this.'

Bella kissed him. 'Thank you.' He'd just made the journey a thousand times easier and infinitely more comfortable.

Henry rubbed his lips. 'You're welcome. I think.' He rucked an eyebrow at her. 'Of course, you realise the place is haunted.'

'Pennerley?'

He nodded. 'Why do you think he's taken this long to go back there? Estates don't manage themselves, you know. Even if you do the paperwork from afar, you still have to stop by occasionally, just to makes sure all is as it should be.'

Actually, she'd never thought about it. They'd been happy in London until he'd left. There'd never been any need to go anywhere else. They hadn't even been back to Yorkshire.

'It's rumoured they're all cursed, too.' His smile developed a rakish twist. 'It's said the first Marquis of Pennerley, Vaughan being the fifth or sixth, dabbled with witchcraft in foreign lands and brought down some sort of blood curse on the whole line.'

Bella stared at him, incredulous. Then began to laugh. 'You are funny.' She slapped his thigh. 'Are you making this up?'

'It's local legend,' he said, deadly serious. 'My family are from Shropshire too. Mother still lives there. Maybe we'll impose on her for a night.'

'Vaughan is not cursed,' she said. 'Leastways not unless

you count total self-centredness and abominable arrogance.'

Henry rolled his cup between his fingers. 'Maybe we should reserve judgement until we've seen him. It might be why he ran off.'

4

'How much further?' Bella complained. They'd been travelling seven days and progress north seemed incredibly slow. Henry insisted the horses weren't overworked and that they enjoyed the luxury of leisurely dining. Bella suspected that for all the discomfort of a public coach, it would have got her north a great deal faster. Last night they'd stayed with Henry's mother, a priggish lady with a dour mouth and frosty expression, who'd eyed Bella with considerable wariness and warned her son never to bring his mistress to call upon her again.

He'd left red-faced and only informed Bella of the remark once they were several miles down the road. It had turned her equally crimson, but with rage rather than embarrassment. Bitter old hag! She'd never once considered bedding Henry. Why would she? She was not so starved of intimacy that she would consider any man other than the one she truly wanted – Vaughan.

Henry sprawled on the seat. 'It's not much further now. We passed Ludlow some time ago. You might look out for the church; we should see that first, with Pennerley beyond.'

Bella strained forwards in her seat to better see from the window. The nearer they got the more nervous she felt, but the pangs in her stomach wouldn't keep her away. 'What sort of house is it, Henry?'

'Lord heavens, woman, you'll see it in a minute.' Indeed,

no sooner were his words out than the coach bore left and the church tower was before them. A moment later, Pennerley itself rose into view.

'Is that it?' Bella slumped back in her seat. She'd seen just a flash of it through the trees: a high timber-framed house like others she'd seen in Ludlow, save this one was painted vibrant mustard-yellow. It seemed too garish for Vaughan, and while impressive, too tiny to contain him.

Henry took her place by the window. 'Come look again.' She leaned over his shoulder. They were past the church now, getting closer to the mustard and black gatehouse. For gatehouse, it was. Not his abode but merely the entrance.

'It's a castle,' Bella gasped. 'He owns a castle and he never even mentioned it. You never mentioned it!' She stared accusingly at Henry, but only for a second before her attention returned to the grey stone edifice.

'I was saving the surprise.'

The coach came to a lurching halt and a groom rushed out of what appeared to be a vast stable block and coach house. Bella jumped down into the churned mud, thankful she'd put on her more sturdy walking shoes rather than her dainty pumps. The air was fresh and clean, and held the first nip of winter. She looked around at the landscape: great hillsides climbed before her, blanketed with dark forests, and the sky all muggy grey above them and roiling with thunderous-looking clouds. There was grassland too, gone orange at the tips, thick spindly bushes and ivy tumbling over the churchyard wall.

She took a big lungful of the air, feeling as though she'd returned home. They weren't in Yorkshire, on the wuthering moors of her youth. The landscape was too lumpy for that, but it called to her all the same.

Henry hung over the bridge before the gatehouse. 'There's a moat,' he squealed in delight. 'And I swear I've just seen the most enormous pike. Are you ready, shall we go in?'

The gatehouse entrance yawned before them, a dark maw between two vertically striped walls over which Adam and Eve stood watch. The gate, a vast cross-planked, iron-pinned construction, was on the courtyard side at the end of a short tunnel. Henry braved his cane against the wood, and a small wicket gate opened in response.

'Are you expected?' asked the gate-guard.

Henry carelessly waved the question away, as if their presence made that clear enough. 'Which way, boy?'

'Straight across, sir.' The servant pointed to a huge arched door across the grassy courtyard. Bella didn't hurry. There was lavender on the breeze and the smell of kitchen herbs; so much detail to take in it was overwhelming. A castle, she kept muttering to herself, as she gazed at the grey stone walls, a castle, although it was clearly a fortified manor house with grand pretensions, considering the Tudor-style timber jetty at the top of nearest tower and the enormous windows. It was as though someone had built a castle for aesthetic purposes rather than defensive ones, which struck her as a little strange considering the location, so close to the Welsh border.

They reached the second oversized door, this one not quite so gigantic but still iron-pinned and sturdy. Again, Henry knocked. They waited. Knocked again, and the door swung inwards. To Bella's complete amazement, she found herself facing Vaughan.

He was dressed in his signature black boots, pantaloons

and open-necked shirt; the only flashes of colour the bright violet of his eyes and a slender gold chain around his neck. In this setting, his simple attire seemed incredibly baroque.

'Welcome to my domain.' He executed a sweeping bow. 'Is Lucerne with you?' He looked right and left around her.

'Um, no.' She gestured towards Henry. Vaughan's eyes flashed, but whatever he was feeling, he quickly masked.

'Tristan.' Vaughan stretched his arms wide, welcoming them into an enormous room, which she realised must run virtually the entire length of the building.

'Since when did you start answering your own door?' she asked, her gaze returning to Vaughan.

He lowered his brows in response. 'Well, we had to lay off the pikemen after Cromwell, and besides, I rather assume that if you've made it past the gatehouse, I'm going to find you agreeable.' He moistened his lips, leaving them shiny.

'Fantastic place,' said Henry, seemingly oblivious to the awkward tension between his host and his companion. 'Where's your pisspot, Pennerley, I'm bursting.'

Vaughan glanced between him and Bella. 'The privy's through there.' He pointed towards a door at the opposite end of the hall. 'Just keep going. You'll find it.'

While Vaughan closed the door, Bella looked around at the vast chamber. It was furnished with a long dining table and several cosy-looking chairs. A staircase climbed to the rafters to her right, while to her left a fireplace dominated. Huge windows lined both walls, each prettily glazed at the top, with shutters below to keep out the wind. Consequently, despite the daylight outside, the hall was lit by huge candelabras, which gave everything a ruddy-orange glow. It reminded Bella of the ancient monasteries and castles of her favourite stories, an effect only enhanced by the towering magnificence of the cruck roof.

'Things must be bad if you're reduced to travelling with Henry Tristan as a companion,' Vaughan said, drawing her attention back to his person. She stared at his sable ringlets where they lay against his shoulders, not daring to meet his eyes, not sure what to say. She supposed she should explain her presence and Lucerne's absence. Ask him why he'd left so suddenly. But the words would dredge up such bitter memories and she wanted to laugh and enjoy his company, not mope and brood.

'He's been kind to me,' she said of Henry, keeping her voice neutral. It felt awkward, this stiff formality. When had they ever been so polite to each other? Damnation! She wanted to fling herself into his arms, share the warmth of his skin and tell him she'd missed him. Instead, they were pacing each other warily. 'He told me all about your delightful first meeting,' she said. 'How you fell upon one another, finding ecstasy in the moment.'

Vaughan folded his arms. 'Please. His wet dream, I assure you. Do I give ecstasy so freely?' His smile sweetened, instantly lightening the mood. 'Perhaps I do. Perhaps that's why you're here.' He artlessly stretched behind him and clasped a chair back. The movement thrust his chest into prominence, making her smile in turn. 'Why have you come, Annabella, my nightingale?'

He touched her face, trailed a finger down to her throat. 'What's the draw, the promise of a gothic nightmare or the bitter-sweet terror of my lips?' His kiss fluttered over her pulse point. Bella closed her eyes and breathed in his scent, rosemary laced with musk. How she'd missed him. How she longed to return his caress. One simple touch and her body was weeping for him, but too often he'd teased her like this and then pushed her away. 'And why no Lucerne? Were you so sure of a welcome without him?' He stepped back suddenly, his tone abruptly cold.

Bella's eyes flickered open. 'Am I not welcome –' she began, and then she caught his smile. He was playing with her, always playing with her.

'But of course. You are both *most* welcome.' He took her hand and traced a slow circle around the palm. Bella watched his long fingers, imagining their trace against a more intimate area of her anatomy. 'Let me give you a proper welcome to Pennerley.' He pulled her, not into his arms for the kiss she longed for, but towards the stairs and down onto all fours.

Bella squealed as her nose pressed to the ancient grain of the wood. It was knotted and splintered in places, worn smooth in the centre where she knelt. Her nose prickled at the smell of dust and linseed. Vaughan threw her skirts over her back. For a moment she felt nothing, then his hand, warm and firm, pressed between her legs and found her wet and eager.

'Why, Annabella,' he drawled, 'I do believe you've missed me.'

'Damn you,' she cursed as the familiar dribble of oil slithered between her cheeks. Nothing had changed. He still didn't care a jot for her feelings or the truth of Lucerne's absence. He cared only for the instant gratification of his own desires.

She shifted indignantly against the intrusive press of his fingers but couldn't stop the anticipatory heat from flaring inside her womb. She'd been waiting for this, longing for him. She knew what was coming, hated it, needed it, this sin. She should have known what to expect.

His fingers stretched her. His cock pushed in, making her empty cunt clench tight. She meant to push back against him, knock him off balance, but instead her bottom rubbed eagerly against his loins. It was so good to feel him inside her again, such welcome relief for the nineteen days of torture she'd spent without him.

'Easy,' he whispered, when she twisted her head to look at him. 'You'll come too fast.' Bella didn't care. She'd been wound too tight and all the emotion and rage she'd felt was spilling out of her. This carnal invasion, this thrusting heat – it was exactly what she wanted. 'Bella,' he hissed between his teeth. A sound broke in her throat in response, a hopeless expression of her longing. He was right. She had missed him, and more than he would ever truly understand. She loved him, but she had no idea how to tell him that or whether he wanted to hear it.

Her head was spinning. Her knees ached. His scent surrounded her, musky and animal beneath the hint of cologne. And at the point of their connection, a pulse was raging, driving her movements, dictating everything in simple, so very simple, animalistic terms.

She came hard, with a long rolling shudder, while Vaughan held himself still within her rear. Once the pulses had faded, he began to move again.

'Again,' he demanded, forcing her hips down with his palm, while the fingers of his other hand teased her still sensitive bud.

'No,' Bella gasped. 'Vaughan, I can't.' She pressed herself to the ancient wood while colour burned her cheeks, feeling both elated and shamed. 'I've been stuck in a coach for days. You could at least offer me a drink before you demand four orgasms in a row.'

'I've only demanded two, and a chance to finish off.' Chuckling, he patted her bottom. 'But very well. Foster!' he bellowed.

Bella's eyes snapped open. 'Your servant!' She scrambled forwards but Vaughan held her tight about her hips.

'Easy now, what's the problem? Your drink's coming.'

Bella hid her head in embarrassment. She'd been here just five minutes and within another five every servant in the place would know their master had swived her in the arse. She heard the screech of a door hinge and Foster appeared by Vaughan's side.

'Bring me the port. My guest's thirsty.'

A moment later, Foster returned with a silver platter holding a decanter and two glasses. Vaughan took the decanter and waved him away. 'That'll be all. Oh, and see that another two rooms are prepared. The North Tower for the lady and the blue room in the gatehouse for Mr Tristan.'

From between her fingers, Bella watched Foster look around as if expecting to find Mr Tristan slouched in one of the chairs spectating. Thankfully he hadn't returned from the privy, although, curiously, Foster also looked up. 'Very good, my lord.' He bowed obsequiously. 'I'll inform cook there will be two extra for dinner,' and he backed away through the arched doorway beneath the stairs.

The moment the door closed, Vaughan began to laugh. His cock flexed inside her and, when she jiggled in response, he slapped her and withdrew.

Bella turned quickly, frantically pulling down her skirts. 'You swine!' she cursed, but he just continued to laugh.

'Nothing more than you expect and far less than you

deserve.' He held out the decanter towards her. 'And no Viscount Marlinscar to rescue you. Something of an oversight on your part, don't you think?'

Bella whitened a little but still reached for the bottle. It was true; Lucerne had always been there to protect her and temper Vaughan's worst excesses. Still, she thought she'd rather be here than face the mess she'd left behind. At some point, of course, she'd have to explain what had happened.

Her fingers touched the side of the decanter, but Vaughan snatched it out of reach and raised it to his own lips instead. He swallowed in greedy gulps, letting the ruby liquid spill over his chin and into the open V of his shirt, until it flowed like a bloody river down his front. She met his eyes and understood, then moved in to lick the rivulets from his skin.

The taste was sharp and sweet. It tingled on her tongue and down her throat, lending additional warmth to the fire already alight in her belly. Lovely wavelets ebbed and built, rushed tingling flames across her body, made her want to feast on his skin. She wanted to strip him bare and trace the silvery scar that wound across his ribs all the way to his heart.

'There's but one mouthful left.' He raised the bottle, then drained it.

Bella fastened her lips over his, and he transferred the liquid to her with his kiss, leaving her giddy and terribly aroused. She couldn't let him go. Instead, she slid her tongue between his parted lips and he kissed her back long and hard. Nobody ever made her feel the same way as Vaughan when he kissed her. There was magic in his slow, hungry embrace, and a magnetic draw that crushed boundaries and pulled her into his chaotic razor-sharp world.

He nipped her lip as he released her, drawing blood.

Bella was too stunned to feel the pain. Clearly, Vaughan in his own dominion was even more dangerous and unpredictable. She licked at the bite as he fastened his pantaloons over his erection. 'You live in a castle,' she said, dazed.

He sniffed. 'It's a toy really. But it does. Shall I show you your room?'

He took her hand. His palm was even warmer than hers, but he'd always had an unnatural heat, and led her up the staircase to a balcony perched just below the rafters. 'Through here.' They turned left along a short gallery into a timber-framed room with windows in three directions, and a decorated stone fireplace with an immense hood. The high timbered room she'd seen from outside.

'This is to be mine?' Bella gasped.

He nodded.

'But it's enormous.' She ran to the central window and looked out at the weathervane on top of the church roof. 'But isn't this the master bedroom?'

Vaughan swung around one of the spindly bedposts and sat upon the bed. 'Don't be silly, or was that wishful thinking?' He held his hand out towards her and, straddling his lap, she tried to seek the comfort of his lips again. When he shook his head, she sucked at her wounded lip.

'You know,' she remarked, 'in three years you've hardly ever taken me like a woman.'

'Never.'

'It's true.' She wriggled against his trapped erection.

Vaughan shook his head and laughed.

'Everywhere else, bottom, bosom, mouth, armpits, even once between my toes, but hardly ever there.' She frowned, traced the curve of his upper lip. 'Why? Is it because you only really like men?'

'Is that what you believe?' He collapsed back against the mattress, rubbed his face, then propped himself back up on his elbows. 'Bella, you are Lucerne's. That's his province, and it's a bloody miracle *he's* never got you with child.'

'Would that have bothered you?' she asked, pressing a hand to his soaked shirt.

He caught her wrist and moved her hand aside. 'You know the answer to that.' He pushed her off his lap and stood. 'Come; let me introduce you to my sister. She'll welcome the company.'

Bella stared after him as he walked to the door. 'Sister! Since when did you have a sister?' She hurried to catch him. 'You've never mentioned her before.'

'Must have slipped my mind. This way.' He trotted back to the stairs. What else had he overlooked mentioning? Did she know anything about him at all? 'I suppose we ought to find Tristan too. We can't have him prying into every corner now, can we.'

Bella paused halfway down. 'What are those?' she asked, pointing to two squares on the opposite wall above the fireplace.

'Windows,' said Vaughan. 'Beyond the solar, which is where we're heading. They're designed so that the lord of the manor can keep a check on his underlings.'

'Spy holes,' she said, and her horror was intense.

5

The solar was breathtaking, entirely oak-panelled with a huge fireplace and a stunning overmantel, intricately carved with half-formed figures and grotesque heads similar to those that graced the outer walls of the gatehouse. It was something, she imagined, straight out of the Elizabethan era, and indeed portraits of gentlemen with sharp beards, dressed in doublets and hose graced several of the walls.

Henry was already seated and chatting amiably to a young lady when they entered, whom Bella instantly took to be Vaughan's sister. Had he left her languishing here all this time?

Two men were standing by the fire. The Vicomte de Maresi, whom she recognised, and a tall, very handsome gentleman, powerfully built with broad shoulders, whose buckskin breeches cleaved to his thighs like a second skin. He turned his head as they entered and looked at her with a languid, easy smile. The sort of smile that was so much more than a greeting. It insinuated intimacy and, more importantly, knowledge. Bella found her gaze riveted upon him. She was certain he was not of her acquaintance.

'Ah, here she is with our host,' said Henry. He stood and waved his glass in her direction. Clearly he'd settled in already, having discarded his topcoat and helped himself to Vaughan's port. 'Have you met Lord Devonshire, Bella?'

'Miss Rushdale.' Devonshire came away from the fireside and accepted her hand. He bowed deeply, though he also peeped along her arm in a rather less gentlemanly fashion. There was a playful gleam in his eyes, but the steely bite of his grip hinted there was a lot more to him than his façade implied. She would have to watch out for this one, she realised. Likely that was true of all Vaughan's associates. Even Henry occasionally made a riposte that knocked her sideways, reeling and breathless, and blushing like a virgin.

'Enjoying yourself, Raffe?' Vaughan asked.

Bella pulled free of Lord Devonshire's grip, still wary of his peculiarly familiar smile.

'Immensely, Pennerley, as, I observed, are you.'

The timbre of his voice lanced her with his meaning. Bella's gaze shot to the alcoves either side of the fire, which contained the small windows she'd observed from the hall. The shutter on the left one, which surely overlooked the stairs, was open.

Lord Devonshire caught her gaze again, and this time his smile was unmistakeable. He'd been watching, she realised, although at least he seemed to have kept it from the others.

A savage blush chased across her skin. If she left here with one ounce of respectability intact it'd be a miracle. She'd have to be more careful around Vaughan and hope for Devonshire's discretion. There'd be no going back to London and civilised society if her name were ruined. She'd risked enough living with Lucerne, Vaughan and her mock chaperone, but then the only reason she'd ever been accepted was due to Vaughan's influence. He wouldn't hear a word said against her. Woe betide the few who'd tried.

'Miss Rushdale,' said Vaughan's sister, coming to her

rescue. 'Would you walk with me? We can leave the gentlemen to their rakery until dinner.' She clasped Bella's hand tight.

She had none of her brother's unnatural heat. In fact, her hands were rather cool and a deal more delicate. Still, there was no mistaking that she was anything other than Vaughan's sibling. She was every inch as beautiful, with fair skin, fine elfin features and curling sable locks. Her eyes, though, were quite different to Vaughan's, being a piercing icy blue. They turned upon Bella, laughing and eager as they made their way out onto the courtyard lawn. 'Thank heavens you've come. It was starting to feel like Udolpho with so many men about the place.'

'Your favourite?' asked Bella, pleased to find they had some common ground other than Vaughan to discuss.

Her hostess nodded. 'How could it not be when I'm stuck in this crumbling ruin, but you do know that my brother has put you in the haunted room?'

Bella gulped. She loved ghost stories and had always dreamed of some gothic adventure, but the vengeful ghosts of Vaughan's ancestors were more than she wanted.

'The first marchioness, driven mad by her husband's infidelity and perversions, fell to her death in the moat, yet haunts the room still, cursing adulterers.'

Bella shifted uncomfortably.

'Oh, but if you know my brother, you can guess that most of the hauntings are just cruel tricks by the lords of Pennerley at the expense of their guests. But let's not talk of such things ... Forgive me. It's so good to have you here. It's so like my brother to forget to invite some women along with all his friends, although he has promised me the Allenthorpes.'

She certainly seemed starved for company and was making up for it with what she thought was amiable chatter.

'I don't know if he was really expecting me,' said Bella. They might as well get that straight from the outset.

'No.' Vaughan's sister smiled impishly. 'But he wanted you here all the same. Don't think I don't know my brother, Miss Rushdale. He hides much from me but he can't hide everything. I know he stayed with you and Viscount Marlinscar in London, and he's pleased to see you.'

Bella felt her heart clench at the thought; she truly hoped that was true. Oh, he'd welcomed her in his fashion, but you could never be sure with Vaughan if his expression and his words matched his inner thoughts.

'Forgive me,' said Bella, remembering her manners. 'I'm afraid you have me at a distinct advantage, for I don't know what to call you. Vaughan only told me of your existence five minutes ago.'

'Brothers,' she scoffed, and showed her lovely smile. 'I'm Niamh. Lady, if the gentlemen are listening.'

'Then you must call me Bella, and I expect the gentlemen will follow your brother's lead and do as they please.' She didn't add that Vaughan only ever called her Miss Rushdale when he was teasing her.

They strolled across a lawn and followed an oyster-shell pathway among the flowerbeds to the perimeter wall. Bella stared over it, down into the muggy green water of the moat. It was a long drop, much further than she had anticipated. 'It must be strange having him home again, after all this time,' she observed. 'Has he changed much?'

Niamh plucked the head of a late rose. 'Vaughan! Dear, no. He never changes. He's always the perfect older brother; spiteful and completely devoted.'

'Sounds exactly like my own.' Joshua had so liked to tease her as they were growing up. Now, he probably just despaired of her and hoped she'd some day send him a wedding invitation. If she married Lucerne, at least she'd be accepted in polite Yorkshire society again. Presently she was considered a disgrace and Joshua a bad example. 'But for all his faults, he's never gainsaid me or reined me in.'

'Oh, Vaughan would pursue me to the ends of the earth if I were to try anything.' Niamh sighed and irritably plucked the petals off the beheaded rose. She let them sail over the wall and into the water, where they formed a myriad of tiny boats. 'Though how he would know I'd gone most of the time is beyond me. Sometimes I swear he has a magic mirror to spy on me, for he always knows what I'm about. Mind you, he does write exceedingly long letters and expects the same in return, so I imagine I just give myself away between the lines.'

Bella grinned broadly, imagining Vaughan pouring over a letter for hints of insurgence. 'You speak as if you have something to hide.'

'Maybe I do.' She linked arms with Bella. 'Are you and Mr Tristan together?'

Bella turned her head sharply. 'No! Why does everyone think that?'

'Oh, I'm sorry.' She pressed her hand to her mouth. 'I just assumed as you arrived together, and without Lord Marlinscar. But I'm pleased that you're not.'

Bella drew her brows together, not at all sure what assumptions her hostess had made or how much she knew about her brother's relationships.

'I wasn't trying to implicate anything.' She clapped her hands together and pressed her fingertips to her lips, a gesture frighteningly reminiscent of her brother. 'It's just . . . Dear Bella, you shall think me quite ridiculous, but his stockings are so shocking, they are magnificent.' She artlessly swirled on the spot. 'I think I shall have some made to match. Do you think I shall look handsome with salmon-pink bands about my calves?' She raised her hem a little, displaying perfectly ordinary stockings, with tiny floral sprigs embroidered onto the ankles. 'Vaughan will hate them but I think I shall insist, and he won't refuse me this.' Her expression sobered. Bella tried to catch her gaze, but Niamh shook her head warily and dipped her chin. They were not close enough friends yet.

The silence lasted but a moment. 'Shall I show you the rest of the castle?'

'That would be nice. I should like to see the keep and get a view of the land around. The earth where I live is rolling and bleak, not like this great hummock before us.'

'To the south tower, then. We'll go up onto the roof. You can see into Wales on one side and across to the Long Mynd on the other.'

They crossed a drawbridge to get into the south tower, and climbed a staircase barely one person wide that ran inside the thick outer walls. Bella was forced to hold her skirts at knee height to stop herself tripping, while Niamh seemed to know every stone individually.

They soon emerged onto a small landing that led straight into the master bedroom. Bella stopped on the threshold while Niamh crossed to where the stairs wound their way up again.

'This is your brother's room. We shouldn't be in here.'

'Don't be silly. It's the only way up, and it's not as if he's in the bed, and he wouldn't mind even if he were. He'd have his curtains about him.' She returned to Bella and tugged her sleeve.

Aware that she was being hypocritical, considering the nights she'd spent in his London bed recently, Bella allowed herself to be pulled into the room. Still, it felt wrong being here without permission. This was *his* room, not just some lodging somewhere but his most private space.

It was a curious chamber, vast, roughly heart-shaped, with five inset window-seats, and full of light and air. Despite all the shimmery light, it was also more overtly Vaughan than any other room she'd known him occupy. The furniture was all dark wood, elaborately carved like the overmantel in the solar and the figures on the gatehouse exterior. The bed was of twisted blackened oak, the head and footboards writhing with grotesque demons, chimeras and sobbing fallen angels. One especially sorrowful fellow sat in prayer with his legs curled before him, and his one remaining wing hanging forlornly from his back. Yet there was something fearful about him, perhaps the quaint curl of his lips or the sense of questioning defiance in his sightless eyes.

He drew her closer, calling for her to reach out and touch the polished wooden surface, to trace the curve of his jaw.

'Bella!' Niamh beckoned her towards the stairwell. 'Unless you're seriously contemplating bouncing on the bed.'

Bella immediately scuttled away from its monstrous allure. Bouncing had not entered her thoughts at all. No, instead her mind was filled with fantasies of Vaughan, blood-smeared and bound across the stark white sheets, his cock erect and his mouth slack from too many kisses. She'd had such fantasies before, but this was different. There was no Lucerne present, and there was such an intense fire in her belly. Her heart was beating far too fast.

'Miss Rushdale.'

The repetition of her name pulled her from the trance and she sprinted up the second flight of stairs as if the devil were on her tail.

Bella waded into the wall of cold air on the roof, panting from the exertion. These fantasies, this desire for him was pointless. Eventually she'd have to tell him why Lucerne hadn't come, how he was faithless and inconstant, and quite unconcerned that their relationship was falling apart.

He wouldn't take it well. When did Vaughan ever take anything well? And then ... And then she guessed she'd learn how much he really cared for her.

The room fell sickeningly quiet after the women left. Vaughan let himself into the library beyond. He didn't care much for company at the moment, especially not the strained conversation that seemed to be brewing. Devonshire was crudely hinting at what he'd seen, as if it was a joke they'd shared, which was more of an acquaintance than the man had a right to presume to. It merely served Vaughan's purpose at the moment to keep the young man sweet. He'd never been that enamoured of being watched. Oh, he'd performed on occasion, but the thought of being spied on was far from a turn on in itself. He'd learned to live with Bella's voyeuristic intrusions on his lovemaking with Lucerne, but she'd rarely just sat and watched. She liked to touch, to be a part of things.

There was one memory of her that he kept hidden away. A time she'd caught him by surprise and made him come so hard he was shaking afterwards. He'd never admitted that it was her doing, and he doubted either she or Lucerne remembered the occasion. She'd been out making social calls and arrived home to find them christening the new loveseat for the parlour. Lucerne had been poised across it, while Vaughan simultaneously masturbated and buggered him. Bella had simply traced a finger down his naked back from his neck to his anus.

The shock of her intrusion and the shivers the simple touch raised had tipped him over into a long juddering climax, that for once had had little to do with the pleasure he derived from Lucerne's body and everything to do with the woman who was a constant thorn in their relationship.

The library door opened behind him and de Maresi shuffled in. He could tell who it was without looking, purely from the waft of floral scent. Since the Vicomte's arrival at Pennerley, Vaughan had managed to get him to wear a little less eau de toilette, but he still smelled like a tulip.

The slender Frenchman's hands alighted upon Vaughan's hips. He pressed up close so that his loins caressed the back seam of Vaughan's black pantaloons, and his cheek pressed to Vaughan's shoulder.

'Don't touch me,' Vaughan snapped. While he'd enjoyed the fragile pleasures of the Vicomte's body, he wasn't in the mood for the Frenchman's effete form of male loving. He didn't want delicacy and flowers. He wanted someone he could wrestle with. Someone whose hair he could pull, someone who would try to top him and pin him down in return, someone he could fuck without breaking.

He missed Lucerne.

Damn him, he missed him. He should have been here. He was supposed to arrive with Bella.

De Maresi backed away, snuffling into his lacy kerchief. 'Later, perhaps?'

Vaughan didn't respond, but when the man failed to excuse himself, he gave a low growl that immediately sent him scuttling back into the solar.

Vaughan grasped the bookcase. He shook his head, unable to stop himself chuckling. His silent laughter faded quickly and he pressed his brow to the cool wood of the shelf. His cock still felt tight from his encounter with Bella. He breathed deeply, willing it to fade, but a moment later he was forced to rearrange himself. The breathing exercises just weren't having the desired effect. Maybe he should have made use of the Frenchman's mouth. They could have locked the door and made sure no one walked in. Sound didn't travel far through the thick walls, although de Maresi would have been effectively silenced, and he was perfectly capable of coming without making a sound. Still, it was never wise to court complacency.

Too late for that now.

The library door opened again. Vaughan swung round, ready to throw a book or pounce if necessary, but the intruder was neither Raffe nor de Maresi. It was Henry Tristan.

Vaughan took in his outrageous banded stockings and pressed his fingers into his eyes. The vision wasn't any less lurid when he removed them.

Henry closed the door with a quiet click.

'Where's Lucerne?' asked Vaughan.

'Ah, yes!' Henry's lips stretched into an uneasy grimace. 'I wondered when you'd get to that. I had to come with Bella, you understand. She was going to come anyway.'

'Lucerne?' Vaughan prompted. He steepled his fingers and tapped his index fingers to his lips.

'Well, yes ... quite.' Lapsing into nervous traits, Henry fumbled in his pocket for his snuffbox. 'You don't really need me to say, do you?'

'You mean he's still with that trollop, Georgiana St John. Dammit! Doesn't the man have any taste?'

Henry raised his hand to his nose. 'Apparently not, or he'd still be sandwiched between you and Bella.' He took a large sniff, then sneezed violently, scattering snuff across the floorboards.

Vaughan allowed his lips to curl. Once, riled by Lucerne's inability to keep his cock in his trousers and out of the mouth of whichever courtesan he was blinkeredly following about, Vaughan had taken action by molesting poor Henry behind a screen at a music recital. His intention had been to shock Lucerne out his complacency; the result was that he'd acquired a new hanger-on.

Henry had been shocked, but quite unable to resist the skill of Vaughan's lips. The way he had crumbled into submission had given an extra high to the satisfaction he'd felt at cracking Lucerne's belief that their relationship was indestructible. Now he closed the gap between himself and Henry, and grabbed him either side of his preposterous cravat just to prove to himself that he could still feel that raw surge of desire and triumph.

The man's mottled-green eyes opened impossibly wide. His back stiffened, pulling his shoulders back and to attention.

'You know you wouldn't survive five minutes with me, and Bella would break you,' Vaughan hissed. Their hips collided, bringing his erection into contact with Henry's loins. Startled, Henry jerked back, his exhalation sharp and desperate. He grasped the doorknob and hung on tight.

'You were supposed to bring Lucerne, Henry.'

Henry swallowed audibly. 'I know ... but ... Bella ...' Frog-like, he gulped air. 'She's a nice girl, can't see why you don't just content yourself with her, eh?'

If he looked any more like a scared rabbit, Vaughan thought he might die from mirth. The laughter that surged up from his belly bubbled on his tongue, but he bit back the smile and forced his expression to remain outwardly neutral. 'She's very far from a nice girl, Henry.' His humour faded abruptly with his words. 'And I'm not a very nice man.'

Vaughan turned on his heels and resumed his position by the bookcase. He felt Henry's gaze but didn't turn to confront it. Instead, he traced the links of the gold chain around his neck down to the locket that lay against his heart.

6

Dinner that evening was served in the drafty great hall. To her relief, Bella was given a chair facing away from the foot of the stairs upon which she'd debased herself earlier. She had spent a pleasant afternoon in Niamh's company exploring the castle and its grounds. It was not as big as Lauwine but, in its own way, far grander.

The Forvasham family, she had learned, had been granted a licence to crenellate for services to the crown centuries before, but had only gained the Pennerley title in 1662 for their help in restoring the monarchy. The tower and moat were vanities, which would never have withstood a real siege, but the effect was beautiful. She positively adored her tower room, its leaded windows overlooking the countryside, and the way it overhung the walls below supported on great wooden arms. She and Vaughan's sister had even taken a turn about the moat on a little wooden punt.

Still, she had missed Vaughan's company. She had hoped he'd show her around himself. Instead, he'd locked himself in the library, before disappearing into the lowest floor of the south tower with Henry and the Vicomte.

Like Bluebeard's chamber, that room had not comprised part of the tour and Niamh had warned her off prying. Apparently, Niamh had confided with squeamish enthusiasm, it was where he was preparing all the spine-chilling horrors for the coming party.

'Are you not hungry?' asked Lord Devonshire, who was sat to her left, tucking into a huge plate of meat. 'I thought you'd have worked up quite an appetite after all that robust activity.' A flame of lusty mirth flickered deep within his eyes.

Bella lifted her fork, but didn't eat. She found she had no appetite for anything but Vaughan. 'I'm quite content, Lord Devonshire –'

'Raffe,' he insisted.

'The exertion was quite minor, and welcome after the close confines of the carriage.'

'Ah, yes. You know, I admire a girl with a sense of adventure.' There was no mistaking exactly what he was admiring. Bella felt a blush spread across her skin and an unexpected flare of heat lower down. So that was it. Her reputation was safe while he held the hope of a similar favour. 'I've never been one for dainties myself.' His gaze flickered briefly towards Niamh who, while not dainty in the traditional sense, was rather more slender and fine-featured than Bella.

Vaughan caught her gaze and lifted one eyebrow, making it all too clear that he could hear their conversation.

'Do you like to ride, Miss Rushdale?'

'I do,' she replied, her head bowed, and all too conscious of Vaughan's watchful gaze.

'Excellent. We must go out together. I'm sure you could teach me a trick or two in the saddle.' He flashed his languid smile to defuse the innuendo.

Across the table, Henry snorted while the Vicomte pushed his nose in the air in snooty disapproval. Bella batted Lord Devonshire with her napkin. She was accustomed to ribald language and the drawing-room riposte, but men rarely practised their wit while Vaughan was watching. They knew better than to attempt to take what was clearly his. She felt her cheeks burn and sneaked a look at Vaughan. He was poised in his chair with a sort of indolent grace that made her want to climb onto his lap, kiss him, bite him, shake him ... and maybe even make vows in a church with him. She wanted to bind herself to him that tight. It would never happen but the thought, unbidden, would not lie. 'Vaughan,' she mouthed. Even the taste of his name upon her lips stirred her blood.

He swept back his chair in response and stood. 'We'll take our port in the solar, gentlemen.'

They rose in unison, leaving just her and Niamh at the table. The Vicomte sneered at her as he passed, showing his teeth. Bella recoiled. She'd met him only twice and they hadn't exchanged a word. His attitude was a mystery. Slowly, she sipped her wine and tried to shrug off the tension that stiffened her limbs, only for her gaze to settle upon Vaughan's plate.

He'd eaten less than she had.

'Vaughan!' She rose immediately and ran after him. It was no good just fretting. She guessed he was concerned by Lucerne's absence. Hell, it concerned her too, and she still had no idea why Vaughan had left London.

Vaughan was halfway up the stairs when she caught up, his hand pressed to the overindulgent brocade of Vicomte de Maresi's frock coat. Bella paled as she watched the tight pinstriped silk pull tight across the Frenchman's arse, but then pushed the display of affection to the back of her mind. 'Vaughan,' she said again. He turned slowly so the skirt of his coat fanned around him, then fell so that, combined with his waistcoat, it emphasised his narrow hips.

Bella peered up at him, trying hard not to focus on his loins, feeling only intense desire. Even once she managed to drag her gaze to his face, the feeling didn't subside. He was as beautiful as ever, and several weeks apart had only served to reminder her how intangible that beauty was. There was a sudden tightening in her chest, echoed a moment later in her womb. 'Love me, Vaughan,' she wanted to plead, but he would never do that. Leastways, not in the way she desired. All his affection was reserved for Lucerne. Still, in that moment, even a touch would suffice.

'Bella?' He raised a delicately arched eyebrow. 'Was there something?'

Nervously, she licked her lips, no longer sure what she intended to say. She didn't want to talk of Lucerne, she simply wanted to press herself into his arms, feel his quick fingers traverse her skin and raise shivers of delight.

'You've been avoiding me all afternoon. I mean, I hoped ... I thought ...'

'Your company was unexpected. I've had other matters to attend. As I do, now.' He turned his wrist and pointed towards the gentlemen awaiting him at the top of the stair. 'Go ahead,' he bade them. 'I'll be up in moment.'

'Is that why you left London, because of your estate?'

He came down the steps towards her, his head inclined so that his dark ringlets spilled over his shoulders, his eyes ever so slightly narrowing beneath their dark lashes. 'You missed me, didn't you, Bella?' he said, ignoring her question.

'I believe I already said I did.'

'Missed me far more than you anticipated?' He fanned his long fingers across the grain of the banister. 'And how did you enjoy having Lucerne to yourself? Was he a nice playmate or not quite all you hoped for?'

The edge to his words raised her hackles. A malevolent gleam shone in his eyes and his lips curled into an aggressive sneer. He'd always loved to goad her, but this obvious tormenting angered her more than usual. Bella struggled for words that would hurt him back. She wanted to hurl Lucerne's love in his face. A thousand lies lay glibly on her tongue, but none of them reached her lips.

Instead, the truth roiled inside her. After the initial act of rebellion with Lucerne on Vaughan's bed, the excitement between them had simply melted away. It had been beastly of Lucerne to bring Georgiana to the house, but it had been the truth when he'd acknowledged that the passion between them was dead.

Vaughan drew a finger up her throat, forcing her to lift her chin and meet his gaze. 'Nothing to impart? How exquisitely dull.'

Vexation tingled in the tip of her nose. That he should tease her like this was intolerable. They'd been apart nearly three weeks, and every day she had ached for him, while he . . . Maybe he'd felt nothing? The gulf between them had always been vast despite them being lovers, but now it seemed to stretch into infinity. What relationship did they have without Lucerne?

'Come, Bella, let's have no secrets between us.' He drew his teeth over his lower lip, gave a wry smile, then wrapped an arm around her shoulder. The embrace soothed her, and she snuggled into his warmth. 'As I recall, you were gagging for some time alone. I gave you it. The least you can do is share the details.'

'That's not really why you left.'

'Is it not?' His eyebrows arched a fraction higher. 'The details, Bella.'

Deliberately flaunting himself, he raised one foot onto the next step. Bella's palms itched with the urge to touch him. She rubbed them together desperate to curb her desire, but the cloth covering his thigh was soft and inviting, and she knew the muscle beneath to be firm. Unable to resist, she edged her fingers up the inner seam. Too often she'd dreamed of him and woken cocooned in his embrace, only to discover she was really alone, bound tight in the rumpled bedclothes. Tentatively, she skirted his loins. 'It wasn't the same without you.' She traced the line of his cock.

'No.' His hand locked around her wrist. 'I don't suppose it was.' His breath lifted the wisps of hair that framed her face. 'And for that,' he lifted her palm and placed a kiss upon its centre, 'you'll have to wait, as I have no intention of bedding you on the stairs again for an audience. Go back to my sister, Bella. She longs for a companion.' He extracted himself from her touch and continued up the stairs, leaving her confused by the edge of his anger.

Bella watched him until he reached the solar door, then reluctantly returned to the hall, where she found Niamh awaiting her by the enormous blaze. 'Are you in love with him?' she asked bluntly.

Bella opened her mouth to speak, but no words would come out.

'Don't be. He'll only break your heart as he's already broken countless others.' She raised a delicate hand. 'Please, don't provide me with the details. My brother is a rakehell among rakehells. I don't care to learn how many beds he has availed himself of. Although I know in my heart it is far too many. You mustn't fall for him, Bella. You must promise me.'

Alas, it was already too late for that. Bella turned her head away, hoping she could blame the colour in her cheeks on the roaring fire. She could not unravel three whole years on a warning, especially as she wasn't entirely sure when in that time he'd usurped Lucerne.

Vaughan continued up the stairs to the solar, his mood considerably darkened by Bella's obvious need for affection. Clearly, whatever had happened between her and Lucerne had played on her vulnerabilities. She needed to know that her position was still secure, but until Lucerne arrived, he couldn't provide that answer.

Raffe was waiting for him just inside the solar. 'Pretty wench,' he observed, 'and goes as if she cracks nuts with her tail from what I've seen.'

'Go to hell and help your mother make bitch pie!' Vaughan snarled. He wouldn't hear her spoken of like that, regardless of anything else. 'And watch your tongue. Or better still go court my sister. It's what you're here for, isn't it? I did get that letter from Lady Devonshire – or did I misunderstand the point of your visit?'

Raffe stiffened and gave a rather terse bow. 'No. No mistake,' he said.

'Excellent. Then we understand each other.'

Vaughan pushed past him.

The solar was stiflingly, so warm that he was obliged to strip off his coat and roll up his shirtsleeves, much to de Maresi's horror and entertainment. Vaughan threw his coat over a chair back and paced to the far corner, where Henry Tristan had his head stuck in one of the alcoves that overlooked the great hall. He'd changed his hideous salmon-pink stockings for an equally distasteful mint-green pair that matched his slovenly coat. Vaughan paused directly behind him. Tristan's pose meant his cream breeches were pulled tight across his bottom, showing his cheeks to perfection.

'What's so fascinating?' He tapped the upthrust arse.

Henry jerked to attention, nearly knocking himself out on the low lintel in the process. 'Pennerley!' he gasped. 'Nothing, nothing really.' He searched nervously amongst his pockets for his snuffbox which Vaughan retrieved from above the mantelpiece and placed in his hand.

'I'll trust you're not admiring Bella.'

'Erm, no.' Henry looked sheepishly at his toes.

'Then I'll have to assume it's my sister you're ogling.'

'Nothing untoward.' Henry raised his hands. Beneath the layers of powder and paint he was blushing furiously. 'She's a lovely girl, that's all.'

'Correct,' said Vaughan, allowing his lip to curl.

It had the desired effect. Henry's eyes widened in alarm and he scuttled away. Vaughan wanted to laugh. Pitiful little mice, all three of them. He recalled his duties as host and passed around the port, but the conversation was minimal and soon lapsed into pathetic rejoinders.

'I say, Pennerley, can we not have the ladies up here?' Raffe asked, all smiles now he'd recovered his poise. He settled himself on the arm of the fireside chair, causing de Maresi to edge away. 'It's damnable cold in that blasted hall of yours and I'm sure they'd overlook a few glasses in exchange for a bit of warmth.'

'Finally taking me at my word, Raffe? How very unlike you.'

Raffe bowed his head at the rebuke. When he raised it again, he'd fixed on a smile. 'Merely thinking of their welfare. It seems a tad ungallant not to invite them in out of the cold.'

'Very well.' Vaughan dismissed him with an elegant turn of his wrist. 'At least they might have something worthwhile to say for themselves, as well as sparing your necks undue strains.' He twitched his eyebrows at Henry, who sunk even lower into his chair.

Vaughan topped his glass and headed to the window, away from the blast of the fire. Cold was good. It didn't ruin the complexion, or make you sleepy and dim-witted. Besides, he could observe the entire room from here.

Bella restlessly paced the freezing and echoic hall, Niamh's words churning inside her head, around and around and around. 'He'll break your heart.' Well, he'd already done that. 'Just like all the others.' What others, she longed to demand. She wanted to grab Niamh and shake her until the answers tumbled from her lips like confession beads. She already had a nagging suspicion about who one current other might be.

'Has the Vicomte been here long?' she asked.

'De Maresi?' Niamh turned her back to the fire in order to face Bella, pressing her palms together as if in prayer. 'He arrived with my brother. Why do you ask? Is there a problem?'

Bella shook her head. 'Not so far.'

'I confess I find him a little odd myself, but he seems to entertain my brother which is no bad thing. I believe he's helping with the "phantasmagoria".' She gave a puzzled frown. 'It's something to do with the party, some new invention he's brought over from France, I think. Anyway, they've been cackling together about it for days.'

Bella sucked on her lower lip, feeling both vexed and intrigued. Whatever Vaughan was planning with the Frenchman was bound to be ingenious but she doubted that preparing the entertainments was all the pair had been doing.

Damn him. If she'd been able to knit, she'd have made him a cock-warmer. Then perhaps he'd be less inclined to take any fool to his bed while they waited for Lucerne to regain his senses. Assuming he ever did.

'Ladies!' Raffe bounded into the room and gave them a rather heroic bow. 'If you'd like to join us in the warmth, I can offer you an escort.' He planted his hands upon his hips, clearly expecting them each to take an arm. When Niamh did just that, Bella saw no reason to refuse. She clasped his arm, whereupon he swung them both around in a wild circle, then hurried them towards the stairs.

7

The atmosphere in the solar remained subdued despite the ladies' presence. After tea had been served, Vaughan slipped away to play billiards with Henry. Raffe lingered a further half hour making small talk with Niamh before following the gentlemen out with a look of resignation scored across his face.

Niamh remained only a dozen minutes more before announcing her intention to retire. Bella bade her good-night at the top of the stairs and watched her cross the wooden bridge to the south tower before returning to the solar. It was still early compared to the hours she'd grown used to in London, but it was also too late to be wandering about the grounds unescorted. Exploring the surrounding countryside would have to wait until morning, although the notion of creeping about the churchyard in the dark was deliciously enticing. She briefly contemplated searching out the billiards room and peeking in on the men, but quickly dismissed the notion. In his current mood, Vaughan was inclined to be vicious.

De Maresi was slouched in a chair with his legs hooked over the arm when she returned. He stopped her with the press of his red-heeled shoes as she tried to slide past to reach the other fireside chair. 'A moment, *morue*.' He looked at her along the length of his outstretched leg.

Bella stared at his ankle, a grimace on her face, and her

hand raised in a pincer-like shape as if preparing to remove something distasteful. 'What do you want?'

He dug his toe a little deeper into the soft swell of her stomach, forcing her to back into the wing of the leather chair. 'You do not belong here. He's no longer yours, *ma chere*. Better if you left.'

'Better if you kept your nose out of it.' She swiped his foot away from her body and scowled. 'I'll leave when Vaughan asks me to, and not before.'

De Maresi gave a vicious scowl and snapped his teeth at her. Bella snapped her teeth back, then left in a flurry of skirts.

So the nasty scented frog was staking his claim. Well, he was in for a shock if he thought his little display would keep her away. Vaughan was hers. The only person she was going to share him with was Lucerne, and she had little hope of seeing him before the New Year, if at all. Besides, she'd played this game before. Vaughan had tried hard enough to warn her off Lucerne but to no avail. The Vicomte didn't stand a chance.

Her breath surprisingly sharp in her throat, Bella made her way downstairs to the dingy great hall. The candles had long been extinguished and the fire had died down to a bed of embers. She warmed her hands above them and closed her eyes. She had thought that by coming to Pennerley everything would resolve itself, but here she was on her first evening, still alone, still just as ignorant as to why Vaughan had left and no closer to his affections than she'd ever been. In fact, and she couldn't restrain a snort of ironic humour at the thought, she appeared to have a rival. Was she destined always to be competing with one man for another?

She sat on the hearth and poked at the cinders, feeling the night's chill seep into her bones. 'Damn de Maresi, and damn Vaughan for making things so difficult.' She stood and turned her back on the almost dead fire. Silver patches of moonlight shone through the gaps in the shutters and the stained top panes. Darkling shadows crept from the corners and stretched across the floor. She shivered, and wondered if the first Lady Pennerley was the only reputed ghost.

She'd hoped to spend the night with Vaughan; instead she faced a lonely night in a cold bed.

Bella knocked on the door to the kitchens, wondering if any of the servants were still about and could fetch her a hot drink to ward off the cold. When there was no answer, she tried the latch and let herself in.

The kitchens occupied the east wing of the castle, the servants sleeping above. Bella stumbled through the first room, a sort of hallway-cum-buttery, and passed under an archway into a room with a long pitted table. She found a candle on the windowsill and lit it on an ember drawn from the stove.

Soft yellow light bathed her surroundings. Pans and skillets lined the walls and bunched herbs hung from hooks in the ceiling. It reminded her of the homely kitchen at Wyndfell Grange where she'd spent many hours kneading dough and stirring great simmering vats of jam she'd made with berries picked from the hedgerows.

There was jam laid out on the table ready for breakfast, alongside a covered loaf and a jug of milk. Bella poured herself a glass and gulped it down. The dry heat in the solar had left her parched. She found herself a knife next and cut a thick slice of bread.

'You're not at home, you know.'

Bella turned her head mid-bite to find Vaughan poised beneath the archway. How he'd managed to sneak up on her she couldn't fathom, but here he was, sleek and silent as a panther, and she felt a giddy relief at seeing him. She hadn't anticipated his company again tonight. Well, so much for Vicomte de Maresi's assertions that she was surplus to his desires.

Vaughan stepped out of the shadows and threw his coat over a chair back. He always seemed happiest and most dangerous when he was half undressed, as if he was peeling off a layer of civility along with his coat.

'You don't mind, do you?' she said, and held the bread out towards him in an attempt to entice him closer.

Vaughan pursed his lips. His dark eyes twinkled. 'Actually, I do. I like to see maids in the kitchen, not mistresses.' He ignored her offering and picked up the jam jar instead.

'I'm surprised you know where the kitchens are,' she said.

The flickering candlelight played across his skin, highlighting his high cheekbones and the opaline pallor of his skin. He dismissed her remark with a look. 'One should always keep the cook sweet.' He licked his lips, and Bella's breath caught, his languid grace easily throwing her off guard as he drew the silken cravat from around his throat. He drew it across her shoulder, then let it sail into the gloom, where it settled on the stone floor like a silver snake. 'Perhaps I'll entertain you with my intimate knowledge of the kitchens some time.' He bent towards her and the edges of his shirt parted, displaying a tiny sliver of skin.

Bella longed to touch him, to trace the line of exposed flesh from his throat to his breastbone, to run her hands across his chest and feel his tight male nipples harden against the centre of her palms. Her lips parted in anticipation as Vaughan leaned closer, but instead of a kiss, he dipped two fingers into the jam jar and offered them to her to suck.

Her eyes firmly locked upon his, she dabbed his fingers with tip of her tongue. The sweet, tart taste of blackberries mingled with the salty taste of his skin as she sucked, while a knot of apprehension tightened within her belly. Despite his magical allure, Vaughan was not to be trusted. He was far too dangerous.

The sticky sweet jam was soon gone, but Bella continued to circle her tongue around the sensitive pads of his fingers and into the gap between them. 'Getting ideas?' he teased. A smile twitching upon his lips, he pulled his fingers from her mouth with a pop. They dipped straight back into the jar. This time he raised the sticky mess to his own lips.

Viscous drips, reminiscent of the red wine earlier, ran down his bared forearms. He was offering himself again, she realised, her breathing quickening at the thought. Bella lapped a trail up the length of his inner arm. She wanted him for herself tonight. There'd been times without Lucerne, but not so many of them as people like Henry Tristan and Raffe Devonshire imagined. She was not Vaughan's paramour. That honour had belonged to Lucerne. Their relationship had always been a delicate balance, and too much time alone with Vaughan would have quickly destroyed it. Lucerne was the pivot, the constant. Everything revolved around him. She almost expected to find him bound to a spindly chair in the corner waiting his turn. Her relationship with Vaughan only existed through Lucerne.

Vaughan coated his fingers a third time.

Take me to bed, she pleaded with her eyes, while his gleamed with sadistic mischief. He smeared the berries across her mouth and chin.

Bella stared at him, her mouth open, still waiting for the kiss that never came. Vaughan licked his lips. 'Come with me.' He took her by the hand and led her into the pantry.

Row upon row of glittering glass jars lined the deep shelves: clear, green and brown. There were pickles on the bottom, preserves on the top, and other more exotic spices nestled between butter dishes and tea caddies. Vaughan took down a huge jar of spiced marmalade and pushed his whole hand inside. It came out glistening with orange glaze which he tasted then smeared down her neck and across the bib front of her dress.

His tongue slid up the side of her neck. Bella squirmed as he caught her earlobe between his teeth. Hot and thrilling, his breath warmed her ear. The sensation tingled through her body, awakening every nerve, making her want to cling to him. But it was never wise to make it too easy for him. For Vaughan, the fun was in the challenge. He'd lose interest if he thought she was too eager.

'You must be pretty desperate to want me twice in one day,' she said.

'I prefer to think of it as starved of opportunity. Besides, de Maresi bores me.'

So, it wasn't just de Maresi's fantasy. Had she really expected him to live like a monk? The knowledge gave her a sickly thrill, but she contained her rage and let her anger burn cold.

Vaughan tugged his shirt over his head, presented her

with his slender torso and the ragged silver scar that ran across his ribs.

'What makes you think I'm willing? You humiliated me in front of your servant and your guests.'

'What else did you expect?' He grasped her jaw and forced a kiss.

Bella shoved him off. 'I'm your guest.'

'My whore.' His eyebrows arched, daring her to argue.

'Fine. Have it your way.' She grabbed the nearest jar and smeared blackcurrants across his torso.

Vaughan laughed.

Bella took down another jar. His chest looked like an artist's palette by the time she'd finished. Streamers of different colours and textures matted in his dark curls. The pungent smells of exotic spices blended with his own unique scent. Finally, she dashed nutmeg across his loins and rubbed her face into the mess. Through his clothing she felt his erection jump and she tongued along its length.

'Ah, is this the sweetmeat you crave? What would you have done if you'd found another waiting?'

Bella shoved him backwards, her desire for him briefly flaring into anger. She thought of how he rolled around the floor with Lucerne, fists and elbows flying, and of how excited it made her to watch. She wanted to battle with him in the same way. The light caught the silvery length of his old duelling scar again. 'Teach me to fence,' she demanded.

Vaughan shook his head. He pulled her upright to nibble at her lips and chin, and cupped her hand over his cock. 'Oh, I think you're long past the need for lessons.'

Bella smacked him hard across the thigh, leaving a sticky

plum print on his pantaloons. Damn him for his insinuations, but she was hard pressed not to smile. She gave his prick a squeeze and basked in the victory of his sharp intake of breath.

'Besides, ladies don't wield swords.'

'Well, you've already made it clear to everyone that I'm no lady, and since my reputation is already wrecked I may as well reap some benefit.' She squeezed again, watching his cheeks flush. 'Truly, it's a wonder you let me associate with faultless Lady Niamh.'

'Your reputation was wrecked long before you arrived here. Let's not forget the time you've spent in London as Lucerne's doxy, and you were a brazen hussy even before that.'

'That must be your type, then.'

Vaughan licked her cheek. 'As I said, I'm starved. And better you than Tristan or my sister.'

'You wouldn't!'

His eyes glittered like cold fire. Bella jabbed him in the stomach. 'No,' he drawled. 'She's not my type. Too pure, too virginal.'

'That never stopped you with my friend Louisa,' she blurted, completely scandalised. She turned her back on him in disgust, shocked that he could even jest over such a subject.

Vaughan nuzzled up to her bare neck. 'Why, Bella, I do believe you're mad at me.' His tongue dabbed over her pulse point and explored the hollow of her collarbone. The touch was soft and teasing at first. It made her squirm and her toes curl. Slowly, the caress became firmer, until she was sure he would leave his mark upon her skin. Despite that, she still couldn't push him away. It was too exquisite, his touch too precious to her.

She batted half-heartedly at him, but he caught her wrist and pressed a lingering kiss to the back of her hand, before sliding his tongue into the V between her index and middle fingers. 'You know the rules, Miss Rushdale.' More hungry kisses smeared over the curve of her thumb. 'But perhaps you tire of the game. Perhaps you should have stayed in London with Lucerne.' A tooth troubled the delicate skin of her wrist. 'Or did you not share his relish for Miss St John?'

'You knew!' Bella spun around to face him, her eyes blazing. 'You knew and you didn't tell me.'

Vaughan gave a nonchalant shrug.

'You bastard!' She shoved him hard, then flailed at him with her fists. 'You ran away and left me there to find out. How long had it been going on? How long had you known?'

Vaughan wrestled her down onto the tiles, where he rolled on top of her. He trapped one arm between their bodies and held the other above her head in a vice-like grip. 'Listen to me,' he snarled. 'You had to see it for yourself. You'd never have believed it otherwise.' He closed his mouth over hers, stopping her words of denial and protest with the force of his kiss.

Bella fought for breath and release. She wanted to hurt him for his betrayal. No matter that his erection was pressing hard against her leg, and that her traitorous body was responding with wanton ease. 'It's why you left, isn't it?' She continued to struggle against his torso. 'Because you didn't want to play second fiddle.'

The rainbow of jam and pickles squelched between them,

making his torso slippery. Bella managed to extract her arm and forced a hand against his throat to pry him off.

'I was already playing second fiddle to you.'

'Like hell.' Although ... maybe it was true. Their triune had never been equal. It had always been her and Lucerne, or Vaughan and Lucerne, or frequently her in the middle of the two men, but never Vaughan at the centre.

She let go of him and turned her head aside. Everything was hopelessly wrong, tearing her apart, and she had no idea how to make things right again before their relationship was no more than tattered shreds.

Vaughan idly traced his fingers through the mess upon her breast, his expression unusually guarded. He troubled one nipple and painted jam around the areola. Bella dug her teeth into her lip, caught on a knife-edge of arousal with tears pricking her eyes. Her white dress was ruined. The mottling of crushed berries would never come out of the delicate muslin. 'You've ruined it,' she snapped, seeking an outlet for her fluctuating emotions.

'Then I'll buy you two, one scarlet and one gold. None of this virginal white rubbish for you.'

'It's the fashion.'

'It's a lie.' There was a burr of heat behind his words.

Bella scowled.

'And while we're speaking so plainly, you can rid yourself of this ridiculous knot of hair piled on your head.' He tugged out the pins that held it in place until it tumbled over her shoulders and breasts in a wavy cascade.

Bella turned her head away from him. There were tears bound to her eyelashes. One solitary bead escaped and rolled down her cheek where Vaughan caught it upon his fingertips.

'Bella.'

The pain of her future loss sliced through her. She couldn't hope to keep him. Once he realised Lucerne wasn't joining them, his interest in her would vanish. She'd never really been anything other than a compromise he'd made in order to have Lucerne.

'Shh-hh!' Vaughan licked at the tiny bed of moisture on his fingertips. 'Is he worth your tears?'

She shook her head. He thought she was weeping over Lucerne.

'Am I?'

Bella dug her teeth into her swollen lips. He'd probably be horrified if he realised how many tears she'd shed for him over the last few weeks. 'Vaughan.' Her voice cracked, and escaped as barely a whisper. She pushed her face into the crook of his neck. 'It's all going wrong, isn't it?'

'No, my nightingale, it's just going differently.'

He pushed himself up so that he was straddling her hips, and drew lewd doodles in the jam on her skin. Despite the playfulness of his touch, she sensed he too was questioning their relationship. She didn't dare look up into his eyes for fear of what she would find in their violet depths. When she finally braved a glimpse, she found him licking his lips.

Vaughan leaned forwards and licked the jam from her nipple. He sucked the dark teat deep into his mouth, then released it with a smack. 'Why, Bella, I do believe you're the tastiest jam tart I've ever eaten.' He caught up the hem of her dress and impatiently pushed it up her thighs.

'Vaughan!' She batted at him ineffectually, but his wicked grin was infectious.

'Yes, Bella.' He trickled honey across her exposed belly and thighs, then moulded spikes into her downy thatch.

'No-o, don't. It'll be hell to get out.'

'I'll let you borrow my razor.'

She couldn't stop her eyes from bulging at the thought. It wasn't the first time he'd threatened to denude her quim. The proposition was both frightening and thrilling. The heel of his hand pressed over her mons. One finger pushed into her heat and found her clitoris, then fiery hunger poured through her body and her fears were neatly pushed aside. Her nipples stood proud, her nubbin aching for him to do more than just press. She felt his cock jump against her thigh and wriggled to get him closer.

'Ah, ah,' he teased, his fingers working the slick folds of her quaint. 'Say please.'

'Pretty please.'

'I don't think you want it enough yet.'

'I do.' She lifted her hips towards him. 'Don't tease, Vaughan. Please ...' She craved the closeness, the sliding together of their bodies and the feel of him hard and vital within her. For the rest of the night she wanted to drown in his fire and feel wanted and loved. 'Please.'

'Tempt me a little first.' He sat back again, wrenched open his pantaloons and poured. Honey dribbled down his shaft. Bella stared at the golden drops, arousal thickening more keenly in her throat. Vaughan guided her hands up and down the length of his shaft, and the sugary glaze mingled with his own pearlescent icing. 'Yes, good. Like that, Bella. Like that.'

'No. I want to suck you.' She curled her fingers around the shaft and teased her tongue around the tip. 'Mmm.' He laced his fingers through her dark hair and urged her closer. His length slid into her throat. Bella almost gagged before she relaxed and let him fuck her mouth.

His hips moved with an increasingly jerky rhythm. Bella fanned her fingers out across his hipbones. She traced his balls with her thumbs, and pre-come flooded onto her tongue.

Oh, yes, you like that, don't you, she thought, and slowed her sucks, pulling him back from the brink. He groaned in protest, his cock impatiently buffeting her lips, but Bella simply lay back and shook her head. 'Not nice to be left wanting, is it, my lord?' She pressed his hand between her thighs again.

'I've a mind to spend on your tongue for that.' He scowled, but his fingers still worked their magic, setting her crooning against his chest.

'Take me, Vaughan,' she whispered into the sparse black hair between his nipples.

'I don't think so.'

'Why not?'

'You know why not.'

I'm not Lucerne's any more, she thought, but she couldn't will herself to say it. It was too final. 'Please, Vaughan. I need it . . . hard.'

He rolled her onto her stomach, with his hand still covering her cunt. 'The answer's still no.' His cock pushed between her closed thighs. 'And since your delectable rear is probably still sore from the journey, I think we'll just content ourselves with a little friction.' He pushed up into the slippery warmth of her vulva. Bella wriggled and whimpered at his closeness. He was almost inside her, nudging her clit and teasing her with the potential of the slick rhythm. Just a slight change of angle and he'd slide deep, right where she wanted him. She didn't think he'd pull out. It would feel too good. They both knew how good it felt. In the past at Lauwine he'd taken her like that and hadn't cared for the consequences. He'd been softer, more vulnerable then as well. She lifted her hips again, begging with the jerks of her body as their pace became more frantic. 'Please, please ...'

'Don't be foolish.' He was still shaking his head even as he came. His hot seed bathed her, making everything more slippery. Simultaneously, it seemed to ignite sparks in her clit. The weird eddy spread, tightened in her womb and flexed her spine. Giddy with pleasure, Bella screamed out her climax, then collapsed against the quarry tiles.

Vaughan rolled off her. There was always something sleek and unbearably sexy about him after he'd just come. It was his scent and the glow of his skin, she thought, and the way his hair curled into tighter ringlets. How his nipples stood proud long after his erection faded.

Where would they stand come morning? He crouched over her and gave her cunt a single wet lick. 'Tart,' he teased. He fastened his pantaloons and was gone, leaving her sprawled across the pantry floor in a pool of preserves.

8

Bella lay for several minutes starring into the blackness of the pantry roof. The nearest thing to hand to clean herself on was his shirt. Once she'd wiped away the worst of the mess she rose shakily to her feet. The housekeeper would have a fit about the mess in the morning, but dealing with the master's foibles was par for the course. No one would mention it, though he might suffer a few aggrieved looks. Stained and dishevelled, she tiptoed out of the pantry to find Raffe waiting for her, his thighs spread wide and his elbows propped on the back of one of the spindly chairs.

'Bravo.' He applauded.

Shocked, Bella just stared at him. There was no question that he'd seen everything, or that Vaughan had known. Of course he'd known or he'd have laid out Raffe like a buttered goose.

'You were magnificent. I can see why Pennerley appreciates you so.' His eyes crinkled as he smiled.

Bella folded her arms across her breasts and glowered at him. Why was he always there to spy on her?

'Though maybe,' Raffe continued, his grin hopelessly and annoyingly charming, 'he doesn't appreciate you enough.'

'Beast.' She scooped up the half-burned candle from the table and swept out of the kitchens. Ah! The arrogance of the man, acting as if she was performing purely for his amusement.

Though she was quite flattered as well.

It was chilly at the top of the north tower. Bella peeled off her ruined dress and sponged herself down with cold water from the washstand. She soaped her sticky thatch with a sliver of rose-scented soap, but even that wasn't enough and she was forced to trim away her downy curls with a pair of embroidery scissors. No doubt Vaughan would comment on that the next time.

Damn him! She wondered if Devonshire was still downstairs, and what sort of infernal innuendo she could expect from him tomorrow. At least there was no puritanical ghost to haunt her for her licentiousness.

Bella tugged on a clean shift and sunk onto the edge of the soft mattress. She should have thought everything through more thoroughly before coming here, and arrived with a strategy instead of relying on fate to guide her. She wasn't even sure what had just happened downstairs. Had he wanted to fight, to show off in front of Devonshire, or something else? One thing she was certain of, she needed Lucerne here, not for protection but because he was the lynchpin of their precarious relationship. Without him, they were just passing time.

'Bella. Bella Rushdale.'

Devonshire, she thought for one horrid moment and pulled the coverlet tight about her shoulders. To her relief, it was Henry who peered around the door instead. 'Can I come in?'

He promptly slid across the threshold with his easy catlike grace.

'What did you want at this hour, Henry?' She found her hairbrush and sat in front of the mirror to work it through her mattered locks. Vaughan might not like it pinned on top of her head, but if he wanted to see it flying about her shoulders, riddling it with jam hadn't been the smartest move.

Henry lifted her ruined dress from the floor and twirled it around to examine the damage. 'What in God's name have you been up to?'

'You're not exactly pretty either, Henry.'

Henry fluffed his preposterously curled hair. He was still dressed in his hideous mint-greens, to which he'd added an intricately embroidered smock as a dressing-gown. In terms of colour explosion, there was little to choose between them. 'I'll have you know, I had this sent all the way from India.'

'Well, mine's a Pennerley original.' Bella smiled and attacked another knot of hair.

'That much I'd already ascertained. I assume it is just jam and nothing else.'

Bella threw the brush at him. 'What else would it be?'

'I'm sure I can't imagine. Here, let me.' He scooped up the hairbrush which had fallen short of hitting him and carefully divided her sticky hair into sections before starting on the knots. 'Obviously you've no regrets about coming here.'

'Jealous?'

'Not in the way you imagine. I like to keep abreast of change and Pennerley's so mutable I'd spend all day whirling like a top.'

'You're just frightened he'll gobble you up.'

'As I observe he's just done to you.'

Bella nervously wet her lips. 'It just got a little heated, and messy.'

Henry met her gaze in the mirror, his moss-green eyes hard and glassy. 'You do realise that not all is well between them, don't you, Bella?'

The remaining strength seemed to seep out of her body. Of course she knew, but having him say it made it seem far more serious. 'Vaughan's just angry about Georgiana, that's all.'

'But that isn't all.'

'Did you deliberately come here to vex me?'

Henry raised his hands. 'Of course not. I'm simply pointing out that Lucerne isn't here, and he's unlikely to willingly walk onto a battlefield when he can content himself in London with Miss St John.'

'He'll get bored soon enough.' She dismissed his statement with a bat of her wrist.

Henry put down the hairbrush and squeezed her shoulders. 'He's been seeing her since New Year, Bella. I think that with you and Vaughan gone, he'll find himself a bride.'

'What?' Bella lurched up off the stool. 'He wouldn't.' He was supposed to marry her. She'd been waiting long enough. It took a moment for her to realise she wasn't at all sure she'd accept his proposal now.

Henry gently took her hands and clasped them tight within his own, but the affectionate squeeze did little to assuage her feelings of doubt and displacement. 'The matrons will have their daughters lined up before him. He's a good catch, Bella. It won't take long for him to find a dainty little miss with a fortune or a title who's prepared to bear him a whole nursery full of children while he humps half the county.'

'Lucerne's not like that. He's kind.' What was she saying? The Lucerne she'd known at Lauwine wasn't like that, but the Lucerne she'd known in London the last six months was very much like that. He was no longer the same man who worried over her lost in a thunderstorm. No matter what Vaughan thought, Henry was right. It was all horribly, horribly wrong. It wasn't just different. It was rotten.

Bella turned away from Henry again. The tears that had threatened in the pantry prickled in her eyes again. 'But he loves Vaughan,' she gasped.

'Ah,' Henry put an arm around her shoulder, 'but does he? Has he ever said it?'

Her head sagged. Of course he hadn't. Lucerne never told anyone he loved them. He was incapable of it. That's where people had them all wrong. They thought Vaughan was the cold-hearted one, when really he was an emotional hurricane. Lucerne was the one who couldn't articulate his feelings. Three years she'd believed he'd loved her, but he'd never said it. Not once.

Weary and bitter, she pushed Henry's hand from her shoulder. 'Leave me. I need to sleep.'

'Of course. Everything is simpler in daylight.' He headed to the door, his stride curiously steady and manly without his cane rattling about his ankles. 'Goodnight, Bella.' He went out, only to return a moment later. 'There was just one thing. Devonshire. Has Lady Niamh mentioned him?'

'No, Henry. Not a thing.'

He grinned and disappeared into the shadows again.

'Wait.' Bella scampered across the room to catch up with him. 'Have you met before?'

'Oh, ages ago, when she was about twelve,' he said, his wistful gaze telling as it slid towards the cruck roof.

'Not as such, then,' she remarked. Actually, she'd meant Devonshire, not Niamh.

'That's Vaughan's fault for keeping her locked up here like Rapunzel.'

Bella tactfully remained silent. Poor Henry, he was clearly besotted after one afternoon. 'Goodnight, Henry,' she said with an anxious smile. She just hoped for his sake that Vaughan approved of his suit, because she didn't want to see him hurt.

Raffe sat in the kitchen a long while after Bella fled. He wondered if it had been wise to reveal himself to her. Perhaps not, but his applause had been genuine. He couldn't help but admire her spirit and appetite for sex. A pity she was wasting herself on Pennerley. Clearly, there was something deep between them, though he hesitated to call it love. He wasn't sure Pennerley was capable of that.

On which subject, he supposed he'd have to up his suit of Lady Niamh tomorrow in order to calm the waters. Pennerley hadn't actually invited him to watch their little tableau, although he'd been aware of his presence. Raffe ran his hands through his short hair and scratched. He knew he should be grateful to his mother and to Pennerley for the opportunity to court Niamh, but lord, he had no desire to bed her. Oh, she was beautiful and would bring a handsome dowry, but Raffe hoped that when he married, if he had to marry, it would be to someone who would reciprocate his desires, not send him to the maids and mistresses for solace.

He reached over, grasped the jam jar from the table and dipped in a spoon. Bella Rushdale was far more to his taste: curvy, wilful and determined. He curled his tongue around the back of the spoon, imagining licking the soft underswell of her breast. She was perfect. He could almost sense her beneath him, as she'd been with Vaughan, soiled and panting out her orgasm against the cold stone tiles. Niamh, he was certain, would only entertain the notion of sexual intimacy fully clothed in a big white bed, while Bella would be equally game in a hayloft, on the muddy banks of a river or even halfway up the stairs.

His breathing sharp, Raffe stood awkwardly and made his way back through the darkened kitchen and up the steps into the great hall. Great shafts of moonlight still streaked the stone floor and painted a latticework across the enormous dining table. He stood for several minutes just staring at the bottom four steps of the staircase. The image of her, bent over with her skirts cast about her shoulders and her pale plump cheeks bared haunted him. It would certainly trouble his dreams tonight.

9

Bella woke the following morning to find her sleep had been profound. There was a maid standing by the end of her bed when she opened her eyes, holding an old-fashioned riding habit with a skirt that actually sat around the waist. 'It's Lady Niamh's, miss. She said I should bring it you, because she wasn't sure if you had anything, and she wondered if you'd join her for a canter.'

A chance to explore sounded just the thing to blow the grit of the city away, and to escape from Devonshire. Bella yawned and stretched. 'What time is it?' Beyond the quarrel windows the air was thick with mist, the church spire just a hazy outline.

'About ten o'clock, miss. Lady Niamh's awaiting you in the great hall. You were missed at breakfast.'

'Ah!' Bella threw back the covers and rolled out of bed in what she hoped wasn't too ungainly a manner. Ten o'clock! Lucerne had taught her some very bad habits.

The water in the jug was warm. Bella washed the last traces of jam from her body, then let the girl fuss over her hair and attire. The former she bound up in elaborate loops before pinning a minute feathered hat on top. Bella stared bemusedly at her transforming image. Vaughan would hate it, but then he hadn't invited her riding. At least he'd approve of the dress. It was bottle green and shaped like a long riding coat, which buttoned down the front almost to her ankles, and showed only a glimpse of the fawn underskirt. She wondered if Niamh had ever worn it.

'It's a little tight about the bust,' said the girl. 'I can let out the seams.'

'No, leave it.' Bella stopped her. She'd simply leave the top few buttons unfastened and show a sliver of her chemise. She took a few turns about the room, pleased with the way the heavy fabric swished about her ankles. Yes, she was definitely ready for a wild chase across the hillside. Ladylike trots about St James's Park just weren't the same.

Niamh was impatiently pacing by the enormous great hall door when Bella came down. 'Stay-a-bed,' she chastened. 'Do come along.' She grabbed her hand and barked at the footman to open the door.

Puzzled, Bella followed her into the weak morning sunlight. Mist still lingered on the hilltops, but there were some patches of bright blue sky nestled between the clouds. 'Has something happened?' she asked.

Niamh paced briskly across the courtyard. 'They weren't supposed to come.' The footman barely had the gate open before she swished past him and stomped onto the moat bridge.

Bella followed rather more carefully. The wooden boards were still shiny from the night's rainfall. 'Has Viscount Marlinscar arrived?'

'Who?' Niamh came to an abrupt halt, so that Bella had to avoid colliding with her. 'Riding. It was supposed to be just you and me this morning, but as is his wont, my brother deigned to interfere.' Her eyes shone like splinters of ice, while her cheeks burned with livid fury. 'Of course he didn't suggest it, but he arranged it all the same. He asked my plans at breakfast and I couldn't keep silent.'

'And then what?' Bella asked, trying to keep up with her tale.

'Why, they invited themselves, of course.' Exasperated, Niamh stamped her foot hard against the rickety boards.

Still not entirely sure who *they* were, Bella looked around the yard for enlightenment. Four horses were tethered in the stable yard, which meant two of the gentlemen must be joining them. She prayed for both Raffe and de Maresi's absence.

'Is that a big problem?'

'Pah!' Niamh snorted in annoyance. Her blue eyes narrowed. 'But lo, forget joy, Tristan und Isolde have arrived.'

'Tristan and who?' Bella coughed and hid her smile, because Devonshire was already through the wicket gate and striding towards them, grinning.

'Lady Niamh, and good morning, Miss Rushdale. I trust you passed a pleasant night.' He swept into an excessively low bow. Bella turned her back on him. He could get down and grovel and she still wouldn't forgive him for spying last night. Suddenly, riding seemed far less appealing.

Henry followed him onto the boards, and gave them both rather less exuberant nods. He was without his cane again this morning, and seemed rather quiet without it clattering about his feet. He smiled warmly when she caught his eye, and cocked his wrist to show her a plaited riding crop dangling artistically in its place. The leather was intertwined with pink and cream ribbons, and perfectly matched his cravat and probably his stockings, although his Hessians prevented an immediate confirmation. He swished the crop through the air just shy of Raffe's backside, which at least raised a snort of mirth from Niamh.

Raffe stiffened and glowered at Henry, who slumped languidly against the wooden railing, the picture of indolence.

'Shall we, ladies? Before the weather breaks.' Raffe pulled himself into the saddle of a dappled gelding.

'Save me from him, please,' Niamh hissed into Bella's ear, before the grooms helped them into their saddles.

Save her? Dammit, she needed saving herself!

The little group followed a twisty lane out from the castle, past the lake to the west, then south. To begin with they rode in single file, not concerning themselves with conversation, but enjoying the wild borderlands and the wind on their faces. It wasn't until the track petered out into open grassland that Bella pushed her mount forwards, eager to spare both herself and Niamh the discomfort of Lord Devonshire's company. After last night's spectacle, she wasn't certain of his discretion. Chances were even now he was undressing her with his eyes and picturing another kind of ride. Alas, as she drew level with the rear of Niamh's mare, Henry cantered past her and moved in, allowing Devonshire the perfect opportunity to trot alongside her.

Well, thank you, Henry, she cursed inwardly.

'I think I have a rival,' Raffe remarked, his voice soft but ladled with a burr of self-deprecating humour.

'For what, impertinence?'

He chuckled. 'Ah, is that how it's to be? Chastised for my simple adoration.' His smile reached his eyes, confirming the truth of his meaning. 'I won't apologise for last night. I won't do you the discourtesy. You were magnificent. A vision to behold.'

'Hmph!' she snorted. Part of her wanted to bring her hand to his face and wipe away his smirk. Another revelled in the compliment. 'You presume too much, sir. We're barely acquainted.'

'That can easily be changed.'

He drove his horse closer in response, so that his knee butted her long skirts. Vexed, Bella pursed her lips and edged her horse away. Raffe simply followed.

'Oh, you're beastly!' But it was impossible to remain angry with him when his laugh was so infectious and his grin endearingly lopsided. There was no malice in his hazel eyes when he looked at her, just bright flecks of honey gold, and the promise of pleasure. They clouded a moment later when Niamh's tinkling laughter drifted back to them on the breeze.

'I think my luck might be running out.'

'For what?'

His sullen pout tugged at the last knots of her resentment.

'For claiming my bride.'

'Niamh!' she gasped, following his gaze to her narrow shoulders. 'No!' Why, they'd hardly spoken the previous evening, and there wasn't even a whisper of friendship between them, let alone affection.

'You don't think we're suited, do you?'

Bella refrained from shaking her head, and instead gazed resolutely ahead.

'It's all right. As a matter of fact, I agree.'

'Then, why?'

Raffe raised his hands palms up. 'Mama expects and I,

being a dutiful son and recumbent on her good will, do as I'm told.' He shrugged. 'She's more than a good match, and there's the title and the estates. Pennerley's not showing any interest in the marriage game, but I guess you'd already know that.'

Bella scowled. As if she needed any reminders of where Vaughan's interests lay. He'd no intention of ever burdening himself with a wife, he'd said so on numerous occasions. A squabble with Lucerne was unlikely to change that.

'Don't you think you should do some wooing?' she said.

Raffe took his reins in one hand. 'I would, you understand. The plan was to ensnare her by Hallowe'en, which gives me what?' He counted the days on his fingers. 'Another two days. But the thing is, I'd much rather not.' His glittering, mischievous eyes met hers. 'Give me an excuse, Miss Rushdale ... Bella, and I'll leave them alone. It's obvious Tristan's as eager as I am not.'

'And I'm quite certain I can't imagine what you're suggesting.'

'Can you not?' His grin only intensified.

Bella pursed her lips and prayed she didn't blush. She could imagine only too well what he was suggesting. Come to my bed and help me escape. Save me from an arrangement I've no stomach for. The arrangement wasn't to her taste either.

'And what of Vaughan?'

'To my mind, he only seems to use you for his pleasure.'

Bella scowled. 'You're being absurd.'

Raffe theatrically raised his hand to his brow. 'Alas then, I'm doomed to my instructions.' He flicked the reins, all set to spur the gelding forwards.

'Wait! Why go along with this charade?'

'Mama can be quite fearsome, Miss Rushdale, and while I'd much rather a wife to my taste, I have to be realistic too. Take a look around. It's all Pennerley's. There are other estates dotted around the country, as well.'

Bella swept her gaze across the cloud-capped hilltops, the dark green woodlands that girdled their slopes and the streaks of barley, yellow amongst the billowing grasslands. Did Vaughan really own all this? Probably. He was a marquis after all, just one step down from a duke, and he lived in a castle. Still, the thought that he'd sell his sister for an allegiance like some feudal lord brought the taste of bile to her throat. She'd always believed Vaughan somewhat nobler than to force a loveless marriage.

'Of course,' Raffe continued, 'if the dame prefers another fool, I might be persuaded to bow out gracefully. Tristan's not a bad sort.'

Bella glanced back towards the castle. That was the difference really; she wasn't prepared to bow out of Vaughan's life, gracefully or otherwise. She should be there, seeking truths and clarifying her situation with Vaughan, not entertaining the advances of this handsome but feckless rogue.

She turned her horse. Enough with the pointless chatter.

'Hey, where are you going?' Raffe called, but Bella ignored him and urged her horse back the way they'd come.

'Said the wrong thing?' she heard Henry shout.

'Evidently,' Raffe replied.

Thankfully, neither followed.

* * *

He was in her room. The scent of her was on the freshly smoothed bedclothes. Vaughan lingered in the entrance until the maids saw him and scattered. He wasn't sure if they were afraid for their virtues or his temper; maybe a touch of both.

Once they were gone, he strode in and surveyed the changes her arrival had brought. Lady's toiletries on the dressing table, fresh flowers by the bedside, a dried streak of jam upon the floor. He bent to examine it with a smile. 'Bella.' Her name slipped from his tongue. There was much they still needed to say, but at least they'd addressed the first hurdle. She knew that he knew about Georgiana.

Vaughan crossed to the west-facing window and cast it wide to the breeze. The early mist was clearing, blown away by the crisp autumnal wind. Sunlight streaked the fields and hedgerows, and painted windows of sky across the surface of the moat. He'd imagined them here together, all three, beneath his roof. He'd never for a moment thought that it wouldn't turn out that way. 'Lucerne,' he hissed into the wind. 'Come to me.' Idly, he toyed with the curtain cord, coiling it around his hands and pulling so that the burgundy loops drew tight. When the stupid bugger did turn up, this was where he'd bring him. He'd tie him tight. Get an artist to paint him horn-mad and ashamed, because Lucerne was deeply ashamed of their bond, despite his rare public flirting.

Vaughan shook his head so his dark hair fell across his face. Bella was still as much of a necessity as she'd ever been. She'd have to be convinced to forgive the fool. Honestly, what had he been thinking, flaunting Georgiana before her? He was lucky she'd merely walked out and not set the house on fire, although part of him wished he'd seen her face. He could imagine the spark. Oh yes, it was cruel and vicious. He loved the way her eyes narrowed when she was riled, how they crinkled at the corners, her mouth becoming a tightly pursed moue and her chin stuck out. 'No,' she'd growl and it was like music to his ears.

'Ah, this is where you're hiding.' The Vicomte de Maresi swanned into the room and collapsed onto the bed. 'I was looking for you. He arranged himself in what he presumed was an enticing manner. Vaughan barely gave him a glance. He was irritated enough to find he'd been sneaked up upon. Too deep in thought, that was the problem. The stairs groaned so much he should have had plenty of warning.

'What do you want?'

The Frenchman's narrow nostrils flared. 'Surely you jest.' He forced a high-pitched laugh. 'They've all gone riding.' He peered up through his eyelashes. 'And I fancied a ride myself.'

'Then you should have joined them.' Vaughan closed the window. He paused for a moment, staring unseeing at the multitude of diamond-shaped pains. He'd made a mistake when he'd salved his lust with François de Maresi.

It had been the evening of the Gillrays' summer ball. For six months he'd tolerated Lucerne's dalliance with Miss St John. When he'd grown tired of watching Bella's attempts to conceal herself with her fan, he'd taken himself off to the garden. The evening had been balmy. He'd stopped in a tranquil piece of lavender-scented wilderness, far from the crowd on the lawn and by the newly fashioned maze. De Maresi hadn't found him. He'd followed him. On his knees he'd begged for a kiss and given so much more.

Vaughan had offered neither encouragement nor rebuke when de Maresi had nuzzled at his breeches, then slipped him out and engulfed his prick. It was only the second time they'd met. The first had been New Year's Eve. Clearly his sharp tongue had made a lasting impression.

After supping down his seed, the silly fool had thanked him for the pleasure and then exposed himself, obviously expecting the favour to be returned. Vaughan had walked away and the Vicomte had shadowed him ever since. He'd finally won his reward when he'd introduced Vaughan to the wonders of the lantern. Ah, yes. He had to humour the Frenchman a little longer, tempting as it was to drop him into the dirty water of the moat and push Raffe Devonshire in alongside.

'You've been ignoring me since she came,' De Maresi whined.

'Since who came?' Vaughan wanted to hear him say it, just to hear him choke upon the name, but de Maresi refused to play, pouting effeminately instead. 'I don't see what the attraction is. She couldn't keep you in London.'

Vaughan smiled, slow and wide, letting his upper lip curl. Leaving London wasn't about Bella. It was about keeping his sanity.

The Vicomte sniffed and threw himself back onto the mattress, an act which rucked up his cream linen breeches and emphasised both his hipbones and the erection that tented the fabric between them. 'Take pity,' he whined, 'you heartless cur.'

'Take pity!' Vaughan snorted. That would involve a pillow and a rather colder heart than he actually had. No, as amusing and annoying as he found the Frenchman, he wasn't ready to commit murder just yet.

De Maresi gave a plaintive and rather enticing wiggle, accompanied by a puppy-dog stare. Nice hard cock, said his gaze. Even nicer easy arse, said the wiggle.

Vaughan's libido sparked, despite his revulsion, although he tried to shrug the feeling off. He knew he was being manipulated. Really the dalliance shouldn't have survived beyond the first precious fuck. The only reason it had was out of boredom and perhaps a hint of loneliness. He wanted Lucerne, but he'd had to walk away. He couldn't sit back in London and watch things stagnate any further. 'If you want me, you'll have to tempt me a lot more than that,' he said. 'Because all I see at the moment is a scrawny overscented frog.'

The Vicomte reached out towards him, but Vaughan backed away. 'No. Don't touch.'

'Then how am I supposed to . . .' His words petered out, but a pale grey spark lit in his eyes just a moment later. 'I know. How about I show you what I'd like you to do?'

'Hmm,' Vaughan responded with a non-committal grunt, then watched the Vicomte peel off his clothes. Canary-yellow coat, cream breeches and waistcoat, stockings and shoes, and enough filigree to decorate five suits. Vaughan was enormously fond of decorative metalwork and beading himself, but he reserved his finery for evening wear. Swanning about in the English, almost Welsh, countryside covered in gold and seed pearls didn't win you any style points. Practicality was what counted and that meant sturdy boots, warm wool and broadcloth. Still, the body beneath wasn't bad, but even that wasn't much of a temptation. He'd seen countless naked bodies over the years, and actually he preferred it when there was still a bit of cloth left on.

De Maresi shuffled up the bed until his head rested upon the pillow, his arms at his sides, then he curled his legs over his head and braced his feet against the wall. Vaughan cocked an eyebrow, vaguely amused by the contortion. It was interesting, but hardly enticing to watch the Frenchman's spine curve and his bottom waving above his head. He was about to remark as much, when de Maresi opened his mouth and did what should have been impossible. He took the whole of his erect cock into his own mouth.

'My God!' Vaughan felt his jaw drop, and the exclamation rolled off his tongue before he could stop it. 'How?' He drew closer to the bed and tilted his head to get a better view. It was incredible, like something from a travelling sideshow. Entranced, he dropped to his knees and rested his elbows upon the bedspread.

He guessed this explained a goodly part of de Maresi's narcissism and his pretty incredible cock-sucking technique. Plenty of individual practice.

Did it feel the same, he wondered? Why wouldn't it?

Crimson circles blossomed around the impressions of de Maresi's fingertips upon his back. His balls stood out, ruddy and proud. Vaughan watched de Maresi's bottom lip rise and fall as he sucked, while his hips rocked, dictating the rhythm of the motion. Credit where it was due, he couldn't deny that he was now interested, if in a somewhat detached way.

He watched de Maresi's lips play along the hardened stem, and felt each glorious suck as if it were played upon his own flute. Still, the flutter of excitement was not quite enough to goad him into action. He wanted de Maresi only in a purely physical sense, while what he really wanted, who he really wanted, was Lucerne.

Vaughan skimmed a finger over the boyish perfection of de Maresi's arse, whose pace immediately quickened. His head rocked from side to side, and his cheeks hollowed with each raspy breath. Slowly, his expression transformed from concentrated panic to serene contentment. Breathless, de Maresi ran his tongue up the length of his shaft to the root. 'Tempted yet?' he asked, while his cock batted merrily at his parted lips. He looked up at Vaughan, his cheeks aglow and his eyes hungry. '*Donnes-moi ton foutre.*'

Vaughan shook his head; he knew more than enough French to understand just how exceedingly crude the request was. 'Why, when the show is so pleasing?'

'Did you want to see me come in my mouth?'

Vaughan climbed onto the bed and ran a finger up de Maresi's curled spine to the tip of his tailbone. 'That would be a sight to see.'

'Bugger me first.' His bottom landed firmly in Vaughan's lap.

'Always so crude, François.'

'Do I have to beg?'

Vaughan raised an eyebrow. 'You'd beg mercy of an Englishman?' He ran his palms down the 'v' of de Maresi's inner thighs, forcing them apart. He reached his cock and drew a single finger up the tumescent length to where the tip, shiny with saliva, was leaving sticky dots upon de Maresi's stomach.

'Better to ask it of you than the fiends in my own land.'

'True. Very true.' Vaughan circled the shiny helm, stoking the fire but not yet delivering enough.

'Don't tease,' pleaded de Maresi.

'Am I teasing?' Vaughan rubbed his covered prick against the man's bared arse, and was rewarded with a satisfying groan. It was all too easy. He needed challenge, something to react against, not this pitiful acquiescence. De Maresi had no fight in him, and it never seemed to occur to him to simply take what he so desperately wanted. Curious, since the rest of his countrymen seemed rather adept at laying siege to whatever they wanted.

'Finish your show, François.' He patted him on the arse and Vaughan held his gaze until de Maresi curled up and began to suck tenderly upon his prick again.

His initial intention had simply been to sit back and enjoy the display, but there was something compelling about the way his motion splayed his beautiful white bottom. Maybe he'd give a little of himself after all.

Vaughan pulled out the vial of oil he kept in his inner coat pocket and lathed François' winking hole, before slipping him his thumb and destroying his steady rhythm.

De Maresi's motion almost stopped at the intrusion. '*Oui*,' he gasped as his anus swallowed the digit. '*Oui* ... Vaughan ... *merci*.'

The man was wound like a tightly coiled spring on the verge of release. 'We have a problem, you and I.' Vaughan exchanged his thumb for two fingers, which he curled so they rubbed against the sensitive inner wall. 'You see, there's an edge that's missing between us, that renders this whole thing masturbatory.' He grinned at his own joke, before adding. 'It's not enough.'

De Maresi groaned but his intense fixation never wavered. His brow creased, saliva glistened around his mouth and on his cock, precome wetted his chin, but his sucking remained intent.

'I feel nothing.' Vaughan found the firm swell of his prostate and petted it with expert strokes. 'This gains me nothing and I find no joy in swiving your pert little arse.' But de Maresi was no longer listening, if indeed he ever had been. He stopped rocking and released his cock. Eyes closed, bliss contorted his features as he caught his ejaculate on his very pink tongue and swallowed it down.

'Vaughan,' he sighed. He pushed himself into a sitting position on Vaughan's lap. His hands threaded into Vaughan's hair, pulling him forwards for a kiss.

'No.' Vaughan shoved him off. 'I told you not to touch me.' He cleaned his fingers on de Maresi's discarded cravat. 'You may not comprehend this, François, but Bella is no threat to you, because there is nothing between us. There never has been.'

De Maresi propped himself up and gaped. 'Then what is this?' he demanded.

'Torture,' Vaughan remarked, and left the room.

On the balcony, he strove for calm. Had it always been this difficult to walk away, he wondered. He didn't think so. Something had changed. In the past he'd have had his fun with de Maresi and laughed off any awkwardness, but he'd been more easily content then too. Now, he needed more than just a pretty face and the promise of fleeting ecstasy to rouse him. He longed for something greater than that, some kind of stability.

'God's blood!' He sounded as if he was headed for the marriage market. Except it wasn't a woman he wanted.

'Lucerne.' Lauwine seemed such a long time ago, and it hadn't been easy then. How many hours had he spent cajoling Lucerne into his bed? How many days? Bella had just been the final battle in a long campaign, and he'd enjoyed sparring with her. Still did. He loved the uncertainty between them, the fact that he never knew if they would fuck or fight, the frisson that burned between them. She excited him, but it was different, very different – his hand closed over the warm metal oval that lay against his chest – to the way he felt about Lucerne.

He was still starring blankly across the hall when the door swung inwards below. Vaughan's gaze dropped to the entryway to find Bella staring up at him, an expression of grim determination upon her face. And he felt it again, that vital spark between them. Memories burned him. The colour was different, but the effect of the heavy riding coat was the same. Three years fell away and he saw her, curious and defiant on the threshold of Lucerne's library.

She was beautiful.

The wind had whipped the colour back into her cheeks, and while it was clear a maid had spent time arranging her hair, several strands had now escaped the pins and hung in knotted wisps about her face.

'Vaughan,' she breathed, and it seemed to break the spell.

She hurried up the stairs to meet him. 'I came back to talk. We need to . . .' She froze just inches from him and her eyes widened in alarm.

'Miss Rushdale, my lord,' de Maresi drawled in a seedy purr as he tucked in his shirt tails. He nudged past them and pattered away down the stairs.

'You've been with him.' The terse accusation echoed across the hall. 'How dare you? I mean, I knew . . . But in my room!' She shook with barely contained rage. 'You're worse than Lucerne.' She lifted her hand as if she meant to strike him, but simply barged past him instead. Vaughan caught her arm and swung her back round to face him, only for her to spit in his face.

He wiped it away slowly, then pushed her against the wall and forced his mouth down upon her.

Bella clawed at him, her throat choked with emotion. She had known about de Maresi but she hadn't really acknowledged it to herself, hadn't let it touch her as it did now, as a betrayal.

She saw them clearly, entwined upon her bed, as they must have been just moments ago, and the knowledge of it burned until she felt sick in her stomach.

'Let go!' She fought against Vaughan's hold, but remained trapped between the flexing steel of his warm body and the wall. Vaughan quashed her cries, forcing his tongue into her mouth and kissing her hard.

She melted.

Nobody else ever kissed her with the same knee-buckling intensity, with a taste that washed straight to her quaint. She'd never been able to resist his kiss. Never.

'Get off me,' she snarled, when he finally pulled back for air.

'Not yet.' He locked an arm across his chest, while his body still pressed against her as unyielding as pig iron, and with his free hand he lifted her hem.

Her arousal exposed, Bella turned her head away from his scalding breath. 'I'm not your plaything. Not even your mistress.'

'You're my lover.' His breath troubled the pulse point in her throat. 'If not my mistress, what are you, some slattern that needed a bed for a night?'

She snapped her teeth at him, but he merely laughed and pushed his fingers into her heat. His thumb worked bitter circles around her clitoris, driving her onto her toes, gasping for breath. Arousal so thick it felt like bellyache knotted her lower half. Slickly, his fingers worked their magic, driving her to the brink of joy and transforming sharp words into sharper breaths.

She couldn't speak. She felt his cock lying unbearably hard against her hip, so full of promise.

'Sing for me, my nightingale. Come.' He dragged his lips down the side of her neck and sucked. She couldn't fight it. Shards of frosty hatred cracked into sparklers of delight. The swirl of his thumb, the twist of his fingers brought such sweet, swift pleasure, her limbs trembled.

Bella's pulse raced with need and expectation. She managed to win one arm free, and immediately dug her fingers into his bottom. The muscles clenched and unclenched as he rocked against her thigh, taking his pleasure from the friction. The dance of their bodies slowed as her breaths became shallow and ragged. Everything was concentrated in her clit and the tingle of her nipples. The whole world seemed to contract into one point as she gasped into his chest and her orgasm rendered her soft and pliant.

Bella snuggled against his shoulder, her eyes wet with tears, content for a moment to simply exist in his embrace.

'Now you're even.' Vaughan disentangled their bodies and stepped back. 'Don't ever presume to tell me whom I can bed in my own house.'

She felt the blood return to her face. Her eyes narrowed, but so did Vaughan's. Was this battle of wills really what she wanted? She longed for Lucerne's easy smile, the safety of his embrace.

Vaughan was the most exciting, sexually aggressive man she'd ever met. The most perverse, the most infuriating, and it hurt to love him.

God, how it hurt!

'He won't come,' she snarled at his retreating back. 'Lucerne – he won't. He doesn't miss you.' Let him hurt too, she thought. He deserved the pain.

She knew he heard but he didn't react, he simply kept walking through the glittering shards of light that pierced the shutters, and the swirling dust motes, until he was gone.

10

The other riders didn't return until well into the afternoon. Bella had been pacing for what felt like hours, turning over the scene with Vaughan and her own hypocrisy. When Lucerne had brought home his trull, she'd fled in a rage, but when Vaughan flaunted a lover before her, she allowed him to give her a shattering climax. Why had she permitted it?

The difference was Vaughan.

Henry came into the great hall and interrupted her reverie. 'You made a good escape.' He collapsed into a gilt chair and stuck out his booted feet. With an exasperated sigh, Bella grasped one muddy heel and tugged. 'You should have shoved Devonshire into a ditch before you left. Damn fool nearly got us into a fight with the neighbours.' One boot down, he presented Bella with the other foot. 'Some fool rose out of nowhere and grabbed Niamh's horse, so Devonshire took the whip to him. Not so much as a "who are you, and what's your business?"'

'Did he look uncouth?'

'He crawled out of the brook. Though I have to say, Niamh wasn't perturbed until Devonshire laid on with the crop. Then she squealed.'

Free of his boots, Henry stretched out his toes, then looked around. 'Pass that decanter, will you?' He poured them each a dram of rum. Bella turned hers in her hands.

It tasted too raw and fiery for broad daylight, a problem Henry didn't seem to have.

'I'm told there's a history to it, a right old hoo-ha.' He continued, having swallowed the whole of his draught. 'Devonshire's intent on having her, and so is this other fellow.'

'I suppose he's just after the title too?'

Henry wound his hair around his finger and ticked the ends against his lips. 'I can't say as I had a chance to speak to him. Niamh's horse bolted, what with all the commotion. I've been halfway to Clun and back chasing them.'

'And is she all right?'

'Oh, she's in a fine fettle. Can't you hear her?' He cocked his brows towards the solar. 'Up there, with Pennerley and Devonshire. Damn fool's wrecked his chances. If he had any to start with.'

Bella moistened her lips, her eyes locked on the small shuttered square. Considering Raffe's comments earlier, she wondered if he'd wrecked his chances deliberately.

'He's laid himself wide open as a target for *grandes dames*, matchmaking harridans all. Silly fool, thinks his reputation as a rakehell will keep them off, but they ain't scared of him.'

'And where do you fit into the noble order of rakehells, roués and reprobates?'

'Middling.' He chuckled. 'They ain't married me off yet, but they have tried.' He lurched onto his feet again. 'Now, let me get out of this ridiculous clobber.'

Bella handed him his boots and strolled with him to the door.

'Let the storm upstairs blow over before you go rushing in,' he advised. She watched him from the doorway as, barefoot, he nimbly darted between the mud patches that streaked the courtyard lawn. His riding suit was the most conservative thing she'd ever seen him in. Henry's idea of decent left much to the imagination. It would probably entail a candy-striped box coat and shoes with pink-studded buckles and, of course, his ubiquitous stockings.

She glanced again at the solar windows. The shouting had now lapsed into painful silence.

Bella was halfway up the stairs when Niamh came rushing out of the solar, her face streaked with tears, but clearly defiant. She caught hold of Bella's arm and turned her about. 'Walk with me.'

'What happened?'

'I'll tell you once we're away from the castle.'

They crossed the muddy ground and turned left towards the church. 'I don't blame you for leaving. I know you're enamoured of my brother and even a minute of his company must be preferable to hours of Raffe's, but still, Bella, I do wish you'd stayed.' She gave a loud tut. 'I shouldn't have forced him upon you, but I was cross at them inviting themselves, and I couldn't face listening to any more of his hollow endearments. I swear he is the most arrogant man I have ever met, and he's reported everything to Vaughan, who is now seethingly cross.'

'Reported what?' asked Bella.

'About me meeting Edward, of course.'

'Oh! It was deliberate. Yes, I see now why you didn't want them to come.'

They reached the church boundary wall, where a private moss-grown gate led into the churchyard. Niamh wove a pathway through the gravestones to a weathered tomb.

'My grandmother,' she said. 'She always knew how to make everything right. She knew how to handle Vaughan too.'

'She must have been an impressive lady.'

Niamh nodded, her gaze lowered. 'Bella, I realise we hardly know one another, but I hope I can trust your friendship. Lord knows, I need someone to help me make sense of things.'

'Go on. I'll listen.'

They linked arms and began walking again. 'It's Vaughan's fault. He's being such a dreadful pig. I wish he'd never come home.' They turned the corner of the church and followed the path towards the distant gate. 'I tried to do everything properly. Edward called just as soon as Vaughan returned and asked leave to officially court me, but Vaughan wouldn't have it. He accused Edward of being a fortune-hunter and said that if I wanted to sell myself, he'd invite some more suitable candidates along.'

'Hence Raffe?'

'Yes, and Henry, although he's not so bad, and they're bound to be a whole host of others invited to the party. It'll be, here, Niamh, come and entertain the Baron Whatsit, and Lord Layabout, and don't forget the Duke of Down There.'

Bella stifled a laugh. She wondered if the Duke of Down There was any good *down there* and if his skill would stand him in good stead. Alas, he was probably an arrogant autocrat like the rest of his peers, who liked to fiddle with himself at the dinner table, although hopefully one of them would catch Niamh's eye.

Bella pushed aside her mirth and fixed on a serious expression. She did wish people wouldn't confide in her. She was completely the wrong person to ask advice from, and her own actions proved it. Her best suggestion for Niamh was to elope, but Vaughan would never forgive her if she played a part in his sister running off, so she tactfully kept her mouth closed.

'We've hardly seen each other these last few weeks,' Niamh was saying. 'I tried to warn him earlier, but Raffe was on him immediately. I think Vaughan had told him to keep a look-out.' She stopped abruptly, and gave an astonished gasp. 'Edward!'

A gangly man dressed in a fashionable blue coat and cream breeches sat perched upon the lychgate.

Niamh swept up her skirts and ran to him.

Bella caught up her hem too, dashed a few paces, then came to a wary halt. She had no desire to play chaperone; she and Vaughan were at odds already without her becoming muddled up in this torrid affair.

Resolved to keep her distance, she left the path and strolled into the line of trees. It seemed strange to her that Vaughan, who valued his own freedom so much, should so ruthlessly dictate to his own sister.

The graves beneath their shady boughs were arranged in two symmetrical lines, all stone-edged rectangles with grass growing in the centre and posies of flowers at the feet. Further on stood a row of crosses, each hung with an iron ring, as if someone had meant to keep the faeries away. Bella traced the rusted inscriptions and wondered if she should remain here, or stray further from the obscured gate.

'I spy with my little eye a buxom nymph I'd like to try.' Two hands closed over her eyes. Bella yelped and turned sharply, stamping at her assailant's foot in the process.

'Devonshire,' she snarled, faced with his charming visage.

Who had he followed out, her or Niamh? 'I suppose you're pleased with what you've done.'

'You've heard?' He shuffled back a few paces, kicking up the gold and orange leaf mulch as he went. 'In my defence, I was simply obeying the instructions given me by my host.'

'Well, she won't have you now.'

'A loss as you know I'm not about to mourn.'

Bella turned her back on him. Poor Niamh. What was so wrong with Edward that she couldn't have him?

'Do you hate me too, Bella?' His words slipped treacle soft into her ear, while his hand slid across her bottom so that the heavy cloth cleaved to her curves.

'Mr Devonshire,' Bella swirled on the spot again, this time sending a shower of leaves into the air, 'don't presume to touch me.'

She shoved him hard, forcing him backwards until he hit a protruding tree root, lost his balance and collapsed with a thump onto one of the low stone graves.

Autumn leaves swirled around his prone form, red, oranges and sunset yellows, like a patchwork quilt. He moaned and Bella crossed to his side. She wasn't sure if he was really injured or feigning to win sympathy, but she wasn't sorry regardless. He'd hurt Niamh.

'Get up,' she snapped.

Raffe gave a second pitiful groan.

'Mr Devonshire.' She bent over him and prodded his shoulder with two fingers.

'It's Lord.' His eyes fluttered open.

'Not until you deserve it. I should slap you on Niamh's behalf.'

Strong arms wrapped around her back and pulled her down on top of him. 'I'd rather you kissed me on your behalf.' He cocked a leg over hers and rolled her onto her back.

'Will you get off me!'

'Not until I've had my kiss.' He stretched over her like a snake, his loins pressing enticingly against her covered quim.

Shocked, further objection stuck in her throat. How dare he? He was presumptuous in the extreme, although curiously entertaining too.

'Ahem.'

Raffe froze at the quiet cough and Bella scurried out from beneath him. Vaughan stood in the shadow of a weathered angel, indifference at her predicament painted across his face. His dark clothing billowed in the breeze, chasing his dark ringlets around his shoulders.

'Where's my sister?' he asked coldly. 'I saw you pass through the church gate not more than five minutes ago.'

Bella stood. Clearly, he'd come round the church in the opposite direction, else he'd have already seen Niamh. There was no way to warn her. Unconsciously, her gaze drifted towards the wooden shelter, only just discernable through the trees.

'Bella?' Bending over her, Vaughan tilted her chin with the press of his thumb and looked into her eyes. His were indecipherable, clouded with the same secrets she regularly found there.

'I don't know.'

He let her go but she was sure he'd read the deceit. 'Is she with that dandyprat, Edward Holt?'

Certain her tone would betray her, Bella shrugged. Her gaze quickened on the gate again and he saw the movement.

'You're not doing her any favours by protecting her.'

With a scrunch of leaves, he left.

'Edward. Thank the Lord.' The worry in her voice seemed to blister the October air. Niamh threw herself into his arms and held him tight. Edward cradled her back.

'I'm fine. I'm fine.'

Niamh stared up at him in wonder. At twenty-four, Edward Holt was a fine-looking fellow, and well he knew it. His coat, fashioned by Brummell's own tailor and his boots polished to within an inch of their existence, and his valet's. His radiance always lifted her spirits, the same way it had the day they'd met. Alone in the churchyard, they'd stumbled upon one another, each overjoyed at the unforeseen company, and celebrated with a summer picnic among the gravestones. She'd made him a daisy chain, and he'd wound it around their wrists binding them together in friendship.

Not that they had remained simply friends very long. As the summer blooms gave way to autumnal falls, he'd stolen one chaste kiss and then another, until some busybody had taken it upon themselves to inform her brother.

Vaughan returned to Pennerley righteous and crazy. Even before Edward called, Niamh had known the answer would be no. Her brother wasn't happy, and if he wasn't happy, he made damn sure nobody else was.

How she both loathed and loved him. He'd deserted her, left her behind while he toured Europe. He didn't care for her loneliness, though he provided everything else.

Edward promised her society, a house in London, excitement.

Niamh sought the warmth of his compelling brown eyes.

'My love,' he whispered. A long red welt ran along the ridge of his left cheekbone, the result of Raffe's brutality. She would not marry a man who lashed out so.

Her fingers traced the air above the wound. Although the skin was unbroken the bruising was livid.

'It's nothing. A small price for seeing you.'

Niamh stretched upon tiptoes and pressed a delicate kiss to his wound. He turned, capturing her against his chest. Not content with her chaste caresses, he drew her mouth to his, driving his hard lips against her softness.

The sensation poured down her throat like warm mead. Gripped with a kind of fever, her limbs trembled as he pressed his tongue into her willing mouth, and with bold knowing strokes invited her to reciprocate

Previously, when he'd grown amorous like this, she'd drawn back, soothed him with tender words and promises of a wedding night, but today, anger at Raffe and Vaughan possessed her as assuredly as Edward's tongue, and slowly her guard slipped, letting him guide her towards what came next.

Vaughan would not deny her everything. He wouldn't deny her this drunken pull of one body towards another. Intoxicated, she surrendered to Edward. As he unfastened the front of her gown, she gave a soft hiss of appreciation, echoed a moment later as he took her nipple into his mouth.

They would be seen, she knew it, but didn't care. The feel of his hot mouth on her breast was too enticing. He drew back, blowing cool air onto her taut nipples, then slicking them with his tongue.

'Be mine, Niamh. Say you will. I can't wait.' His tongue teased with merciless precision. 'Say you'll come away with me.'

She struggled for breath and clear thought as one knee pressed insistently between her thighs. 'I can't, you know I can't.'

'If he loves you, he'll forgive you.'

'Edward, don't. He'll come round, we just have to be patient.' There was too much risk involved in eloping. Her brother's reputation was no myth. He'd killed before now, and had the scars to prove it. 'Don't ask this of me.'

'Then if not this, give me something else.'

She knew what he meant, and trembled at the thought of it. He meant to claim her, to possess her, and thus bind her to him. For a moment, there was something in his eyes, his stance, the way his muscles tensed that made her tremble with something besides lust, but his lips found hers again and soothed her fears.

His hand found a way through her many skirts. The touch of his fingertips on the bare skin above her stocking tops sent a thrill so sharp through her womb that she almost squealed.

'Shh, my sweet,' he soothed, and silenced her with kisses so hard they seemed to bruise her lips, kisses that rained upon her like a torrent leaving her gasping and overpowered.

He clasped her tight and inched her around the gatepost to the narrow wooden bench that ran the length of the lychgate, and bent her to his will. His hands seemed to be everywhere, pressing into the small of her back, guiding her hips, finding the slit of her stockinet pantaloons and the ripe, swollen prize beneath.

She didn't look when he drew out his prick, velvety soft and curiously male, but crushed her eyes closed as he guided it between her spread thighs.

'There now,' he said, and she felt him at her entrance, so hard, so demanding. She hadn't wanted it like this, out in the open, awkwardly poised. She squirmed against him, no longer sure.

'Easy,' he murmured, but there was impatience in his voice. He tried to lift her, to align her body with his.

'No,' she whimpered, but he pressed a hand to her lips.

His hips jerked as he tried to impale her, but instead he slid past, straight between her legs.

Niamh groaned. For several uncertain moments she knew only the press of Edward's body, and then he gave a surprised yelp and the pressure was gone. Suddenly, she was facing Vaughan, her wantonness exposed, her brother holding Edward by the hair.

The world stood still, then reality crashed in around her. Vaughan thrust Edward into the dirt and levelled a pistol at his head.

'I suggest you run, and damnable fast.'

'Vaughan, no!' she squealed.

Edward, without a backwards glance, sprinted from the churchyard.

Time seemed to slow as Vaughan cocked the trigger, setting it into place with a tiny click. He took aim. Niamh ploughed into his side. The resulting explosion rang in her ears and temples. Horrified, she watched Edward stumble, then hobble on, a hand clasped to his thigh.

'Edward,' she screamed.

Vaughan caught her about the waist, preventing her from following.

'You hit him.'

'You jerked my arm. You're bloody lucky I didn't kill him.' He tugged her dress across her exposed flesh. 'Cover yourself up.'

Fingers trembling, she somehow managed the task of ribbons and buttons. Only when he spun her back towards the church did she realise that both Bella and Raffe were witnesses to her shame.

'You don't understand. You've never loved,' she snapped petulantly.

Vaughan faced her, his eyes alight. 'I understand perfectly. That man is an incorrigible lech, and he wants you for your money. Do you think I refused him purely to spite you?'

'Do you think *he* isn't just after my money?' She glared at Raffe who was leaning against an ivy-shrouded gravestone, feigning fashionable indifference. 'He doesn't even make a pretence of liking me.'

'Exactly. He's never made any pretence, which is all that bastard is.'

Nerves alight with what had just happened, Niamh spat out her rage in a string of expletives she'd learned from Vaughan, but at the end she didn't feel any better, just hardened and numbed.

'Finished?' Vaughan asked.

A sudden sense of earthly weariness washed over her. She nodded.

'Next time someone attempts to delve beneath your skirts have the good sense to knee him in the cobs.'

'I'll remember that, should I ever find a husband to your liking.'

Vaughan raised an eyebrow, amusement twitching upon his lips. 'That, dear sister, is your prerogative.'

'Don't mock me.'

He laughed.

'Stop it. Did you ever consider that I was enjoying it? I wanted him.'

'The hell you did. If there were any real passion between you, you wouldn't have been at it straight-legged against a rotten gatepost. You'd have been rolling in the leaf litter and, pistol or not, he'd have been man enough to face me. Credit me with some expertise.'

'All you know is your own self-centred satisfaction.'

For a moment, Vaughan grew very still. Then a flash of sadistic humour stirred in the depths of his violet eyes. 'I think it's time for a lesson.'

He moved so fast, he'd upended her over his shoulder before she could squeal, and then she could only beat her fists against his back and pray he didn't drop her head first onto the cracked stone path.

'Passion,' he said, laughing. 'Let's see how much I can wring out of you on the way back to the castle.'

'Put me down,' she yelled.

Vaughan ran, heedless of her squirming and her shouts. He spun her around until the stone and grass turned into a blur, and he reeled drunkenly under her weight. Finally, he dropped her onto their grandmother's grave. 'What would she say, Niamh, if she caught you in public like that?'

Dizzy and embarrassed, Niamh shook her head.

'Discretion, dear girl.' He laughed again and slapped his hand against the stone. 'Only do what you can get away with.' He crushed her in his embrace, pressing his forehead against hers. 'You don't have to have Raffe. You don't have to have any of them.' He kissed her. 'Tell me what you want and I'll provide it.'

'Edward,' she mouthed.

Vaughan shook his head. 'No, not him.'

Bella felt her heart turn over when she heard Vaughan laugh. He was a swine sometimes, but she couldn't stay truly angry with him for long. At the moment he seemed to have forgotten her. He hadn't even commented on her position under Raffe.

Behind her, the leaves scrunched as Raffe pushed himself up off a gravestone.

'Leaf litter,' he mused. 'By that token, we're destined for each other.' He brushed her hair away from the back of her neck and pressed his lips to her skin. 'Shall we return to our bower and raise some heat?'

'You never give up, do you?' she said.

'No, alas. I must have you or die.'

She bore his kisses until he reached her collarbone, then she pushed him away. 'Why would I want to soil myself with you?'

Raffe clasped her about the waist. 'Why wouldn't you? Confess, you're a little bit tempted.'

Perhaps she was. He was moderately charming and a lot less complicated than Vaughan. There'd been a time when she would have sank onto him without a second thought, without a care for consequences or anything beyond the salving of her lust. But things had changed. The promise of a swift fulfilment was not enough, no matter how much she craved the penetration that Vaughan denied her.

'I already have an excellent lover.'

She began walking, following Vaughan's footsteps back towards the castle. Raffe followed her.

'And who would that be?' he asked. 'Not Pennerley.'

'Yes, and you know it.'

He bent forwards, hands resting upon his knees, and laughed. 'He's not yours. Not really.'

Anger swept through her and spiked in her skull. Her heavy riding skirt lashed at his ankles and settled in jealous green folds as she bore down upon him. 'Yes,' she growled. 'Yes, he bloody well is.'

Devonshire pursed his lips. 'We'll see.'

11

Bella returned to find the castle alive with voices and a train of servants moving trunks between the carriage house and the gatehouse. Raffe at her heels, she swished past and made for the great hall. Pandemonium reigned there too.

The normally echoic vault had been transformed by a gaggle of girls into a modiste's. Bonnets and shawls lay strewn across furniture and shoeboxes adorned the chairs. Someone had thrown open the long shutters, letting daylight flood in.

'The Allenthorpes,' said Raffe. 'Be relieved they've only fielded the four.'

'Why, how many are there?' Bella asked, overawed by the devastation so few had caused.

'Nine in total, eight girls and Gabriel.' He nodded towards a golden-haired young man supporting a mature woman with beetle-black eyes and a roman nose. 'That's the chaperone, Mrs Alvanley, or Aunt Bea as she's known. Deaf as a post by all accounts, and once a notorious light heel if gossip is to be believed.'

'And do you?'

Raffe shrugged. 'You'd best ask de Maresi, he's thick with them.'

I'd rather not, she thought, and scowled at his back. 'He stayed with them in London, didn't he?'

'That's right. He came over from France on one of their

father's ships and has been obliging himself of their hospitality ever since. Well, until fortnight ago, when he tossed his lot in with Pennerley.'

The remark brought the incident on the stairs back with irritating clarity. The Vicomte, she noticed, had changed. Gone was the cream in exchange for black broadcloth, exquisitely embroidered around the pockets, collar, cuffs and tails.

Henry, too, had put on some decent wear, a pinstriped, glacé silk suit in crimson with a contrasting waistcoat of grey damask. He turned and the light caught the fabric, revealing the pattern of swooning maidens arranged in pairs, a motif replicated on his cloth-covered buttons and cravat.

'Seems I'm a little drab.' Raffe pressed his hand to her shoulder. 'It's early to change for dinner but I do like to blend in.' He took his leave with a quick nod.

Bella watched him up the stairs, wondering if she should also change. Niamh, she was relieved to find, was still in her riding habit, although she stood aside from the melange, her posture uncharacteristically stiff. Vaughan's laughter may have lightened the mood, but he presumably still wouldn't give his consent.

She began to move across the hall but, before she reached Niamh's side, Henry pulled her into the ring of Allenthorpes and began making introductions.

Alicia, Mae and Fortuna she managed to absorb, responding with the requisite greetings, while Niamh moved dolefully around the outside of the circle.

'You must tell us all you know about the party,' gushed Mae, the youngest, a pretty, buxom girl. 'Mr Tristan won't divulge a thing.'

Henry raised his hands, once again dangling his ubiquitous cane. 'I've told you ladies. I'm equally in the dark. I have neither Pennerley's ear nor that of his ghostly ancestors.'

'Vicomte,' Alicia appealed. 'You must know something.'

'Alas, I'm sworn to secrecy.' He retreated to a safe distance with Gabriel and a wine decanter. Bella cynically wondered if he'd had his way with the younger man and whether the new arrival would divert his attention away from Vaughan.

'Blow it!' Mae stamped her foot. 'I only want to know if it's going to be gruesome so I know which of Aunt Bea's smelling salts to bring.'

'Oh, the mildest,' said the eldest in all seriousness. 'It won't hurt for her to be out a fraction longer.' While the girls laughed, Henry raised his eyebrows.

'I won't ask why you're here, Miss Fortuna,' he remarked.

She tapped him coquettishly with her fan. 'You know perfectly well.' She smiled again, showing off her dimples. 'Father was quite against it, said I shouldn't be exposed to a fiend like Pennerley, but Mother and Aunt Beatrice talked him round. I think Mama wanted to come herself but she's far too busy organising Sarah's wedding.'

Henry smiled benignly while the other two girls gave theatrical sighs. 'Are they still holding out for Hector Macleane for you?'

Fortuna's dimpled smile twisted into a petulant moue. 'I shan't have him. I told Father so. The man is a capital bore and a glutton. I said I'd rather have Pennerley. He has far nicer thighs.'

'And a far bigger castle ...'

'And a far badder reputation,' tittered the younger two. 'Tunie just wants to be devoured by a wolf.'

'Or a vampire . . .'

'Or a ghoul . . .'

'Or a ghost . . .' They raised their hands like claws and swooped at her, sending Fortuna shrieking and skittering about the floor.

'Girls,' chastened Aunt Beatrice. 'What will our host think? Calm yourselves immediately, we will have decorum.'

They skidded to a halt, lined up neatly before her for inspection. 'We'll have no more lewd talk. If Lord Pennerley cares to notice you, you may respond in an appropriate manner. Meanwhile you will keep your ridiculous notions of marriage and phantasms to yourselves.'

Although the rebuke was not levelled in her direction, Bella's heart gave a fearful jolt. Joshua's lectures had only ever instilled defiance, but Aunt Beatrice spoke in a tone that cut to the quick, leaving her three charges open-mouthed and scarlet. They each bowed their heads and gave her deferential curtsies.

Niamh slipped her arm around Bella's and drew her to the window. 'Don't worry,' she soothed. 'She doesn't stand a chance. He hasn't even said hello to them yet.'

There was no need to ask whom she meant. Vaughan was conspicuously absent despite the influx of guests.

'At all?'

'I think Gabriel got a vague nod.'

'Well, I suppose he was a bit . . .' She strove for the right term, which failed to appear.

'He was horrid,' supplied Niamh. 'He made a total mockery of my feelings and laughed the whole way back.' She cupped her hands over her face. 'I've never felt so ashamed.'

'Oh, fie,' said Bella. 'The only shame is that he stopped

your Edward pleasuring you. I dare say you'd have more of a smile if he'd had his way.'

'Bella! Must you be so crude?' A delicate coral blush chased across her cheeks and chest. She gave a shy smile which faded far too quickly. 'I do wish Raffe hadn't seen me. I fear for what he'll do.'

'What can he do?'

'He could ruin me. Probably will if I don't agree to marry him. He asked, you know, last night in the solar.'

'You only spoke for a moment.' Bella strained to keep the incredulity from her voice. He'd proposed marriage and tried to procure her as his mistress. She hadn't given him nearly enough credit. He was an absolute scoundrel. Alas, she had a soft spot for scoundrels.

Lips tightly pursed, Bella stepped up into one of the window seats. Niamh followed and they sat, facing one another.

'What does Vaughan say about it?'

'That I needn't have him, but I can't have Edward either, and that he'll be far less gentle if he ever catches me making a fool of myself with a man again.' Frown lines crinkled her brow, which Bella tried to rub away with her thumb.

'Naught to worry about,' she reassured. 'Just make sure he never catches you.'

The remark raised a laugh, forgotten a moment later. Niamh's gaze turned to the window. A gaggle of geese were launching themselves into the moat, sending ripples across the surface. 'I expect he'd find out somehow, and I'm not at all sure I want pursue that course again.'

Bella squinted at the geese, thoroughly confused. 'Whatever do you mean?'

'I never intended it to go that far. I was just pleased to know that Edward was fine after Raffe hit him.'

'Niamh, did he try to force you?'

'No.' She lowered her gaze. 'I'm not at all sure. It was happening so quickly.'

Bella saw that her situation had suddenly become a lot more difficult. If Vaughan had suspected that his sister was in any way unwilling, he would have shot to kill and Niamh must have realised that too. She seemed to react to Bella's perplexity.

'It's all right,' Niamh said. 'Really it is. I'm just confused. I wanted him, truly I did.'

Bella wondered if she was trying to convince herself. Maybe Vaughan was right about Edward. If he'd taken her maidenhead, then he might have felt in a stronger position to claim her hand, while holding her reputation to ransom.

'Well, if you're sure,' she said. She climbed down from the window seat. 'I think I'll go and change for dinner now.' The other guests had left the hall with the exception of Henry who still lingered by the fire. 'Don't fret. It'll come right. I'll speak with Vaughan, see if I can exert any influence.'

The offer was met with mute acceptance and tremulous nod.

As Bella trod the stairs to her room, she reflected on her offer. Talking to Vaughan was hard enough at the moment without raising another touchy subject. But she wanted to hear the truth about Niamh's suitor.

Niamh resumed pacing the floor, once Bella departed. The window seat couldn't contain her. She paced, five paces up, five paces back, ten pace up, ten paces back. Was Edward all right? She thought he'd been hit in the leg but it was hard to tell. Hadn't he stumbled before the gun went off?

She remembered his kiss, the feel of his mobile lips hard against hers, their tongues melding, and further, deeper revelations, knowledge of the act performed by lovers. The unanticipated reluctance on her part.

The shock of Vaughan's arrival had skewed so much. He'd branded them passionless. That was untrue, leastways; it was on Edward's part. He'd risen admirably to the occasion. Any lack of enthusiasm had been all hers.

She enjoyed his kisses, but mostly longed for the simple joy of having a companion whom she could trust and who cared for her. Edward's conversation excited her more assuredly that his touch. His nearness offered comfort and a world devoid of silence. In recent years, Pennerley had been her prison.

'You'll wear holes in your shoes,' Henry remarked of her continued pacing. He clattered towards her and came to a halt before her, taller by a head. Niamh avoided his gaze by staring at his stockings. They were shiny cream with crimson bands, and made her smile. Somehow his ludicrous attire made him a deal less threatening than other men.

'Delightful, aren't they.'

Niamh jerked her gaze upwards to where his expression bore warmth as well as bemusement. He clasped her hand and pressed it firmly to his arm. 'Perhaps a step around the walls would better suffice than all this tiresome pacing.'

She allowed herself to be led outside, remembering how he'd comforted her earlier, after he'd soothed her skittish mare. He hadn't plied her with questions or demanded explanations. He'd simply been there, a solid rock of support.

'Are your earlier woes troubling you, or are there further developments?' He didn't press for an immediate answer as Raffe or even Edward would have done, didn't press for an answer at all. 'I find advice in these situations is general worthless, for only you know the whole story, but for what it's worth, I'd suggest you don't pick unnecessary fights with your brother. He's too stubborn and fond of winning to allow you any real victory, especially in his present frame of mind. Better to find more subtle means to win his approval.'

'That could take years.'

Henry acknowledged the fact with a sweep of his cane that knocked the heads off several late flowers. 'Not necessarily. Besides, what's a little perseverance in the face of a lifetime's commitment, eh?'

'Naught, I guess.'

'Exactly. Let matters lie a few days, get this carnival of souls over with, and then see what can be negotiated.'

She nodded her acceptance, and taking out her scissors began to trim a few of the fallen blooms which she presented to him as a nosegay.

'There's still Raffe.'

Henry gave her a devilish smile. 'Oh, confound that fool. It's not as if he wants you anyway.'

'He could ruin me.'

He frowned at her as she pinned the flowers to his monumental lapel. 'That's a fact of the society we live in. A man can destroy in a few words what a woman can only build with a lifetime of goodness, but only a truly despicable rogue would do so.' His lips parted and the tip of his tongue wetted their surface. 'Devonshire isn't that rogue. He's his mama's pawn and she knows how spreading rumours can backfire.'

Niamh looked up at him for details, but Henry shook his head and smiled.

'Ancient history, my dear, and I'm not a gossipmonger.'

12

The atmosphere at Pennerley changed completely with the arrival of Mrs Alvanley. While she was indulgent and compassionate to her adoring nieces, she also took her role as chaperone and the business of their virtue very seriously. Upon learning that Vaughan had omitted to provide a suitably mature hostess for his party, she took it upon herself to ensure decorum and a social pecking order. Thus Bella arrived at dinner to find herself seated well down the table, between Henry Tristan and Mae Allenthorpe, with Fortuna at the top of the table by Vaughan.

Her position usurped, Bella glowered at the silverware, dumbstruck by the woman's interfering but at a loss what to do about it. She could only appeal to Vaughan later, assuming they were still permitted to talk to one another. Bella had scared off a good many governesses, but this was outside her experience and therefore unbearable.

Niamh, scurrying to the table late, came to an abrupt halt behind Aunt Beatrice's chair, her pretty face contorted with rage. 'Who has placed me here?' she demanded.

'Why I have, dear,' said Mrs Alvanley.

'No.' She stared at her position next to Raffe Devonshire in disgust. 'Vaughan,' she appealed.

'Swap,' he said.

Niamh turned immediately to Bella, who hopped up and scampered around the table overjoyed at the vexation she'd cause Fortuna and her aunt. The former scowled hatefully into her soup, and Bella suspected her influence in the seating arrangements. The little gold-digger was out to snare herself a husband.

With Niamh happily positioned between Mae and Henry, the meal commenced, and an early silence slowly gave way to crisp requests and finally to conversation.

'It was very good of you to invite us,' Fortuna said to Vaughan. She had dressed in a pale-gold evening dress with a low, rounded neckline, which slipped off her shoulder as she leaned towards her prey.

Vaughan's gaze lingered a moment on her rather bony shoulder, then sat back in his chair. 'You must thank my sister, Miss Allenthorpe. She positively insisted I invite some ladies. Apparently, I'd omitted to do so on the original guest list.'

'Now you jest,' she accused, tapping his fingers where they lay upon the table edge. 'How could you forget to invite any women?'

Vaughan caught Bella's gaze and smiled. 'Oh, I assure you there were many I'd considered, but none entirely suitable according to my sister. Though they all had some admirable qualities.' His focus shifted to the neckline of her dress. She'd left on the stays she'd worn beneath her riding gown, but had them laced tighter, so that her breasts seemed full and round. Compared with Fortuna, she felt positively overendowed.

'Yes, a truly accomplished lady is hard to come by,' said Fortuna.

Further down the table, Henry snorted.

'I cannot disagree,' said Vaughan, 'and one might say I've made it a special study.'

'I see you have competition.' Raffe's breath tickled Bella's ear, as annoying as it was intimate. His presence was the unfortunate side effect of a position at the head of the table. 'Do you enjoy watching him flirt with other women or are you contemplating stabbing her with a fork?'

Once again his astonishing directness. If he hadn't been such an incorrigible lecher, they might even have been friends for that.

'Neither.' Bella brushed him away. She did find Fortuna's flirting irritating but suspected that Vaughan would be thoroughly bored by the small talk before long.

Fortuna sidled closer still to the edge of the table, a wary look cast in Aunt Beatrice's direction. But the meddlesome chaperone was deeply engaged with Gabriel and Henry Tristan on some matter of public affairs. With a small gasp of relief, Fortuna reapplied her attention to Vaughan.

'Do you always tease so mercilessly, my lord?'

Yes, thought Bella. You can't begin to imagine. He could play everyone at this table like an instrument, rouse passions, break hearts and dash hopes, and he was undoubtedly plotting something, for there was a twinkle in his dark eyes and a slyness about his smile. For a horrid moment, she remembered her last conversation with Lucerne, yelling that she would never perform with a woman, not even for Vaughan. Was that where this conversation was leading? Was he planning a show for his own amusement, just to see how far she would go to gain his favour?

'Getting worried?' Raffe sighed into her ear.

'No.'

'Yes, you are.' He squeezed her thigh beneath the cover of the tablecloth. 'You'll have to act. Do something to distract him.' He squeezed her leg again, this time more firmly. 'I suggest you toss him.'

'What!' For a moment she completely misunderstood his meaning, but realisation didn't make her any less scandalised.

'Now, beneath the tablecloth. I guarantee it'll get you his attention.'

'Is this one of your sick fantasies?'

His palm edged towards her quaint. 'I wouldn't say no. How about you?'

Bella swiped his hand away and shuffled her chair closer to Vaughan's. Raffe was simply being outrageous in the hopes of provoking a reaction, but his suggestion might be worth a try. Vaughan rarely flaunted himself publicly. He preferred things more furtive which is why he might find such secretive play beneath the table completely diverting.

'Chicken,' Raffe mouthed, holding her gaze.

He couldn't have said anything more persuasive. If there was one thing she detested, it was being called chicken-hearted. Bella stretched out her hand and traced her fingers lightly over Vaughan's thigh.

He stiffened, light flaring in his eyes, but his focus remained firmly on Fortuna, who had given up all pretence of eating and was now leaning so far over the table she was in danger of losing her dress.

Enthralled with her naughtiness, Bella slid her palm upwards until it covered Vaughan's sleeping cock and gave him an encouraging pat. She half expected him to push her away. Instead, he settled comfortably with his legs apart, allowing her more space in which to work.

'And what should we expect from your spectacle, my lord?' Fortuna asked.

Bella unfastened his breeches. The skin beneath was warm, his soft cock slumbering. It perked at her touch, thickening with only the smallest amount of coaxing.

'Aah!' He hid a sharp intake of breath behind the exclamation. 'Telling you would only spoil the surprise. You must allow me my secrets, Miss Allenthorpe, the better to entertain you.'

He pressed his tongue to his teeth and suppressed another hiss.

Bella continued the torment. How surprised they'd all be, the faces around the table, if they realised what she was doing. Mrs Alvanley would be scandalised, Gabriel and Niamh would blush, the younger girls would likely faint. She struggled not to grin at the thought of them collapsing, only to wake with a bird's eye view of her hand working his cock.

Henry would shake his head, perhaps feigning boredom, while de Maresi, she was sure, would be totally disgusted. Just payback, she considered, for his earlier smugness. As for poor Fortuna, she would realise how successfully her attempts at flirting were being undermined. Vaughan was hers.

His stomach muscles twitched and his breathing, willed into regularity, faltered. She was getting to him. She could sense his urgency in the line of heat above his cravat.

'Would you pass me a napkin?' he asked rather abruptly.

Fortuna happily obliged.

Vaughan dabbed his lips, then pressed the linen into Bella's hand, so that it covered the head of his cock. Mere moments and a few tormenting strokes later, he spent into the silver-blue folds, a sharp cough the only visible expressions of his peak.

Beaming proudly, Bella withdrew her hand and was about to turn to Henry and Niamh when Raffe's hand alighted upon her knee again, having found a way beneath her petticoats. The cool touch was shocking against her bare thigh. 'Very impressive.' He dipped two fingers into the moist heat of her cleft, causing Bella to shift her chair back sharply. It grated loudly, turning heads.

'Sorry,' she murmured.

Once they'd turned away again, Bella glared at Raffe. She was slick with need and cock-hungry, but not for him. She squirmed against his fingers but he withdrew the touch and twanged her garter.

'Read it,' he said, and she felt the scratch of paper beneath her stocking top. 'I need to see you later.' Eyes a-sparkle, he addressed the table at large. 'What say we hold a contest this evening?'

'Oh, yes!' gasped all four female Allenthorpes.

Vaughan dropped his abused napkin onto the table. 'What manner of contest are you proposing, Devonshire?'

'Oh, nothing too eventful, just a little silliness to entertain the ladies.'

'Not apple-bobbing,' sighed Henry, carefully daubing sauce from a powdered cheek. 'I refuse to stick my head in any bucket you've been near.'

'And I refuse to stick my head in any pail,' remarked de Maresi. 'I left my own country to avoid such inconveniences.'

'Oh, yes, very good, sir,' remarked Aunt Beatrice tactlessly. She smoothed the lace collar of her dress, looking back and forth along the line of gentlemen. 'What think you of a sack race? They were much the rage in the past but seem to have fallen somewhat out of favour.'

'A sack race,' drawled Vaughan, his eyebrows raised almost into his hairline.

Bella could imagine his interpretation, but the proposition was being echoed up and down the table with considerable enthusiasm.

'Stakes?' remarked Raffe.

'Oh, you must each champion one of the ladies,' said Aunt Beatrice, quite in her element and beaming in a girlish fashion. 'You will compete for –'

'A dress,' Fortuna interjected. 'A new silk dress. I saw the most beautiful cream moiré at the haberdashers before we left town.'

'Yes,' agreed Aunt Beatrice, 'a dress would be just the thing. The gentlemen may contribute two guineas each.'

'Two guineas,' blurted Gabriel. 'It will be a very fine dress, indeed.'

'Indeed it will,' said Vaughan, and he slapped two coins down upon the table. 'And perhaps the lady might bestow a token of her esteem upon her knight.'

Fortuna practically fainted at his feet.

'Foster. You'll arrange some sacks, please. The gentlemen will retire to the solar for brandy while the course is set. The ladies may make use of the lower parlour. No doubt they will wish to discuss their champions while they take tea. If someone would inform us of the choices.' Vaughan pushed his chair back and stood. 'Gentlemen, your contributions and your presence.'

Bella sniffed at the overwhelming smell of linseed in the lower parlour. The room lay directly beneath the solar but was smaller, with only one narrow window overlooking the moat and a tiny fireplace. A pianoforte took up much of the space, to which Alicia immediately applied herself.

Mrs Alvanley surveyed her new domain from the comfort of the horsehair settee and drew out her pocketbook. 'Lady Niamh, we'll begin with you. Am I to assume, not Lord Devonshire?'

Niamh winced at the name, drawing a look of disapproval from Aunt Beatrice. 'I should prefer Mr Tristan.' She leaned towards Bella and added, 'Not that I shall have him procure a dress, for I have plenty.'

Bella shared her smile, imagining the most fantastical stockings ever created. She was quite bewildered when Aunt Beatrice turned to her next. 'Miss Rushdale. Lady Niamh informs me you are an heiress, therefore, as status demands.'

'Marquis Pennerley,' she said in a loud clear voice, instantly wiping the smile from Fortuna's face, but her petulance changed nothing. Aunt Beatrice was satisfied.

'Oh, drat,' sighed Mae, verbally expressing her sister's frustration. 'That means one of us shall have to have Gabriel.'

'Indeed it does, and that honour shall be yours as you are the youngest.' The older woman made several marks in her pocketbook, though what she felt she needed to record, Bella couldn't fathom.

'Bother!' Mae complained. 'Gabriel has two left feet. He can't dance. He's bound to be atrocious in the sack.'

'Mae!'

Bella clamped both hands over her mouth to stifle her laughter, while poor, bewildered Mae stared open-mouthed at her aunt. 'What did I say?'

'Never mind.'

Contrite, Mae turned away from her aunt but she caught both Bella and Niamh's gazes, and grinned. The little minx had said it deliberately to provoke her aunt. She joined them by the window, skipping in merry delight.

'Fortuna, Alicia, that leaves the Vicomte and Lord Devonshire, either of whom your mother would be most pleased with.'

Alicia stopped playing and shook her blonde head in dismay. 'Aunt Bea, it's only a sack race. Can't it be a bit of fun rather than a matchmaking exercise?'

'Only if you wish to remain a spinster, my dear.'

With a sigh, Alicia began the tinkling music again. 'You choose, Tunie. I've no preference for either.'

Fortuna glowered at the music scores over her sister's shoulder while her fan tapped repetitively out of time with the beat. 'Lord Devonshire, I suppose. The Vicomte's only interested in Gabriel.'

Mae grasped her around the waist and swung her around in a wide circle so that they tumbled in a swirl of muslin. 'Cheer up, Tunie. I'll wager my best bonnet that Henry Tristan falls over more often than your Lord Devonshire.'

Her sister staggered dizzily to the settee and sat beside her aunt. 'If you mean your new poke bonnet, then I agree, and if he doesn't you shall have my cashmere shawl.'

By the time they all returned to the great hall, several other such 'chicken stakes' had been placed. Devonshire was deemed the favourite for his athleticism, with Vaughan as second. The furniture had largely been cleared and stacked in the southwest corner, with the exception of the long dining table, which now stood in the centre of the room with the track marked around it with rope.

While Mrs Alvanley inspected the sacks, she allowed the ladies a few moments with their champions to offer charms and encouragements, and in pairs they drifted to various corners.

To Bella's delight, Vaughan insisted on the privacy of the lower parlour where she followed the moment Aunt Beatrice's back was turned.

'You look absolutely dashing in your sack,' she observed, her tongue pressed firmly into her cheek. Vaughan raised an eyebrow. The coarsely woven cloth encompassed him from foot to throat, where it had been tied with a fiendish knot.

'Not half so handsome as you look out of yours, and it would seem Devonshire feels the same way.'

Bella blushed. 'Raffe jumped on me. You scared him off. Anyway, you're out of touch. I haven't worn a sacque in years.'

'Hmm.' He hopped towards her, eyes bright. 'Shame, I was always enormously fond of them. Plenty to hold onto and lots of space beneath.'

'Yes, I expect you've spent a fair amount of time canopied by skirts.'

Vaughan pursed his lips, his gaze drawn in contemplation towards the bowed ceiling. 'An uncommon amount of the nineties as I recall. Shall I have him flogged?'

'There's no need. I can handle him.'

Bella stroked his face. She didn't know how he managed it but even tied to his neck in sackcloth he was impossibly handsome. One finger traced the dark curves of his brows, ran down his cheekbone and smoothed over his lips. He smiled and leaned into the caress.

'I confess I'm surprised. I thought Miss Allenthorpe would have beaten you.'

She blinked and shook her head. 'I had the choice, thanks to your sister. Apparently I'm an heiress.'

'Is that so?' He tilted his head, causing his dark hair to fan across his shoulders. Bella drew it back off his face and captured the strands in a ribbon drawn from her reticule.

'Probably best if you can see if you're going to win me that dress,' she said. It felt strangely strained between them, the banter just a mask for all the things that really needed to be said.

He turned his head again, freeing several inky strands, which curled around his jaw. 'How many do you need? Didn't I promise you two the other night?' He had, scarlet and gold, as he'd coated her in jam and honey.

'How many coats does Lucerne own?'

'Ah!'

It was the first time they'd mentioned his name in normal conversation. Bella sucked her upper lip and turned away. The thought of the bitter parting brought the burn of anger to her chest, yet she missed him, missed the closeness the three of them shared. She wanted more than just a sparring partner in Vaughan but could tell just from the way he said 'ah' that she was no closer to winning his affection than she'd ever been.

'Are you going to tell me what happened?' Vaughan asked.

'I left.'

He made an ungainly hop towards her. 'You mean you ran away.'

'He was tumbling her on the parlour floor. What else could I do? I couldn't stay and watch.'

With a second hop Vaughan reached her. There was a stiffness to his shoulders. He had stayed, she realised. He'd watched her and Lucerne make love plenty of times, sat apart from them, his black eyes glittering in the dark, and in the end he'd run away. Come here to Pennerley.

Bella buried her face in his chest and clung to his body. The sacking smelled of oats and horses, pleasant reminders of past joys and furious couplings, of times when things had seemed simpler.

'Vaughan,' she crooked her chin up to see him and sought the comfort of his lips, 'would you do something for me?'

'I can't drown Raffe, if that's what you're thinking. He's a guest.'

'No, not that.' She nuzzled against his shoulder. 'Make me yours.'

'And how do you envisage me doing that? My hands are tied, Bella.' He dipped his head and pressed a kiss to each plump breast.

'That's never stopped you before.' She stepped back and raised her skirts. Wanting this reassurance, this comfort. The excitement.

The ruby lips of her quim were slick and swollen, ripe for his touch. 'Please.' For a long excruciating moment, he simply looked at her, no hint of his intent upon his face. Had she asked too much?

Finally, his lips quirked. 'You're practically bare,' he observed. She wasn't, but what he'd done with the jam had necessitated a considerable amount of trimming.

Vaughan sank onto his knees for a closer inspection.

If there was one thing he was truly gifted with, it had to be his tongue. The first light touch of its tip against her nub raised a gasp. The second drove her up onto tiptoes. 'Yes,' she mewled, straining against him, as each bold knowing stroke whipped her towards fever point. Her hips tilted as she opened deeper for his caress. One hand slid into his hair, clutched convulsively, sought to pull him closer.

'You're a greedy whore, Miss Rushdale,' he said, and she nodded in mute agreement. She was that and so much more. She'd be anything for him, do almost anything for him. 'If my hands weren't tied, I'd lay you across my knee and give you the punishment you so desperately deserve.'

She knew he didn't intend to spank her, though the punishment would undoubtedly warm her cheeks. No, his fingers would explore her dark rear passage, would tease delicate nerve-endings. He'd drive her into a state of frenzy with twin penetrations, as his tongue did now.

She had not realised just how deeply her need for him was until that moment. The stresses and excitements of the day had taken their toll, which his tongue now both fanned and soothed.

Bella threw back her head and revelled in the ecstasy of his touch. He supped her. He penetrated her. His tongue drew lazy circles around her throbbing flesh. He tantalised her until she was sobbing with need for him, and the ribbon she'd used to bind his hair hung limply in her fingers.

And all too quickly she was coming down. Satisfied in a fashion, but far from sated. 'More,' she urged, bucking against him.

'Greedy slut.' He shuffled away from her and climbed unsteadily to his feet, gazing at her from the sanctity of his sack, a bemused smile quivering upon his lips.

Bella rushed to him and threw her arms around him. 'Will you come to me tonight?'

Narrow-eyed, he looked down at her. 'You already have an assignation.'

Raffe! She'd forgotten his note tucked into her garter. How the hell did Vaughan know about that?

'You should go,' he said, as if he were approving a social engagement. 'He'll thrust his nice big prick up you, just like you want.'

The catty remark cut deep, sliced away all her fantasies, reminded her again of the truth. She was simply a diversion to him, like de Maresi, while he waited for Lucerne.

'Maybe I will,' she snarled, hoping to see him flinch. Vaughan merely nodded and, following a curt bow, hopped to the door, leaving her staring in frustration at his back.

Vaughan paused in the passageway and pressed his brow the wall. The cool stone soothed him. He wished he could wipe her juices from his chin. She infuriated him, but he couldn't help himself. She strained his patience in ways she'd never comprehend. Everything about them being together was wrong, yet his very clear, physical reaction to her lay hidden within the sack.

He wanted her. And he was no longer sure the reaction was entirely physical.

Each encounter, it grew harder to deny her, and deny himself. The urge to lose himself in her soft warmth was increasingly overpowering.

Vaughan smoothed his hands against his groin and swore. Nothing he ever did scared her off. He'd tried all sorts over the years, and always she came back for more.

He'd watched Raffe scribble his note. He doubted the

man could truly satisfy Bella. For a brief vain moment he saw himself as Bella's incubus, cursing her never to be content by another man again. He shook his head to free himself of the image. 'Where are you, Lucerne?' he whispered into the wainscotting. 'I need you here. Help me make sense of this mess.'

'Ah, so you've decided to delight us with your presence after all,' said Mrs Alvanley when Bella finally reached the great hall. The race had begun, and already Gabriel and de Maresi lay floundering on the floor just yards from the starting line. 'You might show more respect to your host and the other ladies. If the exercise means so very little to you, it would have been thoughtful to allow my niece her chosen champion.'

Bella saw the fan laid across the older woman's lap like a warning and tactfully kept both her silence and her expression in check until she turned around.

'Hideous old bat.'

She joined Niamh and Alicia at the finish line.

'She's not so very bad,' said Alicia in her aunt's defence. 'Some chaperones won't let their charges four paces from their sides, for any reason.' Bella was vividly reminded of her friend Louisa's problems with her aunt. Of course, she'd eventually escaped such scrutiny by marrying.

'And there are some,' Alicia continued, 'who consider any conversation with a man a prelude to marriage.'

'That's ridiculous,' snapped Bella, her encounter with Vaughan having left her irritable. 'Why, you'd never be able to dance or anything.'

'Oh, but dancing is very risqué, you know,' Niamh said in all seriousness. 'Come on, Henry.' She clapped her hands in delight as he briefly stole the lead. 'Frightful things can happen to a girl if she so much as brushes her skirt against a man.'

'Such as discovering he has an erection,' said Bella.

The two other women blushed and giggled. Alicia flicked open her fan and waved it ferociously. 'That's hopelessly impolite,' she hissed, her eyes all a-sparkle. She strained forward so her looped ringlets almost brushed Bella's own, eager for more forbidden insights.

'Alicia, come here, dear,' called Mrs Alvanley, clearly sensing an unsuitable turn to the conversation. Her niece complied with a weary sigh.

'Are you my brother's mistress, Bella?' Niamh asked once Alicia was out of earshot. The fading blush upon her cheeks glowed again, deep crimson.

The question seemed to spring out of nowhere. Surely their relationship was obvious. Bella glanced over her shoulder at Vaughan and the sculpted plains of his face. 'He doesn't keep me, if that's what you mean,' she said. 'If, however, you're asking me if he gives me his cock, then I should say that more often he keeps it to himself.'

Niamh's eyes shone as clearly blue as her brother's were dark. Bella sucked her tongue, conscious that perhaps in this instance she'd said too much, and a little more tact might have served her better.

'You're far too forthright,' Niamh said eventually. She pressed a finger to her lips. 'I feel I should faint or make a dramatic scene every time you say something shocking. Although, God knows, my own reputation is equally tarnished.'

Bella shook her head. 'We're not remotely the same.'

Niamh frowned and they allowed themselves to be distracted by the race for several minutes. The contenders were rambunctious and rough, jostling each other as they hopped and waddled around the course. 'How does Lord Marlinscar fit into this?' Niamh eventually asked. 'I was told that you were engaged to him.'

Practising tact, Bella kept her eyes averted from Niamh's face and buried all thoughts of the two men together as deep as she could. 'We were never engaged,' she replied. 'They shared me sometimes.'

'And now?'

'I'm in limbo, while they decide my fate.'

It was truth of sorts, but she still felt guilty over the deception; she wasn't going to be the one who explained Vaughan's proclivities to his sister.

Thankfully, Fortuna pushed her way between them at that point to giddily cheer the men on as they rounded the bottom of the dining table. They started the final lap, Vaughan and Raffe neck and neck, with a particularly florid Henry trailing close behind.

'Keep going, my lord,' Fortuna shouted, fooling no one over who she meant. Bella added her own support and watched dismay and determination wash across Raffe's handsome face. He lurched right, towards Vaughan, and his elbow jutted against the seam of the sack, straight into Vaughan's ribs.

For several breathless moments, the blow met with no discernable effect, then Vaughan stumbled, his rhythm disrupted. He staggered forwards, tripped over Gabriel, who still lay sprawled where he'd first fallen, and landed face down upon de Maresi.

The Frenchman grunted in shock, then laughter bubbled from his lips, joyous and lewd, but his mirth lasted but a second, as blood dripped from Vaughan's nose onto his lily-white cheek.

The ladies scrambled around them in shock.

'Get me out of this damn sack,' Vaughan bellowed, and Bella applied herself to the knot.

Raffe paused to look back, fear in his grey eyes. He began to apologise, only for Henry to leap past him into the lead. 'Goddammit, man!' He lurched forwards in pursuit, but his heart wasn't in it or his legs were too tired, for although he wheezed like a consumptive miner, Henry increasingly lengthened the gap between them. He bounded over the finish line, just as Bella succeeded in releasing Vaughan from the sack.

Handkerchief pressed to his bloody nose, Vaughan scrambled over de Maresi and Gabriel with little thought to their discomfort and stalked from the hall, with a muffled curse of 'Damn fool game.'

Bella longed to follow him to make sure he was all right. She'd never seen him injured before, and the sight of his blood made her heart beat with a rapid cadence. Fortuna, she noticed, had turned a distinctly sallow colour and had flopped into an armchair where Aunt Beatrice was soothingly fanning her.

'Bella, he'll be fine,' Niamh called, and beckoned her to her side. 'He's survived far worse.'

Bella joined her on the fireside chaise alongside the victorious Henry, who was gulping a celebratory glass of Madeira, while Niamh surreptitiously washed away the remains of his streaky cosmetics.

Bella gaped at him. There was something unnervingly intimate about seeing him thus exposed without his paint and his patches and his thick layer of powder to hide behind. Niamh, on the other hand, seemed enchanted with the revelation, as if she'd found something she'd been looking for, but hadn't quite realised until that point.

'I hope you won't be offended if I decline the offer of a dress,' she said. Bella didn't catch the rest of her words, for she leaned close and whispered into Henry's ear but she could guess.

'Fortuna, Fortuna, dear.' Mrs Alvanley continued to waft her noxious smelling salts beneath the nose of her eldest niece who Bella swore was faking her distress, purely for attention.

She crossed to where Raffe stood by the fireplace, now free of his sack. 'Idiot,' she scolded. 'Best pray you haven't broken his nose.'

His smoky grey eyes thinned to enraged slits. 'He belted me a few good ones too. If you'd paid more attention you'd have noticed, and the other three were far from innocent. Why do you think de Maresi and Gabriel ended up on the floor?'

Bella could think of a whole host of reasons, but grudgingly admitted that it hadn't exactly been fair play all round.

Raffe threw a few more logs on the fire, and prodded them into place with the poker.

'I can't meet you,' she said.

Grimly, he raised his head and conceded with a nod.

Bella fished the note from her sleeve where she'd placed it after reading it and fed it to the flames.

'I trust he brings sweeter satisfaction,' he said, as the paper crumbled to ash.

13

Bella left the house immediately after breakfast so as to avoid Mrs Alvanley's accomplishments' practice. The chaperone had decided the morning would be best spent capturing the southern transcript of the church on canvas and Bella, who barely knew one end of a paintbrush from the other, excused herself on the pretence of riding, the one activity she was apparently allowed to enjoy unchaperoned and unaccompanied. Unfortunately she arrived at the stable to discover Gabriel and de Maresi had arrived ahead of her.

Morosely, she watched them leave the yard, then ventured into the coach house to hide until Mrs Alvanley's entourage had passed.

'Vaughan!' she said. He was standing in a dark corner, his back to her.

He spun to face her, a fishing rod and what appeared to be a tatty brown blanket clutched to his chest. 'Bella! Not improving yourself with the ladies?'

'Might I join you?' She nodded at his accessories.

Vaughan wrinkled his nose which she was relieved to see was not even bruised. 'Ah! Well, I'm not actually doing any fishing. I was just sorting a few things out.'

Bella eyed him sceptically. Gentlemen, in her experience, didn't 'just sort things out'.

'We could walk instead.' He stuffed the rod and blanket

into a box of horse tackle and took her hand. 'I'll show you the lake.'

Bella stared at his fingers laced with hers, remaining rooted to the spot. This was all surprisingly charming, which meant he was almost certainly up to something.

'Where do you want this . . . ?' Henry Tristan swished into the coach house, stopped abruptly, then backed out as rapidly as he'd entered. 'No matter. I'm sure Jenkins can help sort it out.'

'Is that the straw delivery?' Vaughan called.

'Erm, yes.'

'Excellent. Stack it in the hayloft!'

Bella watched the performance in stupefied silence. Excellent! Since when did Vaughan describe anything as excellent? 'What are you up to?'

Vaughan gave her a guileless smile. 'Absolutely nothing.' He clapped his hands. 'Now, about that walk, or would you prefer to spend the morning embroidering one of Aunt Beatrice's tammys?'

The lake was not far from the castle. It fed the moat via an underground stream, which Vaughan helpfully pointed out as they strode over the springy turf. Nearer the bank, the long grass gave way to reeds, and birdsong to the chirp of crickets. He took her out in a little blue boat. Bella sat in the bow, watching ripples spreading out in concentric circles as the paddle dipped in and out of the water.

Near the centre, he stopped paddling and let them drift.

'You should have brought your fishing rod,' she said.

'Hmm.' He leaned forwards and put an arm around her shoulder. He pulled her against his chest. 'I was never much for fishing.' Bella settled against him, listening to his heartbeat, content to remain for ever, or at least until a crick formed in her neck and the sun went down.

'Vaughan, is this where you grew up?'

'Mostly.'

She almost caught a glimpse of him: a thin pale youth, with a mass of black hair and an indolent smile, but the image wouldn't solidify into anything tangible. 'Where else?'

Cheek pressed to her head, he began to work the pins from her hair. 'Don't you know enough about me already?'

'Actually, I know very little, despite having shared your bed for three years.'

'Shared Lucerne's bed.' One shiny pin went sailing into the air and vanished below the surface of the pond. 'You've never shared mine.'

A moment's silence stretched between them. Bella toyed with the buttons of his waistcoat. 'But there are other houses, aren't there?'

'A few,' he responded. 'Why the sudden interest? You're not eyeing me up as a potential husband, I trust.'

'No, of course not. It's just that you're not a gentleman, are you? You're a nobleman. It never sunk in before.'

With a snort of disgust, Vaughan pushed himself into an upright position. 'I'm so gratified you clarified that remark. Not a gentleman.' He snorted again. Eyes narrowed under long dark lashes, his lips twitched as a salacious smile crinkled the corners of his eyes, and he pushed a hand inside the front of her dress. 'You can darn well say that again.'

'Vaughan.' She batted him away, conscious that her action caused the little boat to rock unsteadily.

'Bella.' He eyed her curiously, his violet eyes calculating and intense.

'Are there other titles as well as houses?'

'Lord and master.' The remark set her eyes rolling and earned him a dismissive tut.

'Very well, sixth Marquis of Pennerley, Earl of Oswestry, Earl of Craven and yes, there are other estates, one in Rutland, one in Cheshire and one in North Yorkshire near Middleham. Satisfied? Oh, and the house in London.'

'That's yours,' she gasped. 'I thought it was –'

'Lucerne's. Well, you thought wrong. Lucerne rented his previous quarters, which were hardly a suitable abode for a lady.'

'Oh!' So she'd lived in his house and hadn't even realised. The knowledge made her feel strangely excluded as if they'd been keeping secrets from her, which was probably just silly. It was her own fault for making assumptions.

The wind blew and ruffled her clothing. Vaughan drummed his fingers on the side of the boat. 'Stop sulking. I want to hear what you got up to with Raffe.'

Bella scowled. 'Nothing. I didn't meet him.'

Vaughan rolled his eyes, and clasped his hands before him, so the tips pressed to his sensual lips. That mannerism again. 'How exquisitely dull.'

Really, he was the most impossible man. If she hadn't been stuck in a blasted boat with him she'd have stormed off. To think how he raged over Niamh being with the man she loved, and then calmly expected her to bed down with whomever, for his entertainment, that was too much. She lowered her head and pressed the heels of her hands over her eyes.

She felt the boat tip as he shifted position. The resulting waves lapped merrily at the sides. Vaughan's breath whispered across the back of her neck, causing the hairs to stand on end. 'You're thinking about my sister.' Moist lips pressed to the sensitive skin, sending a shiver of anticipation rolling through her suddenly tensed body. Unconsciously, she leaned into the caress.

'It's not as if I can actually do anything to stop her. She's of age, Bella.'

'But you're making her life hell.' As he continually made hers.

'No, I'm saving her from a life of hell. He doesn't love her, he's using her for her assets.'

His lips continued to trouble the curve of her throat, gliding over her skin like a dragonfly over the surface of the lake, in flighty, delicate little bursts, which nevertheless raised a heat, both across her skin and in her belly.

'You seem very sure. How can you know that?'

'Shh!' He pressed his index finger to her lips.

'It's just a game to you.' She batted his hand away and turned her head to better see him. 'Is what's going on with Lucerne a game too?''

Vaughan rested his cheek upon her shoulder. 'That is no game. There's too much at stake. I ran. I hoped he'd follow.' He rubbed a circle against her skin with his cheek. 'Maybe I even hoped you'd follow. There is something quite delicious about you.' He stuck out his tongue and drew it up the side of her neck, creating a cold, tingly trail that culminated in the nip of his teeth upon her earlobe.

'I doubt you thought of me at all.'

'On that, too, you're wrong. I thought of you an awful lot. I'm thinking of you now.' His hands slipped around her until they cupped her breasts. The sensation of his fingers spread across her sensitive flesh, holding her, supporting her, making the fire he'd raised burn a little fiercer. But there was a certain irritability to what he was doing too. He was using her, and she didn't want to be used. She didn't want to be his whore; she wanted to be more than that. She wanted to be in that place in his heart he reserved entirely for Lucerne.

'Oh, Christ!' he muttered. 'Don't go maudlin on me in the middle of a lake. We were just starting to have fun. What's the matter? You're up and down like the wind.'

'Can't you figure it out?' she snarled as the bubble of irritability burst.

Vaughan shuffled round to face her. He stared at her long and hard. 'Maybe I don't want to. Maybe, I'd rather just shag you until you smile. It seems a lot simpler, somehow.'

Bella shoved him, and he toppled back against the prow, causing the boat to rear and dip into the lake. 'You've vile and cruel, and if I had any sense I'd make you take me ashore and take up with Devonshire instead. Likely he'd see me better off.'

Vaughan gave an incredulous snort that quickly developed into a full-blown laugh. 'Better with Raffe, oh, that's good. You don't even like him enough to meet him when you're gagging for it.'

Bella scowled, but Vaughan wasn't finished. His voice dropped an octave, and crawled across her senses making each nerve vibrate. 'That and you're forgetting. You like it when I'm cruel.'

'I like it when you satisfy me,' she growled.

Vaughan maintained his mordant smile. 'Do I not always satisfy you, ultimately?'

Perhaps he did. Maybe that was the reason she kept coming back for more, no matter how infuriating she found him, or how much he swung her emotions.

'What do you want?' he hissed.

Bella's gaze flitted nervously across his face. Would he give or do the opposite of what she asked? She pursed her lips. What did she want? She thought she wanted him, wholly and completely, but hadn't she once thought that about Lucerne too? What if all she really craved was what she couldn't have?

'Very well, Miss Unforthcoming, how about I tell you what I think you want?'

Her mind conjured an array of images, one illustration after another, of things he might do, of things she wanted. Clearest came a vision of him prone in the bottom of the boat, his pantaloons unfastened to reveal his erection and her straddled across his hips, her skirts covering his face as she rose and fell upon his cock, driving them to mutual ecstasy.

Tentatively, she placed a hand upon his thigh. 'Take me as a woman.'

'No.'

'Why not?'

Vaughan licked his lips. 'Because until he tells me otherwise, you're Lucerne's.'

'What if he never tells you? What if he doesn't come?'

Vaughan's eyes darkened. 'Then you'll have to wait a long time.'

'I've waited long enough already. Take me ashore.'

Vaughan resumed his seat but, instead of taking up the oars, he simply stretched with his hands on his head and closed his eyes.

Furious, Bella grabbed the oars and struggled to row but couldn't seem to get them to work in unison. She succeeded only in turning the boat one hundred and eighty degrees, whereupon she dropped them in disgust. Vaughan peeped at her from below his eyelashes. 'Guess you should have met Raffe. He's desperate to stick it up you.'

Bella prodded him in the stomach with the wet end of one oar.

Vaughan sat abruptly and batted at the wet patch on his waistcoat. 'That was uncalled for.' The little boat lurched as he tipped her backwards beneath him. Water crashed over the sides, soaking them both. One oar went overboard and sailed off towards the reed beds on the back of a wave.

In terror, Bella clung to him. Wet clothes pressed to her skin, pinned her just as surely as his body. Water dripped from his ringlets onto her face, where they ran like tears over her cheeks. The ridge of his cock warmed her thigh, then his kiss came, carnal and forceful. It stole her breath and her thoughts, so that all she could do was moan and respond.

Her hair was wet. She lay in a puddle, but his scent was so strong, her emotions so tangled, that her resistance faltered.

Vaughan drew back, his smile hinting at mischief. 'I could take you now, as per your request, but the boat's already swimming and I'm in no mood for subtleties. It's your choice, Bella. Shall I raise these sodden skirts and plough you deep, until the boat sinks and we're dragged to the murky depths?'

'Take me on the shore.'

He shook his head. 'Where would be the thrill in that?'

'Vaughan ... please.' She pushed her hand between their

bodies and kneaded his cock where it lay trapped beneath his tight pantaloons.

'Here or nothing,' he said, stilling her wrist.

'I can't swim.'

'Ah! And I gather I'm not worth drowning for?'

Bella frowned and tightened a hand over his bottom, but he merely raised both eyebrows to reiterate the question. 'Fine,' she snarled. 'Take me ashore.'

Vaughan took up the remaining oar and paddled back to the boathouse. 'Where do you think you're going?' he said, when she climbed out onto the stone steps. He clasped his arms about her waist and lifted her back into the boat.

Bella squealed, but didn't dare kick, as he deposited her in the centre of the boat.

Precariously balanced, with his legs spread wide, Vaughan unfastened her dress and let it fall in a soggy heap at their feet, where it instantly soaked up much of the water sluicing about. Her shift was also wet, but he left that on and tucked it up into the bottom of her stays at the front. The top four hooks on her stays were next, just enough so that her breasts spilled over the top, warm and soft into his palms.

'What now, my wanton nymph? Should I take you standing up in this floating bathtub?'

Bella wriggled as much as she dared, feeling the wet cloth of his coat cold against her skin. 'You weren't intending to take me, as I recall.'

'No.' He shrugged off his coat, which landed with a soggy plop, sending the boat juddering. 'I said I wouldn't come in your cunt.'

Now his loins pressed teasingly against her rear, wetting

her appetite for him a little more. 'Dammit, Bella, I'm as ripe as a plum for you.'

'Are you?' She stepped out of the boat again and this time he followed her out of the shadowy boathouse, with its watery echo and green-tinged internal hue, into the meadow that bordered the lake. 'Take me, then.' There was only one way he could take her here, in daylight in a field overlooked by the castle, without risking arrest.

Vaughan stared at her naked quim, an untroubled smile playing upon his lips. 'The grass is long. Don't assume you've outwitted me. Besides, the only windows that look this way are in my room and Niamh's, and she knows when to turn her head. Although, Lord knows, maybe if she took notes occasionally she might have half an idea about men.'

'I thought you liked her innocent.'

The damp cloth of his shirt peeled away slowly as she pushed a hand beneath his shirt. Through the sodden lawn she could make out a dark patch of hair and the glint of gold. The metal lay warm in her hand a moment, then her fingers closed tight about it and she tugged.

The catch gave and the chain slithered over the back of her hand.

Vaughan grabbed for it, but too late. 'Give it back.'

Bella jerked away from him. 'You can have it once you've given me what I want.'

'Don't be foolish, Bella. Give it back.'

She laughed and sprinted into the long grass, the golden locket clasped tight within her hand. She knew he'd follow. The precious oval was his link to Lucerne. Lucerne – who probably didn't even know of its existence. She was the only person who knew just how much it meant to him.

Yellowing grass and wildflowers lashed at her bare legs as she ran. The hem of her shift worked itself loose of her stays and tumbled, clammy and cold, over her nakedness to lap at her ankles. Still she ran, until her chest felt tight and her stomach cramped with fatigue.

He caught her at the field boundary and tipped her over a drystone wall on her stomach. 'Give me that.'

'Take me like a woman first,' she teased, holding the locket out of reach on the far side of the wall.

'I'll do more than swive you if you don't hand it over.' Voice hoarse from running, his words carried the force of his anger, something his palm carried through a mere moment later as his hand came down hard across her rear.

Bella jerked in shock as the pain flared across her cheeks and indignation coloured her face. He landed another, and she kicked, causing her wet chemise to pull taut across her bottom.

'Give me the pendant.'

'Give me your prick, my lord.'

Heat bloomed and spread out from the point of impact of his palm. Each successive smack stole her breath and raised a delayed squeal.

Her nipples hardened, steepled against the cold rocks. Moans of agony transformed into pants of pure longing. As the rocks dug into her belly, her desire to come only increased.

Cold air bathed her heated skin as he raised her shift. 'You're very wet,' he remarked. 'Not to mention a particularly lovely shade of fuchsia.' His palm spread her wide and brushed up between her thighs. Juicy and open, she responded to his touch with more moisture.

Bella felt her breath mist before her face as her heart

beat a cacophony against the stone wall beneath her. She felt empty, craved the feeling of him hard between her legs, filling her, bringing sweet fulfilment.

'The locket,' he demanded.

'No,' she hissed.

Vaughan stuck his thumb up her arse, all pretence of niceties gone. 'Don't play with me, Bella.' Her nipples rubbed the rough stone. Vaughan pushed another finger into her cunt alongside the two already giving her pleasure.

'I'm not asking for much.' She wriggled against the intrusion as if a torture such as this would ever persuade her. Didn't he know her by now? It sometimes shamed her but she revelled in his style of torment.

'And I'm not playing.' Another finger, another push. 'Give me the locket, Bella, or I'm going to stick my whole hand in there.'

Bella spluttered her next words, a curse, onto the grass. How would that make her feel? Would it fill her as well as his cock? Was it even a punishment, when his fingers brought such pleasure? She couldn't stop herself groaning. Four fingers slipped in and out of her with incredible ease.

'Such effort,' she teased. 'Using your cock would have been much easier and we'd both have reaped the rewards.'

Vaughan folded his thumb alongside his fingers and pushed, not very far, but enough for her to feel him stretching her. 'Vaughan,' she whimpered.

'Last chance to surrender.'

Bella lifted her hand and let the chain slide through her fingers. It swung merrily at the extent of its chain, just out of reach. 'I'll take my punishment.'

'Damn you!'

No doubt his face was like thunder, a dark brooding

mask, enough to scare most people into submission, but not her.

He cupped his thumb to his fingers and swived her with the length of his fingers, not really giving what he'd promised at all. The pleasure was diverting, but more infuriating than intense. Each stroke promised, but didn't quite deliver. What she wanted was deep and rough, not slow and cautious. The pace made her buck. Vaughan licked a trail of sweat from her tailbone, his breath rasping against her splayed cheeks.

'Are you hard?' she gasped.

'Like iron.'

Her breath hitched. 'Please, Vaughan.' They both needed this. What was the point in this endless denial? To her surprise, he slowly withdrew his fingers, allowing her to roll off the wall and onto her back with her thighs spread. As if gripped by an unfathomable dilemma, his face was hard, eyes glittering, not with obvious passion but something brittle. Bella held his gaze, the locket poised above her breasts. She let the chain run into his open palm which was still sticky with her juices.

'Please.'

Despite her pretty pout, Vaughan shook his head, although he drove his hard lips against her soft yielding ones. 'You want this. You want me,' she hissed when he allowed her a moment to breathe.

'Yes,' he agreed. 'But unless you tie me down I'll deny it. I can restrain myself.'

'Why?' What was the point? 'Vaughan, for God's sake, and for mine.' She'd never take him by force. The last time she'd tried it had taken several grown men to restrain him. She rubbed her glistening pubis against the ridge of his erection, felt him leap and stiffen at the contact, but instead of rousing him to action, it prompted him to pull away.

Vaughan sank onto his knees between her thighs and blew a long intimate whisper across her clit. 'No,' she sobbed, feeling her body spark. A single touch of his tongue was all it took to push her over and set her thrashing.

When she reopened her eyes, Vaughan was above her once more, the locket back in place around his neck. He blinked slowly and she looked into his violet eyes as confused as ever. Why? The question stuck on her tongue. 'When did you last come?' she asked instead.

Vaughan shrugged. He straightened and began to smooth his clothes. 'Dinner last night, by your hand as I recall.'

'And before that?'

'In the pantry.'

'Not with de Maresi?'

He shook his head. Bella tweaked some grass from the gaps in the wall and twirled it in her fingers, contemplating his answer, confounded by his intentions.

'Doesn't he make you feel?' she asked.

The question earned her another shrug.

Wet petticoats tumbled into place and stuck to her legs as she stood. She ran her hand over the lozenge-shaped swell of his cock, clasped tight by his figure-hugging pantaloons. 'Adds up to a lot of self-denial,' she said. 'I'm not sure it's good for you.'

Expertly, she freed his erection and ran teasing fingers over his tip. She felt his back go rigid, watched his jaw lock, but he didn't push her away and he came very quickly.

'He'll come,' she whispered into his hair as he further messed her chemise with the culmination of her efforts.

'He loves you.' She didn't add that she felt the same way. There was little point; it wasn't what he wanted to hear.

They went back to the boathouse after that and gathered their wet clothes. 'I'll see you at dinner,' Vaughan said, on reaching the gatehouse. 'I have business to see to.'

The ladies were gathered in the great hall as Bella was on her way to her room. Aunt Beatrice took one look at Bella's wet gown and dismissed her with an imperious frown. Bella marched up to the stairs not caring one whit. The Allenthorpes and their annoying chaperone could think of her what they liked. That she had Vaughan was what mattered. She just wished for his sake, that he had Lucerne. It seemed he needed that comfort.

14

As expected, Bella didn't see Vaughan again until dinner that evening, where she was forced to endure another of Fortuna's eyelash-fluttering overtures. Quite unexpectedly, the girl had conjured a scarlet dress cut in the very latest style. It sheathed her slender figure to perfection, enhancing delicate curves. To Bella's relief, Vaughan hadn't noticed as he was too busy ducking her feathered headdress.

He was perfectly turned out in charcoal Florentine silk, which emphasised his broad shoulders and slender waist. Bella drank down the sight of him, wishing she'd had the presence of mind to bring a few more dresses with her from London.

'Can't say as I'm much for feathers,' said Raffe, slipping into the seat to Bella's left. 'Damned ticklish, and the red's a little brazen.'

'I thought you liked brazen.'

Raffe considered this as he unfurled his napkin. 'There's brazen, and then there's shameless. She's trying too hard which is precisely the reason she's failing. He likes a challenge.'

'Don't all men?' Bella asked, still observing the pair.

'Oh, I don't know. I wouldn't object to you throwing yourself at me.'

Rolling her eyes, Bella picked up her knife and fork. 'It won't happen.' She tucked into the meal before her, ignoring the complaints and endearments he delivered through a mouthful of peas.

'Viscount Marlinscar,' Foster announced. The words didn't register until she heard the great iron-pinned door swing closed. That end of the hall was in near darkness but a single glance at Vaughan confirmed what her eyesight alone couldn't. Lucerne had arrived.

Vaughan's eyes burned with anticipation. His lips, normally red, seemed swollen with the expectation of kisses.

The rest of the table noticed him rising and followed suit. Vaughan stilled the scraping of chairs with a imperious flick of his wrist. 'Enjoy,' he said, strolling towards his lover.

Bella strained to witness their reunion.

Lucerne was in the shadows below the stairs. Vaughan curbed the urge to run, forcing himself to walk. Three weeks. It'd been too long, but the relief now he'd arrived. He couldn't express it, not in company. Ever since he'd left London, he'd longed for this moment. The moment when everything fell into place again.

It had been imperative that he'd woken Bella to the realities of their relationship, and given Lucerne a jolt, but more important still to remove them to the country. London was draining their vitality. Here at Pennerley, he could make things right again. With or without Bella. Except . . .

Foster applied a taper to the guttered candles and light spilled over Lucerne's golden hair. He glowed, and Vaughan feasted upon the sight of him. Despite the coach journey, he was resplendent in caped greatcoat and every bit as angelically perfect as the first time they'd met.

'Lucerne.' Somehow he made his voice sound normal. He

politely extended a hand, though what he wanted to do was push the stupid bugger against the wall and toss him into a state of feverish excitement, to lock their bodies together and fill him and never let go.

'Vaughan.' Lucerne's voice carried an unexpected edge. 'Is Bella here? I need to find her.'

Bella! Vaughan's eyes narrowed, all this time apart and he thought of her first. The jealousy he never managed to kill licked flames beneath his skin. He should make him wait until after dinner, but he had no appetite any more, if he'd had any to begin with.

He guessed that Lucerne sensed his anger, for he leaned a fraction closer. 'It's not what you think, Vaughan.' His chest rose with a heavy sigh. 'I have pressing news for her.'

'So pressing it won't wait a minute or two?' Vaughan nodded for Foster to open the door, and he backed Lucerne outside and up against the kitchen wall. 'We have pressing matters of our own.'

Lucerne stiffened, but not in a good way. His blue eyes gleamed with spellbinding intensity. 'I'm not here for this,' he growled.

'Aren't you?' Vaughan tenderly traced his fingertips over the curve of Lucerne's cheek. He leaned in for a kiss, but Lucerne turned his head away.

'Bella first.'

The rebuke hurt more than any physical slap. Bella. Always destined to come between them. 'Very well.' He drew back. 'Miss Rushdale,' he yelled. Their eyes locked upon one another, unspeaking until she came, then he retreated inside and shut the door on the pair of them.

* * *

Bella stared uneasily at the studded door before turning to Lucerne. She didn't look at him. Vaughan was angry which didn't bode well. He should have been happy to see Lucerne, as a tiny part of her was. She nipped out the glow of warmth. Lucerne would have to earn his forgiveness. He had to understand how deeply she'd been hurt before she once again gave in to her desire for him.

Determined to make the few moments alone count, Bella swished passed him across the darkened courtyard to the curtain wall. Only a thin sliver of daylight remained as a yellow-pink band fell across the base of the valley. The air smelled of faded summer and the coming frost. Her nose twitched as he came up behind her.

'Bella.' Lucerne placed his greatcoat around her shoulder. Ever the gentleman, she thought, tempted to shake it off. Practicality won out. It was too cold to be outside in just a muslin dress. Besides, the wool was warm and fragrant and her anger had faded in the week since their parting. She wanted an apology from him but, more importantly, she wanted everything right between the three of them again. Vaughan needed him, which meant she did too.

'You said you wouldn't come.'

A cold leather glove curled around her shoulder. 'I know. Nothing's changed in that respect. I still need time . . . It's not why I came.'

The lack of an apology rankled. Incensed, she turned and struck him hard about the ear. The impact stung her palm but it made her feel better. It was what she should have done the night she left. 'Time to cosset Miss St John,' she hissed. 'How dare you come here and expect me to even see you?'

Lucerne flinched, but it was hard to tell if it was at her

words or the slap. To his credit, he didn't try to rub away the sting.

'You call yourself a gentleman but you don't act like one. You let me walk into the night while you mated with a doxy.'

'No!' His fists locked around her wrists. 'That's not true. I looked for you.' His posture was rigid. There was no freeing herself from him. 'Listen to me. I didn't come here to argue with you or Vaughan. A letter came . . .'

'A letter?' Struggles subsiding, she looked up at him with guarded interest.

Time had changed him. Charcoal smudges shadowed the skin beneath his eyes and he was almost consumptive in his pallor, an effect not helped by the blackness of his clothing.

He handed her a package of letters.

Bella frowned in recognition of the familiar hand and the length of yellow ribbon that bound the papers together. 'Why have you brought me these?'

Unable to maintain eye contact, Lucerne stared at the polish on his own Hessians. 'Wakefield's returning to England. Louisa's dead.'

The spark of joy that leaped at the thought of being reunited with her friend was quenched equally abruptly, her exclamation of delight transformed into a howl of denial. 'She can't be . . . The baby?'

'Is fine. A healthy girl.' Lucerne's grip slid reassuringly to her shoulders. In better times, he'd have crushed her with his embrace. 'It was nothing to do with the birth. Wakefield said it was fever, very quick, very sudden. She was never the most robust . . .' He shook his head, unable to complete the sentence. Instead, he thrust another letter upon her.

Bella stared at the page but couldn't focus on the words. 'When did this come?'

'I came home to it after I'd searched the whole of Mayfair and Marylebone for you. I left the moment I'd established you weren't still in London. Then I knew I'd find you here.' His voice cracked and he hauled in a shallow breath. 'I know how you feel about him. It's been plain for a long time.' His lips pressed tightly together. 'I'm sorry. I should have talked to you sooner instead of trying to ignore it.'

It was her turn to feel guilty. The shift in her affections was what this was all about. It had destroyed the balance in their relationship. Instead of Lucerne being pivotal, he'd become a pawn, a means of reaching Vaughan. His feelings had been pushed aside. He'd tried to tell her that too, but she hadn't listened. 'I'm sorry too.'

Lucerne rubbed his thumb across her lips. 'Has he been good to you, Bella? Has he given you what you want?'

She shrugged. 'He's been Vaughan.' Her lips felt dry and cracked, but wetting them would mean tracing Lucerne's fingertip with her tongue. 'It's not me he wants. It never was or will be. He's been waiting for you.'

Uncertainty clouded his blue eyes. She watched him struggle through the mire of memories. There was still love there but it came at a high price. Could he stand being the object of Vaughan's affections but not hers?

'I'm sorry. He just . . .' Lucerne pressed a silencing finger to her lips. In that moment, he looked so fragile and dreadfully alone.

'I ought to go to him. Explain Wakefield's loss, not that he'll care.'

'He liked Louisa.'

'He hates Wakefield.'

Bella's eyes swam with tears, but she was too numb to stop them spilling. 'When is he back?' She sniffed.

'I'm not sure.' Lucerne smeared the tears across her cheeks with his thumbs. 'He's coming to Lauwine. I'll meet him there. If he goes to his sisters, they'll oust him from the nursery and his daughter and then he'll have nothing.' Perhaps a fraction of the devastation Wakefield was surely feeling touched Lucerne's pallid face. He dragged his hands through his hair. 'I've made a mess of everything. I should have ...' He shook his head. 'No.' His gaze drifted to the grey stone of the great hall with its three majestic arched windows. Light gleamed through the shutters. His jaw set, grimly determined.

'I'm so sorry, Bella.' His mouth, warm and bitter, crushed hers. 'So, very, desperately sorry.'

Vaughan left his guests and went up to the solar. He couldn't hide behind a mask of indifference. His rage burned like a bloody haze. He'd waited too long for this moment. The moment when he'd entwine Lucerne in his arms again, feel his hard body against his, his kisses killing him. Ever since he'd left London, he'd longed, pined for him, and now ... All that mattered to Lucerne was Bella.

Women! He grabbed the poker and jabbed it into the coals. Three years he'd tried to ignore the fact, but he couldn't any longer. Lucerne preferred women. He would always be second best, to Bella, to whichever belle fluttered her eyelashes in Lucerne's direction. But he couldn't be second best any longer. The arrangement had to change. He wanted someone who loved him exclusively, with the same intensity he felt for them.

'Lucerne,' he breathed into the darkness. 'It can't be this way any more.'

'Vaughan.'

Lucerne entered the solar to find his lover staring resolutely into the flames. He'd been in this room before, years ago, before London, before the time in Rome. It had been the dowager's domain in those days – Vaughan's grandmother. Her old bones parked before the fire, her beauty withered, but her hair coiffed and powdered and her décolletage just as low as it had been in her youth. He smiled at the memory of her, wrinkled, powdery, and smelling of ginger and sherry, a feeble guard for two determined young rakehells. They'd sneaked out of the castle, scaled the walls and crossed the moat on an improvised punt made from an old door and a clothes prop, then abducted two local beauties and taken them to the Craven Arms Inn for the night. All he really remembered was a sea of linen and entwined limbs, as the four of them shared the same flea-bitten bed.

Had Vaughan's palms brushed the backs of his thighs that night, he wondered, as they'd lain alongside one another smothered in female flesh. Had he thought of leaning over and claiming the night as their own? Even then he'd been courting scandal. That was the reason he'd been summoned back to Pennerley and the watchful eye of the dowager.

Shortly after that, the 5th Marquis of Pennerley had passed away and Vaughan had taken off for the Continent.

Lucerne sighed, his smile fading along with the memories of their youth. Sometimes, he wondered just how much easier life would have been if they'd simply remained friends who shared lovers, but not each other.

'Vaughan.' Not sure what else to say, he hung back for a moment, then cautiously placed his hand upon Vaughan's shoulder.

Lucerne felt the shiver roll down Vaughan's back and curled his fingers into the muscle. He'd never envisaged this as an easy meeting. He knew too well how vengeful and emotional Vaughan could be. The slightest thing might set him laughing or tumble him into the foulest pit of despair. He didn't dare attempt a caress but without some form of prompt they might be staring into the flames until only cold ashes remained.

Frustrated, Lucerne rubbed his jaw. Why was it always necessary to go through this drama, this torture? All they ever needed to do was say what they actually meant to one another.

'Are you forgiven?' Vaughan eventually asked, breaking the uncomfortable silence.

Yet more dancing. Lucerne sighed. 'I don't know. We didn't really speak of it.' Taking a risk, he edged his fingers under the collar of Vaughan's shirt. Despite what he'd told Bella back in London, he did miss Vaughan's touch. The man could make him come so hard he thought the top of his head would fly off. Besides, life was just plain more interesting with him around ... It was just the agony that went with it.

Vaughan raised both hands and shrugged him off. 'Then what, pray, did you speak of that was so damn urgent?' Finally, he turned his head, revealing a carefully constructed mask of indifference, emotions and desires locked away behind a front of conceit and arrogance. But Lucerne had learned to read him long ago. Those eyes, you could fall into Vaughan's eyes and get lost for days. Every slight, every moment of pain and every fragment of bliss was writ there. Jealousy flicked across their shiny surface. Blind panic troubled their depths.

'Louisa's dead,' Lucerne said frankly. He hadn't wanted to break that particular piece of news just yet; there were issues enough to address without muddying things further but the situation demanded an explanation.

A sliver of sadness melted into Vaughan's gaze, brightening their liquid intensity. 'I see,' he said, voice chipped and brittle. He paced to the window overlooking the moat. 'Stupid bastard should never have taken her to India. She was far too delicate to be a soldier's wife.'

Lucerne followed him. 'What would you have him do, Vaughan? Give up his commission?'

'There was no need for them to go. Louisa brought plenty of money to the marriage. Accept it, Lucerne. The man liked playing soldiers and his fixation has cost him his wife.'

Lucerne felt his head throb. Not this argument, not again. 'Not now,' he growled. His two friends had never got along but now was not the time for criticism and blame or for rehashing old slights. A wave of grief washed over him. Lucerne bowed his head. The sorrow wasn't all for Louisa; at least some of it was for himself and the jumbled mess his life had become. 'You made your peace with him before they left. Let's not reopen old wounds.'

Vaughan shook his head. 'I made my peace with Louisa. I tolerated him for her sake and for yours. Otherwise . . .' He rolled his eyes towards the ceiling. The rest remained unsaid.

Lucerne opened his mouth, then changed his mind and let the words of Wakefield's defence wash away too. 'Perhaps we shouldn't speak of it any more,' he said diplomatically.

'Perhaps not.' Vaughan twisted the rings on his fingers until the stones lay straight. 'What do you suggest instead? Miss St John's charms, perhaps?'

'Georgiana's announced her engagement.'

'Really.'

'To Sir Nathaniel Glenbervie.'

Vaughan sneered. 'To that rancid macaroni! Clearly, your prowess as a lover is under dispute if you can lose out to him.'

Lucerne felt his temperature rise. He was not by nature quick to anger but he'd taken quite enough stick recently and he wasn't going to take any more. 'You're pleased she's gone, so don't mock.'

'I never doubted she'd leave. I told you all long that she wouldn't wait as patiently as Bella.'

That was it. Lucerne smashed his fist into the back of a nearby chair. The impact smarted, made his knuckles throb. The chair faired somewhat better. It merely skittered over the polished boards and banged against the oak panelling. 'We both know the only reason I haven't married Bella is because you wouldn't have it!'

There were times over the last few years when he had thought to hell with Vaughan and been on the very verge of a proposal, but always something had stopped him. During that whole time, he'd been constantly riled by interfering matrons, his peers and her brother over his intentions. Goddamn Joshua! But he could hardly blame the man.

Vaughan calmly rubbed his finger over the new dent in

the wainscotting. 'I left London three weeks ago, Lucerne. How much time do you need? You could have married by special licence within the week.'

'You'd never have spoken to either of us again.'

Vaughan shrugged. 'We all face difficult choices.'

'That was a choice you know I'm not prepared to make. Besides,' he whipped about, causing his coat-tails to flap, 'she'd have refused me. She lost interest in me the moment you left the house. All she cared about was how quickly she could get you back between her thighs.' He pushed his hands through his hair and clenched his fist, but the discomfort didn't help. 'Oh, but she never gets you between her thighs. I know about the times at Lauwine, but that was before you cared, wasn't it, Vaughan?'

He slapped Vaughan's hands away from the wood and grabbed him by the shoulders. 'You never gave a thought to the countless other women you've risked getting with child. But you couldn't be quite so heartless on her account. Couldn't risk fathering a bastard.'

Vaughan shifted uncomfortably beneath the vice-like grip. 'Let go, Lucerne,' he growled. 'She was yours.'

Lucerne snorted in disgust but held on. 'She stopped being mine a long time ago.'

'Then why the hell is she still lying between us?'

'I'm not the one who invited her.'

'But you are the one who claims he needs a woman for satisfaction, despite the fact I can make you come with just my little finger.'

Rage almost blinding him, Lucerne shoved him away. He found the brandy decanter and poured himself a large glass which he knocked back. The second burned on his tongue before he swallowed.

Vaughan's eyes glittered as he watched Lucerne, hatred, passion and terror, all there in his gaze. He drew his long hair back into a ponytail then let the dark strands fall slowly through his splayed fingers. Then he raised his other hand and mockingly wiggled his little finger.

The glass shattered against the hearthstone.

Lucerne pounced. 'Damn you!' he growled as he forced his mouth down over Vaughan's. He slid one hand up Vaughan's back and into his hairline as he ground their hips together. He'd make this simple.

Vaughan snarled as he kissed him but his lips were curiously immobile. Lucerne squeezed his arse and felt a kick of excitement as he felt Vaughan's cock jerk in response. But he was still resisting. 'Kiss me, damn you.' Riled and aroused, he cupped Vaughan's jaw and forced him to make eye contact again. 'You left so I'd chase. Well, I'm here now. This is what you want, isn't it?'

'Not like this,' Vaughan hissed between clenched teeth. 'I can't be forever second best. I don't want to share you. I don't want to fuck you for Bella's pleasure.' His fingers bit hard into the arm of Lucerne's coat. 'I want it to be just us. I've tried your way.' He took a deep breath, and released it with shudder. 'I convinced myself that if we just left London, it would somehow be fine. Without the distractions and the pressure, if it were just her again ...'

'Oh, for God's sake, just because I spoke to her first. Her best friend is dead, Vaughan.'

'It's not that,' Vaughan yelled back. His eyes were liquid and bright. Painfully open. Emotions he normally kept hidden were painted with unnerving clarity in the violet depths. Lucerne refused to look into them, resorted, instead, to a third glass of brandy.

'I can see the truth, Lucerne. You didn't want to come. You did it out of necessity, nothing else.' He drew his teeth over his lower lip, shaking his head. 'I love you. I wish to God I didn't, but I can't do it if I have to share you any more. That time is past.'

It was true, Lucerne acknowledged. He hadn't wanted to come. He'd told Bella as much. He'd intended to stay away until the New Year or later. 'I just needed some time alone,' he said. 'I'm exhausted. You pass me between you, pin me down, tie me up. It's not even for my pleasure any more. It's a game of one-upmanship between you. You're both so busy fighting, you forget I'm there. Is it any wonder I seek comfort elsewhere?' He put the glass down before the urge to shatter it as well became too strong. 'Not that you've any right to lecture me on faithfulness. How many times have you shafted de Maresi recently?'

'Not half as many as you'd like to think.'

'And Bella?'

He shrugged.

'Just can't keep your hands off her, can you?' Their rapid breaths seemed to bruise the air between them as he let his words sink in.

'Make your choice, Lucerne.'

'The choice has already been made for me.'

Vaughan bit his thumbnail. 'She'll leave with you.'

Lucerne forced a laugh. 'You think so. You really think so. Have you taken in a damn thing I've said? She's in love with you, Vaughan, and we both know it. Lord knows it's probably for the best. You're far better suited.'

'You're being absurd.'

'Am I now,' Lucerne mouthed, his throat choked by a

bitter lump. He swallowed hard. 'Or are you just scared because really you feel exactly the same way?'

Vaughan lifted his chin. His lips were thin and set, and his eyes, moments ago so open, were narrowed and glassy. 'Go. Leave.' He crossed the room again, this time heading for the door.

Just a few paces short of it, Lucerne grabbed the back of his coat. 'No! Admit it.'

Vaughan's elbow jabbed hard into Lucerne's stomach, leaving him bent double, gasping for air; still his fingers remained locked around the thick fabric of Vaughan's coat. Vaughan shucked it off. 'I only ever wanted you.'

Breathless, Lucerne launched himself forwards, hit Vaughan squarely in the midriff and sent them both crashing into the wall. His ears rang with the impact. The oak groaned beneath their weight as they both scuffled for balance and dominance, feet and fists delivering equally vicious jabs. Lucerne snaked his arms around his lover's body and squeezed until he grew still. The world seemed to tumble in on itself. Everything that mattered was focused on the space in which their breath mingled. 'I'm not leaving. Not yet.' His heart was beating wildly and he could feel Vaughan's too, drumming against his chest where they were pressed together. Desire coiled in his loins. Why did this always have to be the way? The rush he got when they tussled like this ran straight to his groin. For the second time, Lucerne forced his mouth down upon Vaughan's.

This time the kiss was salty and aggressive. It claimed. It demanded. When he pulled back to take a breath, Vaughan's eyes were closed and his mouth slack from the vicious kiss. 'I know what you need.' He covered Vaughan's prick with his hand and kneaded him with thumb and curled fingers.

'No,' Vaughan whimpered.

'I'm going to fuck you,' Lucerne said. 'Just try and resist. And then tell me to walk away.'

'Don't.'

Lucerne bent his head, licked and nipped Vaughan's nipples through his waistcoat and his shirt. He slipped the buttons at his waistband and began to masturbate him with practised ease, his thumb and fingers curled around the shaft. This was what had been missing between them recently: the raw edge of intensity that left him reeling like a drunkard. Their fighting had become a pantomime for Bella's amusement, not an expression of the frustration and desire they both felt. Society would not let them be together, not without her as a decoy. That was strain enough, without Bella's desire to add to the mix.

Vaughan's mouth was hot and sweet, his nipples two taut little peaks. It wasn't enough to ravage them through the fabric. Lucerne wanted to taste his skin, to know the heat of Vaughan's flesh.

Buttons! There were always too many damn buttons. Lucerne unfastened Vaughan's, while his partner tried to reciprocate. After the first five, he knocked Vaughan's hands away and concentrated on unfastening them himself.

Waistcoats dealt with, his attention turned to their cravats. Lucerne wrenched his off and chucked it aside. Vaughan's, he drew from him slowly, gently tugging open the knot, then pulling the white linen downwards until it unravelled and slithered to the floor.

Within just a few heartbeats, Vaughan's body was quivering in anticipation, his hips rocking to the rhythm of Lucerne's hand, which cupped them both.

'I need to get inside you, Vaughan,' Lucerne panted into Vaughan's rosemary-scented hair. 'This isn't close enough. You know that, don't you?'

Vaughan squeezed his eyes tight shut.

Lucerne wetted his fingers and rubbed saliva between Vaughan's cheeks.

Vaughan's breath hissed past his ear in response. His mouth fell open and his head tilted back. 'Use the oil. Right pocket.'

'Use it yourself.' Lucerne slipped him the tip of one digit.

Vaughan fumbled in his coat pocket. He bit the cap off the bottle and spat it out, then upended the contents into his palm.

The glinting golden droplets rolled past his shirt cuff and down his arm. It was cold against Lucerne's cock but warmed quickly.

Using the wall for balance, Lucerne lifted Vaughan. He cupped his buttocks, found his anus and worked him loose with two fingers.

The moment of penetration stole his breath. The tight heat, the sensation of being squeezed, coupled with the novelty of having Vaughan in his arms, their chests pressed together, it was too hot, too amazingly good. 'Oh, God!' Acutely aware of Vaughan's every murmur, every hiss he made between his teeth, Lucerne inched a little deeper.

The closeness he felt at having him like this surprised him. He should have done this more often. Been active instead of passive.

Their mouths locked as Vaughan's hands splayed across his bottom, and teased him. He fluttered his muscles around Lucerne's cock, tilted his pelvis, making the slide deeper.

Lucerne groaned, already feeling himself beginning to soar. It was all about the rhythm ... He could just about focus on that. Deeper. The strokes becoming longer. Vaughan's sighs, sharper.

Nothing else mattered when they were locked together like this, only the fluttery sensation in his groin and the streamers of bliss that poured along his shaft. Just a little more, and he was going to come.

Vaughan's moans were a barely coherent jumble of syllables against his shoulder. He sucked his breath in deep, his voice rising on the out breath. Hot semen warmed his abdomen. Muscles clasped him tight, then he too was jerking and groaning with the force of his own climax.

Slowly his head cleared. Lucerne brushed the hair out of his eyes, where the blond strands lay plastered to his skin. Vaughan's head lolled warm and precious against his shoulder. He clasped him tight. Just holding him, knowing that what he had to do next would be the hardest thing he'd ever done in his life. Expressing his feelings had never been something that came easily. He knew how he felt, but actually saying it was something else.

'I love you,' he whispered. 'But I love Bella too. And I can't choose between you.' Gently, he lowered Vaughan back to the floor. 'Take care of her for me.' He cleaned himself with a handkerchief, then fastened his breeches and waistcoat. He could feel tears pooling in his own eyes. He didn't dare look at Vaughan who stood rigidly before him, his clothing still strewn about and unfastened, his stomach shiny with come. If he met his eyes, he knew he'd lose his resolve, and this was the only way he could make either of them truly happy. They might agree to forgive and forget, to begin their ménage à trois afresh, but the poison would still be there. They'd have the same problems over again.

At the door he paused. His resolve almost faltered. They'd shared so much, the three of them. He wanted them to share so much more, but he knew it was all in tattered ruins. He had to let his two lovers find each other. Maybe then they'd find him again.

He wasn't hopeful. He wasn't that much of a fool.

One foot across the threshold, he risked a glance back. Vaughan's eyes were wild in the darkness, their brilliance pronounced against the damp pallor of his skin. His lips were deep red, bruised from too many kisses. Lucerne wanted nothing more than to crush him to his body and spend the night on the rug before the fire, streaking one another with ash and semen, but it wasn't to be. He took a deep breath. There would never be another Vaughan. No equal to his wit, his beauty, his raw sexuality ...

There were no words ...

Lucerne closed the door quietly and made his way down the steps and into the night.

Bella stood on the edge of the kitchen garden, surrounded by the scent of damp earth, of garlic and wet mint. The light had faded since Lucerne had gone in, and her tears ran thick and fast. The more she mopped them, the more readily they seemed to spill. She was half-frozen, even draped in Lucerne's heavy greatcoat, but she couldn't face company, the stares and the questions, and there was no way to get to her room without first passing through the great hall.

'Louisa,' she sobbed into Lucerne's coat sleeve. It wasn't

fair. Her friend should have been enjoying the child she'd just brought into the world, not lying in the cold earth in a foreign land.

She could picture her so clearly, so petite and perfect, standing on the lawn of Wyndfell Grange on her wedding day, her head cocked delicately to one side as she wondered aloud how she would explain to her new husband that she wasn't destitute after all.

It was the last time they'd seen one another.

The sound of a door slamming across the courtyard brought her thoughts back to the present. Bella licked the salt from her bee-stung lips. A lone figure emerged onto the grass. 'Lucerne.'

Desperate for the comfort of his embrace, Bella started towards him.

His pace was equally determined in her direction. They met beneath the timber frame that sheltered the well. 'Lucerne.' He opened his arms for her only after an awkward pause, and even then his face was so stripped of emotion, she paused before snuggling up to his heat. His collar was askew and he smelled of sex and Vaughan. 'What happened?'

He tensed.

A loud thud came from the direction of the castle. Vaughan rushed onto the south tower drawbridge. 'Lucerne!' he yelled.

His dark ringlets danced in the breeze.

Lucerne held himself rigid in her arms. Bella's gaze flickered between the two men, taking in the rigid stoicism of Lucerne's face, the raw pain in Vaughan's, clear even from a distance. 'No,' she said. 'No . . . Lucerne . . .'

He closed his eyes, ever so slightly inclining his head.

'No,' she shrieked in disbelief. It couldn't be. He was supposed to mend things . . .

He turned away from her. Bella clung to his sleeve as he strode out through the wicket gate and across the moat. In the shadow of his crested carriage he stopped and gently pried her fingers from his arm.

'It's the only way, Bella. I can't make things right.' His man opened the carriage door. 'I'd ask you to come, but I know the answer.'

Her nose tingled. The tears ran cold across her cheeks and down her throat. 'You can't,' she squeaked. 'I can't leave him.' The burning passion she'd once felt for Lucerne was but dying embers to what she felt for Vaughan. Perhaps, given other circumstances, they'd have rekindled, but for now she belonged at Pennerley with Vaughan, not with Lucerne in the north.

Lucerne took his greatcoat from her shoulders and pushed his arms through the sleeves.

'Don't go.'

'I have to, Bella. It's for the best.' He enfolded her in his arms. 'I'm sorry.' There it was again, that apology, as if all the wrongs of their relationship were somehow his. As if this was entirely his fault. He pressed a kiss to her forehead and another to the back of her hand. 'Tell him . . . tell him . . .' He shook his head. Let her fingers slip. 'Goodbye, Bella.' He forced a smile, then mounted the carriage steps. 'Farewell.'

Bella stood in the dark and watched the carriage rattle away until it was an infinitesimal blot on the horizon and her tears had dried in tight streaks across her face. Slowly, terrified of Vaughan's reaction and numbed with sorrow, she turned back towards the gatehouse.

15

Vaughan pulled the bottle from the rack and rubbed the dust off it with his sleeve. Sherry, port, Madeira. What did it matter? He just needed something to rid himself of the taste of Lucerne. He wasn't sure how long he'd sat before the fire watching the flames dance and cinders fall across the hearthstone, maybe minutes, maybe hours. The room had grown dark, the candles burning out one by one, and then the brandy had run out too, which was why he was fishing around the cellar in the dark.

He drew the cork from the dusty bottle with his teeth and spat it across the room. The liquid within was syrupy and a fraction too sweet. Not one of the castle's best, although he wasn't sure anything would ever take away Lucerne's kisses.

The wine, or whatever it was, hit his stomach like vitriol. Vaughan bent double, clasping his sides. He knew it was his fault Lucerne had left. He'd pushed him to it. And now it was real, he had to live with it. Had to continue somehow, with half his heart torn out.

'God damn you, Lucerne,' he cursed. 'You weren't supposed to walk away.' Especially after an encounter like that. The memory of Lucerne's cock stretching him, of his kisses, so aggressive and demanding, necessitated another swig from the bottle. His stomach immediately protested, but he continued to swallow regardless, only to retch the moment he stopped. There wasn't anything to come up apart from alcohol, which thankfully stayed put. He hadn't really been able to face food since Tuesday night. Not since he'd painted Bella with jam.

Vaughan pitched forwards onto his knees. His eyes felt like they'd sunken into his sockets and his jaw ached. His lips were tender too, scratched raw by the faint growth of Lucerne's stubble. They hadn't made love like that for months.

'Fuck!' Still holding the bottle, he slammed his fist into the nearby wall, driving fragments of splintered glass into his palm and splattering his clothing with wine. The thick red liquid pooled by his knee, fed by his own blood.

Cold seeped into his brow, numbing his thoughts as he sagged against the pitted stone wall. Was there nothing left except memories now? They all tasted bitter. Salt water mingled with the memories. Vaughan brushed the streaks away with his hand. What was he supposed to do now? Pretend nothing had happened? It wasn't as if their relationship was openly acknowledged. How could it be, when the King's law forbade such loving. Even the intercourse he shared with Bella was considered a crime of nature. Judging by her recent pleas, she was beginning to think that too.

Bella ... He'd have to ask her to leave if she hadn't already flown with Lucerne. She couldn't stay here, a constant reminder of what he'd lost, and why he'd lost it. Lucerne was wrong, there was nothing between them. He conceded that he'd been pleased to see her at first. She was the only woman who ever stood up to him, and they sparked nicely off each other. But it wasn't love.

He tucked up his legs before him, and picked the shards

of broken glass from his bloody palm. His blood tasted cloying and thick as he sucked the wound clean.

He'd let her stay until the party. Then he'd send her away with the other guests. Pack her off with Devonshire if he had to.

'Who's there?'

Vaughan glanced up from beneath his eyebrows. An orange flame bobbed in the darkness by the cellar steps. 'Vaughan, is that you?' A moment later, a delicate hand touched his shoulder. Niamh's fingers stroked through the tumbled shroud of his hair. 'What is it? What's happened?'

She knelt before him and pushed at his shoulders until he raised his head. 'Blessed angels!' Her eyes went wide. Already pale, the colour seemed to bleed from her cheeks. She touched one finger to his lips, then stared at the red smear upon her fingertip. 'Blood,' she gasped, and there was a tremble of fear in her voice. 'What have you done?'

Vaughan opened his palm, causing the wound to run freely again. Dark rivulets trickled into his coat cuff. Distractedly, he watched the light play across the streams. They glinted maroon and scarlet, red like his sister's lips, plum like his lover's glans.

Niamh forced an embroidered handkerchief into his palm and watched the stain seep across its surface.

'I'll send for Doctor Kepple.'

'No doctors,' he said, and it felt as if his voice was disembodied. 'It'll heal.'

'But . . .'

He clasped her wrist in an iron grip. 'No doctors. I don't need blistering or bleeding. I can manage both myself.'

She drew away from him, shuddering. The candle flame shone in her pupils, highlighting the sheen of fear within.

Vaughan rose to his feet, causing the shards of broken glass to scrunch noisily beneath his shoes.

'Where are you going?'

He shrugged and pulled another bottle from the rack.

'Wait.' She pressed a hand to his arm.

Vaughan stared at the point of contact. Very few people dared stop him doing as he pleased, but he was finding his sister had developed a certain stubbornness in his absence. He guessed he'd allowed her too much freedom.

'Let me help. I can bind it.'

He shook his head so that his dark hair spilled over his shoulders and stuck to the wetness on his cheeks.

'Just let me come to your room.'

His stomach lurched at the thought. 'Most women have more sense than to suggest such a thing.'

'I'm not most women. I'm your sister in case you've forgotten,' she chastised, and clamped a hand onto her hips in a pose that reminded him far too vividly of Bella. 'What's happened tonight? Bella is milk pale and won't say a thing to anyone, and you ...' She was blocking the stairs. 'You stalk off halfway through dinner and now after midnight when all our guests have retired, I find you skulking about the cellars.'

'It's over,' he said simply. 'I couldn't bear the thought of sharing him any longer.' He didn't want to explain, but how else was he to get rid of her. Unfortunately, the statement only brought more questions.

'Who are you talking about?' She bit her thumbnail. 'I've heard rumours. They say that you and Viscount Marlinscar are lovers.'

'Hmm.'

'Tell me it isn't true. They could hang you!'

'It is true. And they can damn well try.' He swept her aside and headed up the stairs, realising for the first time how drunk he'd made himself.

Niamh scurried after him. 'Vaughan! Did you never think of the risks?'

They reached the top of the cellar steps and she dived ahead of him again, this time blocking the corridor to the lower parlour with her outstretched arms. 'I know what a libertine you've grown into, but did you run out of women to satisfy you?'

'Niamh,' he growled, his temper rising quickly in response to the revulsion in her eyes. 'Be very careful what you say.' He drew his hand towards her and she flinched, drawing herself up against the passage wall. 'Do I disgust you?' he asked, sliding a finger into the coils of one of the ringlets framing her face.

She cowered. 'You frighten me.'

'Hmm,' he murmured, his other hand tightening on the neck of the bottle he'd brought up from the cellar. He wasn't sure what he was feeling, except that it was raw, and he wanted everyone else to feel it to. He wanted her to understand that it wasn't wrong, it was simply how he was, who he was, and no amount of insults would ever change that. But she didn't understand. She'd never felt the same way.

'That fool Edward Holt, do you love him?' he asked.

Bewildered, Niamh stared at him, her elegant lips parted, her nails curled into the wainscotting. It was clear she didn't understand the connection, but there was one.

'Do you?'

Still flustered, she twisted both her head and her body,

trying to escape his touch and his soul-searching gaze. Vaughan cupped her cheek with his injured hand and forced her to meet his stare. The movement hurt, but the pain was minimal to what he felt inside. She made a half-choking sound, her lip trembling. 'I'm not sure.' The statement was delivered as a hesitant stammer.

'You're not sure,' he echoed. 'Well, I'm sure. Don't criticise my feelings until you understand them.' He let go, leaving a bloody handprint on her skin. 'Marry him if you want. I'm done with ruling your life for I can't rule my own. But, Niamh, if, after all, you can't marry for love, 'tis better not to marry at all.'

Her mouth fell open in response to the permission she'd never expected him to give, quickly followed by words of explanation, of justification for her desires. 'He entertains me,' she said.

Vaughan sighed. Had everybody else forgotten how to feel? 'So does "Monk" Lewis, but you're not set on marrying him.'

'He's never offered.'

The quick response shocked a snort of mirth from him. 'I guess I should have invited him instead of Devonshire.'

'Stop it,' she bleated. 'Just stop it. You've always been like this. Just because you're hurting ... It doesn't give you the right ...' She clasped her arms before her like a shield, the same way she'd used her dolls as a barrier in the past. 'I like Edward. I find him agreeable, which is all society demands.'

'Bugger society!' He grabbed hold of her chin. When she squirmed, he jammed her against the lower parlour door with his thigh pressed between her legs. A curious wash of arousal bathed his loins at her exclamation of fear, followed a heartbeat later by a rush of nausea as her startled breaths assaulted his tender lips.

He hadn't wanted it to be like this. He'd tried to shield her, to protect her from men like himself. One of them had to have a chance at being happy. She had to understand, he wasn't the villain.

'Agreeable,' he snarled, his mouth a mere inch from hers. 'How agreeable will you find him after he's forced himself on you every night for a year? What about when he insists on bedding the maids in your place or when he makes a mistress of your best friend?'

'You're sick. You need help, Vaughan.' Her arched eyebrows rose. 'Edward's not like you. He wouldn't do that.'

'Edward already has.'

Her eyes turned glassy with tears. 'You pig. Let go of me.'

'He spent last spring wooing Alicia Allenthorpe, then dropped her when he found out she had a far richer friend languishing all alone in the country.'

She shook her head but he could see the doubt in her eyes. Vaughan released her and watched her depart in a flurry of skirts. Perhaps a better brother would have found a kinder way. If she'd loved Holt, he'd have kept his silence, tolerated him even, but he wasn't going to have her marry a scoundrel for nothing. He sighed. In the morning, she'd go sobbing to Alicia, and the whole sorry story would no doubt spill out. Maybe then she'd realise he'd saved her from a life of misery.

Despite everything, he was still convinced love was an essential requisite for tying yourself to someone. People who didn't even like each other had no business being together. His parents had been a good example of that. Maybe Niamh had been too young to remember.

Up in his bedchamber, the fire had burned low in the grate. Vaughan lay on the warmed bed linen, having bound his injured hand, and stared up into the inky depths of the canopy. His palm stung but the cut was not particularly deep. It would heal far quicker than the other wound he'd sustained.

'Lucerne,' he whispered into the dark. He lifted the gold locket that lay close to his heart and pressed the warm metal to his lips. It was over, but it would never truly be done between them. He rolled onto his side, locket clasped tight within his fist, and willed himself to sleep. But when he closed his eyes, images came to him of Lucerne's Cupid's bow lips, of his blond hair ruffled against the pillowslips, and of Bella curled around his feet.

For some reason, no matter how hard he tried, he couldn't extract her from the vision. He guessed he'd grown accustomed to her presence. Futilely, he kicked at her image, but it merely shimmered and reformed whole again.

After twenty minutes of this torture, Vaughan got up. He stood before the fire and swigged from the bottle he'd brought up from the cellar, only to choke on the acrid poison within. His eyes watered as he spat the vinegar, with a hint of sludgy cork, into the flames. Not only were his lovers deserting him, his cellars were mouldering too. Disgusted, he peered into the bottleneck and found crystals growing around the rim. How in God's name was a man supposed to drown his sorrows when his wine tasted like cat's piss?

Air. He'd take himself for a walk instead.

Shunning the battlements, he headed for one of the castle's curiosities, a door set into the outer wall of the tower. In his youth, he'd assumed it was a relic of the castle's medieval past, but it was unlikely the curtain wall had reached such an impressive height even in the fourteenth century. Instead, he'd been reliably informed by Foster, whose family were another of the castle's relics, that it was simply a means of getting furniture, too bulky for the stairs, into the tower.

The wind battered him as he stepped out onto the narrow ledge, chasing away some of the alcohol haze. To his right, the castle walls fell away into the murky waters of the moat. If he slipped, would he survive or crumple like a rag doll?

His toes dug into the rock for purchase as he stared at the reflection of the heavens spread like a silver rainbow across surface of the moat. The wind was too wild to stand in its grasp for long. It tugged at his shirt and hair, distorted the silver rainbow. Carefully, he lowered himself off the ledge. The effort shot pain through his injured hand and he landed in an ungainly fashion on his rump in a bed of thyme. He flopped back into its fragrant embrace. Tomorrow, All Hallows Eve, the *beau monde* would descend on Pennerley. He had to focus on that, ensure everything was perfect.

De Maresi was confident they'd pull off their little tableau, but his attention had wandered since the arrival of Gabriel Allenthorpe, and he'd had to rely on Henry Tristan for assistance staging several of their props.

Still, it was a relief that François' attention had been diverted. He couldn't face his pawing at the moment, and maybe his calculated disdain had finally done its job. He wondered how long the affair would last, assuming the boy's predilections matched de Maresi's own, and he was by no means certain of that. He looked the sort to run, terrified, into the arms of the Church.

His mind straying towards Lucerne again, Vaughan extracted himself from the thyme bed, slightly sodden with dew, and followed the curve of the south tower to the dungeon door. He'd keep his thoughts from straying by concentrating on the details of the ghastly tale of Sebastian Alastair Elisud, 1st Marquis of Pennerley, a despicable rogue to whom he bore a striking resemblance.

He barely had the key in the lock when a new scent on the breeze caught his attention: strawberries and apple blossom. A moment later he was rewarded with a voice.

'Lord Pennerley.'

Perhaps he wouldn't need Sebastian Alastair Elisud after all.

'Miss Allenthorpe.' She floated towards him in a button-up nightgown with a cashmere shawl pulled tight around her shoulders. 'Isn't it a little late for a stroll, and somewhat indecent without a chaperone and a bonnet?' Her long flaxen hair was flying loose about her shoulders. It curled prettily at the end, although his gaze settled not there, but on the pleasing curve of her belly and the apex of her thighs where the wind blew the flimsy flannel-gown taut against her body.

She had legs a racehorse would envy.

'Have you ever worn a bonnet, my lord?'

'I can't say I've had the pleasure.'

'They're cumbersome, itchy devices, which make you feel as if you're wearing horse blinkers.'

In other words no use for sneaking around in the dark. 'I

see. Does that mean we're to see you abandon your hats as well as your stays?'

Fortuna glanced down at her billowing shift and drew her brows together in a frown. 'Do you consider us indecent for desiring freedom of movement?'

'Quite the opposite. I simply mourn the opportunity tight lacing provides. There's a certain satisfaction to be had from struggling to attain the pleasures held within.'

A vague feeling of arousal stirred in his groin. There was no heaviness yet, no imperative to pounce, but he knew he could lose himself in her for a while. She'd been desperate for his attention from the moment she'd arrived, but his thoughts had been elsewhere and his jaded palate had seen no challenge in her conquest.

Eyes bright, Fortuna took a wary step closer to him and touched the back of his hand where the bandage stretched across it. 'Forgive me.' She looked away, then back up at him from beneath her eyelashes. Her coquetry made him want to laugh, but there was something delightful about her attempted guile. She knew what she wanted, but he was certain she had no experience of getting it.

Why not?

'I'll forgive you when you do something that warrants such a reward.'

She leaned in again, and this time her curled fingers alighted against his cheek. Vaughan shook his head. 'Touch me where you really want to.' He leaned back against the iron pinned door, his hands raised either side of his head.

Her eyes widened until they resembled two great saucers.

She wanted him, he was certain of it, but she'd envisaged her ravishment as the play of his fingers against her skin and the whisper of coaxing words. Instead, he was inviting her to take charge.

Temptation, curiosity and fear each played across her face. Her eyes sparkled, her breasts rose and fell with each breath she took and, when she sighed, it was deep and wanting.

'Come now, don't be shy. No one's watching.'

Her head jerked towards the gatehouse, but the windows were all dark and empty, the occupants asleep in their beds.

When she faced him again, he dipped his head and looked up at her from beneath his eyelashes, mimicking her earlier display. 'Well . . .' He wetted his lips and let his gaze slip slowly down from her eyes to her heaving breasts, where her nipples poked like two stiff towers against her shift, begging for his touch.

Finally, she stepped forwards. Her shift brushed against his chest as she leaned in to him and pressed an intolerably chaste kiss to his lips.

Vaughan sighed, a sound she obviously mistook for pleasure. This was for his pleasure, and that meant complete control. He was not going to make this easy for her. If she wanted easy, she'd chosen the wrong man.

When she lifted her chin for another such chaste kiss, he shook his head. 'Touch me,' he hissed.

'I . . .' Tentatively, she reached towards him, her fingers spread wide, but her palm merely skimmed over the surface of his shirt without ever truly making contact.

'Do it.'

Apparently a little authority went a long way. Both palms immediately fanned across his upper arms, before sliding across his chest and down to his stomach. She hesitated at exploring any lower, her fingers twitching against the waistband of his pantaloons.

'Go on. Don't stop.'

'You're . . .'

So nervous she was quivering, she unwittingly pressed against him.

'Erect,' he helpfully provided. He took her hand and placed it over his cock.

'Erm . . . How does this work exactly?'

He took pity. 'Just touch me a little. Slide your hand up and down. Rub me. Yes-ss, like that!' Her touch was unskilled but nevertheless what he needed to forget, much better than wine to wipe away the taste of Lucerne.

He still smelled of him. Could still taste him. Her hand wasn't enough.

Vaughan forced his mouth down hard upon hers. The kiss was sharp, laced with bitter memories, but still she melted beneath him. He pulled back, only to stop her swooning. He lifted her hand and pressed his lips to her knuckles, then to her palm, and finally to the seam between her index and middle fingers.

Now aroused, he wanted more of her, longed for a firmer touch, and perhaps a soft pliant mouth in which to loose his seed.

Fellatio. Was there anything about it that wasn't perfect?

She'd be unskilled, but so had Lucerne been, once.

Vaughan guided her hand inside the placket of his trousers. His cock pulsed in greeting at her warm touch, and Fortuna squealed.

'Hush.' He clamped a hand over her mouth. 'Do you want to raise the castle?'

She shook her head. 'I'm sorry. I won't do it again. It was

just a surprise.' She glanced nervously down at him. Pretty fingers fluttered over the tip of his glans. 'I'll do whatever you want.'

'Whatever I want.' A low chuckle rolled from his throat. 'My dear, you have no idea what you're saying.'

'I do. I understand.'

'Here?' He drew his tongue across his teeth, and then inclined his head towards the grass.

'Your room.'

He laughed again. Less risk of exposure, it was true. Safer? Only if you didn't mind locking yourself in with a hungry wolf. 'If you come to my room, there's no changing your mind,' he said.

Fortuna inclined her head. 'I know.'

'No.' He refastened his buttons, and placed her hand upon his arm. 'You don't. But you will.'

She was in a kind of trance. Fortuna stumbled along beside him, her hand clasped tight to his shirtsleeve. This was the future she had dreamed of when she'd begged on her knees to be allowed to come. Of course, she'd anticipated, or at least imagined, declarations of love would precede her deflowerment, but at this moment, with this man, such assurances didn't seem to matter.

She was out of breath by the time they climbed the winding stair to his room. The vast chamber occupied the entire floor of the tower and was furnished in a sparse masculine style. Vaughan bolted the door behind them, then crossed to the fire to stoke the flames, leaving her standing awkwardly by his galleon of a bed. It was a monstrous thing, thick carved oak spread with white sheets. Any moment he would throw her upon it, pin her down and ravish her with the weapon she'd barely glimpsed, but which she'd felt hard and vital in her hand.

Finished with the fire, Vaughan stripped the rings from his fingers and left them scattered across the top of an iron bound chest. He was the most beautiful man she'd ever met, exquisitely saturnine, with dark eyes full of secrets and cruelly suggestive lips. Just watching him move did strange things to her. He circled her, making her pulse race as she anticipated his sudden approach.

He didn't pounce. Instead he set a cushioned stool before her. 'Sit.'

Fortuna obeyed, to find herself facing her reflection in the surface of a huge gilt mirror that lay propped against the wall. Vaughan stood behind her; she could smell the musk of his body, muddied with alcohol and something sweet. His shirt hung open to his breastbone, revealing the muscle beneath and a teasing glimpse of a flat male nipple.

His hands were impossibly warm against her shoulders as he drew her shawl from her, then hotter as he worked open the line of buttons that ran from her throat to her breasts.

Her breath seemed to stick in her throat as he pushed a hand through the opening and covered a breast. She fit neatly into his hand, and her nipples steepled. Their soft tissue crinkled and hardened until they were fully erect and arousal seeped through her body, causing the flesh between her legs to tingle with need.

'Lift your skirt,' he said.

Fortuna hesitated, hand on hem, afraid of what pleasures such exposure would yield, but it was impossible to deny him. He didn't coax with words but with fingers, long agile fingers that played upon her nipples drawing squeaks of joy from her.

She shut her eyes and raised her hem to her waist. Her heart fluttered. 'Look,' he said, indicating the mirror before her.

The image she presented was incredibly lewd. Her breasts poked from the open neck of her shift and the rest of the fabric lay bunched around her waist, leaving the full length of her long legs on display. Never had she seen so much of her own skin. Even when she bathed she wore a shift. Her nipples were two dark pink peaks, her legs milky-white.

Vaughan insinuated a hand between her knees and pushed them apart, causing a knot of excitement to tighten in her belly and a flood of moisture to appear between her thighs. Up his palm slithered, forcing her legs wider, until her every secret lay exposed.

Sable curls framed the dusky pink split of her quim. Her moisture glistened on his fingertips as he dipped them into her heat. Without conscious thought she tilted her hips to give him better access and let his teasing fingers slide over her ripe flesh. He rubbed repetitively at her taut swollen nub, until she gasped and writhed against the stool, pushing herself against his hand.

'Take me to bed,' she pleaded.

Vaughan looked down into her face. A dark light flashed in his eyes, cold and unfathomable. 'We're not going to bed. I'm going to fuck you on the floor.' His fingers tightened cruelly on her nipples and squeezed. His long hair brushed against her shoulders as he bent his head to her and licked the curve of her ear. 'I sleep in my bed. I don't break in virgins upon it.'

She burned with shame at his words but she couldn't tear herself away from his touch. She was greedy for it. Wanted more from him: the thrust of his tongue in her mouth and the velvet heat of his weapon inside her.

Her pulse ran fluttery and light just below her skin.

Vaughan tipped her forwards off the stool and she landed on her hands and knees before the mirror, red-cheeked and slack-jawed. She felt the rub of his shirt against her back and the tickle of his ringlets, then two fingers probed her intimately.

His phallus nuzzled against her bottom, impossibly large. Tense with the excitement of it, she merely stared at her reflection. His cock-tip pressed into her quim, stretched her, though he was barely inside her. Then, with a sharp thrust he sheathed himself deep, filled her completely. The sensation – she'd never known anything so breathtaking as that moment. It hurt, but only a little, and in a good way. Everything felt so tight, but even that changed with his thrusts. She opened to him, became increasingly wet.

'Look at yourself,' he insisted. One arm wrapped around her body to reach between her legs. The friction immediately set her gasping.

From the mirror, her image stared back at her in total abandonment. She looked every inch the harlot she'd made herself. Shame washed a further ruddy glow across her exposed skin. Her breasts swung with their motion, as his cock filled her to distraction. She had to make sure her family never found out or they'd have her wed so fast she'd not have time to breathe, let alone say 'no'.

Still, nothing would make her accept Hector Macleane now. Nothing. She wouldn't doom herself to years of doing this with that simpering baboon. She knew it wouldn't be anything like this with him.

Her clitoris tingled. Her thighs were soaked with the juices of their pleasure. Skin slid against skin, as he pushed her higher, then higher still. Rational thought exploded around her, as her orgasm peaked, broke and scattered through every tensed muscle.

Breathless, she flopped forwards against the Persian rug, but Vaughan barely allowed her a moment respite. He moaned, lost in his own need, then, subtlety abandoned, he crushed her breasts beneath his palms and drove into her with increased vigour.

His lips moved on the back of her neck, murmuring endearments she couldn't quite catch. His roughness excited her again, enflamed her, and she rose to meet him, until their bodies slapped against one another and their heat ran together. She came again, and this time she felt him come with her, his cock flexing inside her as a long convulsion rolled down his back.

He jerked above her, his dark hair wild about his shoulders, then collapsed against her body. For several moments, he remained still, just breathing against her shoulder. When he rose, his hair framed his face, but even its shadows couldn't hide the tear track that glinted across his cheek. Bewildered, she stared at his ashen face. He didn't meet her eyes in the glass, just withdrew and turned away.

The feeling of ecstasy she'd felt moments before crumbled away. 'Leave, now,' he said, his voice no more than a whisper.

Hurt, a thousand questions swelled inside her mind. Had

she displeased him in some way? Done something wrong? 'I don't understand.'

'You don't want to be here. I'll use you, more than I've already done.'

He said nothing more. In the end, hurt and confused, she fled the room, leaving him to his demons.

16

Bella rose to a world of grey mist. The air, even at the top of the north tower was damp and sour with the taste of mulched earth. The previous night seemed like a dream. Louisa and Lucerne. She had lost her two dearest friends in one evening. There were no tears left in her, and now she merely felt numb.

She washed in cold water and put on a plain blue dress with a black ribbon tied about the sleeve. It seemed more appropriate than her trunk full of virginal whites.

The clinging mist was even thicker at ground level. It tugged at her with ghostly fingers as she made her way to the corner of the kitchen garden. There in the shelter of the arbour, she sat and reread Louisa's letters. It seemed impossible that her friend was not sitting at a writing desk somewhere penning another epistle. Once she'd read them all, she retied them with the faded yellow ribbon and sat with them clasped within her hands, staring blankly out over the courtyard. She had no letters from Lucerne. They had never been parted long enough to warrant any.

'We should never have left Lauwine, any of us,' she said to the Louisa of her imagination. 'I wish we were all back there: you, Wakefield, Lucerne, Joshua and me.' The thought of her brother raised a wan smile, as did the memories of the ribald gambler, Charles Aubrey. They all faded beside her memories of Vaughan. He was her one remaining link to that time. What would happen if he forced her to let go?

Her gaze strayed to the south tower drawbridge, where she almost expected to find him, still waiting for Lucerne to return through the wicket gate. For days he'd tormented her, hunted her through the castle then tried to push her away, all with the shadow of Lucerne between them. And what did they have now?

Maybe nothing at all.

She'd have to face him. But not right away. Not while their wounds were still so raw.

Breakfast was a mistake, Bella realised, as Raffe slid into the chair beside her. 'A rough night,' he remarked. 'Everyone is walking around as pale as ether this morning. I've just seen Miss Allenthorpe. She has eyes like saucers and clearly hasn't slept a wink, and you look a deal worse than her.'

'Thank you,' Bella remarked, but Raffe seemed oblivious to her sarcasm.

'Nothing a good breakfast won't fix,' he said, offering her a tray of kippers. When she didn't take any, he put two on her plate and heaped mushrooms on top.

Bella looked at the heap of grey and yellow and her stomach lurched. 'I'm not hungry.' She shuddered at the thought of even bringing a morsel to her lips.

'Then at least drink some tea to warm yourself. You were outside far too long last night.'

Bella stared at him in warning, and he appeared to take the hint that the events of the previous evening were off limits.

'Pennerley needs to sort out these windows,' he said blandly. 'It's always bitter in here first thing.'

'I didn't realise you were such an early riser.'

'Always,' he replied.

'He likes to toss himself off before breakfast,' remarked Vaughan by way of a good morning. Suave as Satan, he settled at the head of the table and emptied the teapot. 'That's right, isn't it, Devonshire? I can hear your piteous mewling all around the tower.'

'Milord,' said Raffe, taking his cue with a sickly pale smile. 'If you'll excuse me.' He bowed to Bella and, taking his breakfast with him, left in the direction of the lower parlour.

Bella listened to Raffe's footfalls until he reached the door, then her gaze shifted to Vaughan. His expression was drawn and cruel, his eyes beetle-black and his sensual lips pulled tight and thin.

'You're still here,' he observed, and he stretched his fingers out over the top of his cup, so the steam curled up between his fingers. It must have burned, but he didn't flinch.

'What happened?' she asked.

'Didn't Lucerne explain? You should have left with him.' Finally, he lifted his hand from the cup, to reveal the gash across his palm. She started forward in shock, but he scraped back his chair and stood. 'It's over, Bella. What more do you need to know?'

'Between us, or between you and him?' she asked, her lip trembling, and her arms still stretched out to him.

For an unbearably long moment he stood perfectly still, his head slightly bowed and his eyes lowered to the stretch of oak between them. Bella strained towards him. Part of her wanted to crush him in a tight embrace and refuse to let go, another wanted to shake him, scratch him and damn him for his stubborn pride. The final part held her rigid in fearful anticipation.

'There's never been an us,' he said, and the words raised welts across her soul far more vivid than any he could have striped her body with. He turned away.

'No!' she screamed after him. Her skirts snagged among the chair legs. 'It wasn't just about him. There was more than that.' Her words petered out as he dissolved into the shadows. 'I love you. Don't walk away.'

Hazy drizzle mingled with the mist in the castle courtyard. Bella ran into its cold, cushioned embrace. She would leave tomorrow morning, first thing, and go home to Yorkshire. There was no point in remaining, though she still believed her decision to stay the previous evening had been the right one. She wanted to be with Vaughan far more than she wanted Lucerne. 'Damn it!' She swiped remorselessly at the lavender bush growing by the base of the drawbridge, which revealed an arched pathway beneath it. She'd anticipated Vaughan's rejection. His heart had only ever belonged to Lucerne, the locket was proof enough of that, but she'd hoped he at least felt some measure of affection for her. Not everything between them had been about competing for Lucerne, or even about sharing him. There'd been times – a wan smile teased her lips – some of the best times, when it had been purely about them, when she'd felt warmed by a fraction of the affection he felt for Lucerne.

Vaughan's love was fragile and intimidating, a place of

burning heat and raw, crushing obsession, but it was also full of sweet promise. He'd lie cradling her, his embrace so tight she'd feel claustrophobic. It was always after he'd been particularly savage in their lovemaking, as if once let out, the beast of his emotions was hard to lock back in its cage.

The concealed pathway led into a small quadrangle bordered by the south tower and the solar block, completely concealed from the rest of the courtyard. Bella sat on a weathered stone bench and let the rain glue her hair to her face. There was still this evening. He might change his mind. But the more she brooded, the more angry he made her feel. He'd pushed her away at a time when she needed comfort. Her best friend was dead, Lucerne was gone, and Vaughan was so wrapped up in himself he hadn't even asked how she was.

'Oh, Vaughan,' she sighed, both angry and tearful. But she wouldn't cry again. She'd shed tears enough already for them all.

A window opened to her right, just shy of ground level.

'Bella Rushdale, what the devil are you doing?' Raffe stuck his head out of the narrow window. 'It's pouring down, woman. Get yourself inside.'

She shook her head. 'I'm fine here.'

'The hell you are. Wait there. I'll fetch an umbrella.'

'No, Raffe! Don't come out,' she yelled back at him, but he'd already closed the window. Surely he realised they'd quarrelled after Vaughan had dismissed him.

Bella peered through the glass and found herself looking into the billiards room. She clenched her fist and hammered on the pane, but it was too late. Raffe was already gone. 'Damnation!' She didn't want to explain anything to him, and nor did she want his well-meaning but insidious kindness.

'There you are.' Raffe appeared under the bridge without the promised umbrella.

He was dressed all in cream calico, which the rain quickly turned transparent and plastered to his skin, so the dark hairs upon his chest and the even darker shadow around his loins showed through.

'You should come in before you catch your death,' he said.

'You should mind your own business and go away.'

'And if I don't?' He stepped forwards and took her arm.

Bella smacked him hard across the cheek, sending sprays of glittering droplets flying in all directions, but he didn't let go. He flicked the hair out of his eyes, and then forced her up against the castle wall. 'I don't know what happened last night, but I do know that he doesn't appreciate you.' Raffe's hand closed over her breast, hot and possessive. His cock ground hard against her thigh. 'Forget him. I can give you what you need without having to play games.'

It's not a game, she yelled silently. Oh, but it was a game, an inner voice replied, and a grand one at that. It had always been a game between them from the moment he'd warned her away from Lucerne. The constant challenge was what she thrived upon. What they both thrived upon. She didn't want to stop playing the game.

Besides, wasn't Raffe playing a game with her too?

'He doesn't love you, Bella.'

The rain ran into her eyes. It trickled over her lips and into the neckline of her dress. Her heart was racing. She shook her head, but Raffe pressed in closer still. Wet hard muscle thrust against her softness. 'Don't kiss me,' she warned.

'Or else what?' His cock pressed against her eager and hard. Bella shivered. The rain was torrential now, so that the woollen dress hung from her all clammy and stiff. She snarled and watched his pupils dilate. Wild and furious, her lips plump and her eyes red with anger, she glared at him, her image alive in his pupils. Raffe forced his lips upon her.

Bella fought against his grip, raking her nails into his shoulders, but it wasn't until they bit into the nape of his neck that he released her. 'Bella,' he growled. His jaw remained determinedly set and his eyes burned with lust.

'Get off me, Raffe.'

'No.' He forced his mouth down hard upon hers again, stealing her breath. 'I'm going to fuck you, get right up deep inside you and give you the ride of your life, until you scream with the pleasure of it.'

'I'll scream now if you don't let go.'

'Yes, do, Bella. Make sure he hears you.'

She glanced up the side of the tower, to where one of his windows overlooked the courtyard. 'What have you against him?'

'He has you, but he doesn't see how precious you are. Isn't that enough?'

She slapped him hard. Raffe's boots slid on the wet flagstones but he stayed upright. 'Slap me again and I'll redden your backside.'

Loss and rejection welled up inside her. Raffe wasn't Vaughan, but he was honest and direct and would give her what she craved.

They stood at an impasse for several long heartbeats while their breaths clouded between them. Then they came together with a muffled snarl. Raffe's hand covered her breast again. His tongue penetrated her mouth. Bella fought his grasp, even as she rubbed her belly against his swollen loins and thrust her hands inside the back of his breeches. She was Vaughan's nightingale, but this morning she would sing beneath his window like a lark. Tonight . . . tonight, she would hold her head high and tell him to rot inside his own personal hell for being so cruel.

One hand touched her thigh. It slithered under the wet wool and bunched it between them. Raffe's fingers probed her wetness, rubbed at her hard and needy clitoris. He was going to give her exactly what she needed. Precisely where Vaughan wouldn't.

She was slick with need. Raffe lifted her and pushed his cock deep.

Not waves, but sharp tingling smacks of pleasure coursed through her body as the heat of him filled her core. He was the first man she'd had beside Vaughan and Lucerne since the time with Mark in the stables. It felt different. It felt strange. 'Oh, God!' But it also felt good. He was going to make her come and rapidly.

'I've wanted you since the moment you arrived and I saw you bent over on those stairs with your arse on display. I've wanted your soft curves, wanted the bite of your lips. I've brought myself off imagining how it would feel to plunge myself into your slick wet heat. And it feels good, Bella. Ten thousand times better than I ever imagined.' His lunges became sharper, harder, and he drove her hips downwards to meet his upwards thrusts. 'Take me deep. Take all of me.' His jerks became more rapid, then lapsed into irregularity. 'Oh, hell! Marry me, Bella! Marry me?'

He pulled out and shot his semen into the cold air. Scalding, it hit her thighs, only to be washed away by the rain. Raffe moved his hand up between her thighs, found her clitoris and rubbed and rubbed until she came, howling at the storm like a drunken banshee.

'I was serious,' he whispered into her mouth as she came down. He got down onto one knee, ruining his breeches on the sodden mossy flagstones.

Bella shook her head. 'It's not real. You'd tire of me soon enough.'

'I won't. I want you again already. Give me moment and I'll be hard enough to give it to you.'

Shaking her head, Bella stepped around him, out of his reach.

'I can give you what you want.'

'You don't know what I want.'

'Don't push me away. It's what he's doing to you.'

Bella pressed past the lavender bush under the arch. 'I'll await your answer,' she heard him call as she ran.

'Damn him!' stormed Bella, safe in her room with a blanket around her shoulders and a change of clothes laid out. Could he give her she wanted?

No, never. But he could give her what she needed. He treated her like an equal. He had made no pretence with her. And he could save her reputation at a stroke, if she still cared about such things. If the dream of her life with Vaughan was lost for ever, then she could do far worse than Raffe Devonshire.

* * *

Two hours later, Vaughan stood beneath the arched entrance of the gatehouse as a fifth carriage rolled up the driveway. His guests had been arriving steadily since midday, all eager for the evening's entertainment. The castle hadn't welcomed so many visitors since his father's day or, more accurately, his mother's. The marchioness had so loved to be surrounded by people. He supposed she'd been at the back of his mind as he'd planned this diversion. She'd have loved the grotesque excitement of it, although outwardly she'd have disapproved of the subject. Vaughan shook aside the memories. He fully intended to scare the wits out of his guests and fill the emptiness in himself. If it had worked for his mother, maybe it would work for him too.

'Come on,' he muttered at the carriage as he stomped his feet against the cold. It was taking an interminably long time to get up the last few feet of driveway.

'Foster,' he bellowed. 'Get me a hot toddy, man. It's bloody freezing out here.' The tea he'd swallowed at breakfast seemed a distant memory. Spirits on an empty stomach was probably asking for trouble, but the thought of anything more substantial made his stomach churn.

Henry Tristan appeared at his shoulder. 'Connelly and Dovecote are settled, and Devonshire's entertaining the rest. Who's this coming?' he asked.

Vaughan raised his hand to his eyes, peering through the mist at the red and gold crest. 'Darleston.' He turned to Henry, to find him staring at his now bandaged hand.

'Dare I ask what happened or shall I save my breath and just ask where Marlinscar is this morning?'

'Halfway to goddamn Yorkshire, I imagine.'

Henry twisted a knot into his spotted cravat. 'Amicable, was it?'

'Don't push your luck, Henry. Unless you've a peculiar desire to wrestle with my pike.'

Henry glanced warily at the murky waters of the moat. 'I just like to have my facts straight before the rumours start. The bloods'll notice he's not here.'

Vaughan stiffened. 'Do you think I don't realise that?' he hissed. He pressed his knuckles to his lips, a surge of emotion stinging his eyes. It was far too soon to be entertaining guests, but far too late to cancel. In truth, he wanted to be alone with his thoughts, not entertaining a crowd.

Henry's gaze remained focused on the rain-swollen waters, making the inner workings of his mind unfathomable. 'What's the official line?' he asked.

'Just tell them the bloody truth,' Vaughan growled. 'That he's gone home to play nanny to Wakefield's babe.' What else did they need to know? What had occurred between him and Lucerne was private, none of anyone's goddamned business. His absence didn't have to result in endless speculation.

He flinched as Henry curled a hand around his shoulder. 'I know you don't want to hear it,' the other man said, 'but they're not entirely stupid. They might not dare admit it to your face, but most of them know how it's been between you and Lucerne.'

'Leave it, Henry.' Vaughan pulled away from his grip and stepped out from under the shelter of the gatehouse into the rain.

'You'll have to make a concerted stand with Bella.'

'I said, leave it.' None of them had any real idea how it had been between him and Lucerne. Nobody did. As for Bella! He didn't want to think of Bella. Facing her at breakfast had been difficult enough. She was too much a part of what he'd shared with Lucerne, just a vivid reminder of what he'd lost. If he could have transported her anywhere else at all, he would have, but until the party was over he intended to keep as much distance between them as he could.

'How is she faring?' asked Henry.

'How the hell should I know?' Vaughan snapped. He swung back round to glower at Henry. 'If you're so concerned, go and ask her yourself.'

One snuff-stained finger tapped against Henry's nose, once, twice, three times. For perhaps the first time ever in their acquaintance, he looked genuinely riled. Vaughan took a wary step backwards, his muscles tensed.

'You're a bloody fool, Pennerley.' Henry's whitened face glowed pink. 'And I'll risk your pike to say so. That woman is in love with you. She followed you into this godforsaken wilderness because she'll do anything for you, and she wanted to mend things between you and Lucerne.'

'It's her fault it ended.'

'No.' The sound of Henry's hand hitting the top of the wooden railing rang like a shot through the air. 'It's your fault, yours and Lucerne's. And if you had any sense at all, you'd be apologising to her and doing your damnedest to ensure she stays in your bed.' His eyes swam with unaccustomed rage. 'But as usual, you're too far up your own arse to see what you're doing to her. You're going to lose her, and you'll regret it.'

The carriage finally rumbled to a springy groaning halt.

Vaughan held his palm up to Henry. 'Stop. She was Lucerne's. The world knows it.'

Henry batted the hand aside with his cane. 'She's yours. Even Lucerne realised it. Isn't that why he left? The rest of us knew it long ago. It's clear enough just from the way she moves around you. Hell, I've seen the pair of you dance.'

Whitened to his toes, Vaughan turned stiffly. He didn't need to hear Henry's opinions and he'd damn well stay wrapped up in his grief if he wanted.

At the farther end of the bridge, a footman lowered the carriage step, which belched a lady and two gentleman from its dark interior.

'Pennerley,' said the foremost of the two flame-haired men, forcing Vaughan to draw back his anger and fix on a sociable mask.

'Darleston,' he acknowledged. Heart beating wildly, he briefly returned his attention to Henry. 'If you really want to help, stop lecturing me and go find my damn fool sister. She's supposed to be out here playing hostess, not wallowing in her room.'

Niamh wasn't in her room. She was sitting in the little blue rowing boat inside the boathouse. It was too misty to risk leaving the shore, but she needed space to think, and the castle felt crowded with all the toing and froing of guests. She wasn't used to so many people and couldn't fake a smile like Vaughan.

She'd lain awake most of the night, churning things over and over, Vaughan and Lord Marlinscar, Bella, Alicia and Edward Holt. None of it made any sense. She'd always known Vaughan's relationship with Bella and Lucerne was different, but she'd never tried to flesh out the details of it. She'd naively assumed the men shared Bella, but not at the same time, and not once had she envisaged them touching each other.

Since they were children, Vaughan had never known when to stop. It wasn't that he'd been spoiled. It was simply that he'd refused to accept any limits. Yet his fierce overprotectiveness had meant that limits were all she knew.

He'd given his blessing to her regarding Edward, but sown such seeds of doubt.

At some point soon she'd have to screw up the courage to ask Alicia about her relationship with Edward and find out if what Vaughan had said was true. But even if it wasn't, Vaughan had made her question everything.

Edward had made her smile. He'd filled the otherwise dreary days with joy. Their stolen kisses had added excitement, but she'd never considered it love. Affection, yes. Enough to believe he'd make her happy, yes. But actual physical love, the sort that she saw in Bella's eyes when she looked at her brother? She shook her head. Of that, she wasn't sure. Did it grow or spring out of nowhere? Was love what had made her brother so wild last night, or just the fact that he couldn't have his own way?

You must speak to Alicia, she counselled herself. They'd been exchanging letters all summer, but for some reason she'd always kept Edward's identity a secret. Had he really courted her friend too, and deserted her? Vaughan had no reason to lie.

A twig snapped on the path outside and a moment later the boathouse door opened. 'Niamh?'

Henry stepped onto the mossy step. 'Foster told me I might find you here.'

She watched the water lap about his buckled shoes. They were embroidered with silver threads in an elaborate pattern of swirls. 'Am I wanted?'

He nodded so that his hound's-locks shrouded his face. 'Sorry. Vaughan sent me to find you. I've put it off as long as I could. Did a whole circuit of the lake but I daren't risk any longer for you.'

'I understand.' She rose and accepted his hand to step out of the rowing boat. 'Thank you.'

Henry kept tight hold of her hand until they were safely out of the boathouse. Outside the mist clung to the fields and danced like steam across the surface of the lake. The castle was a fuzzy grey silhouette. With equally soft steps, they began along the pathway. 'You're troubled about something. Anything I can help with?'

Niamh glanced up at him but avoided making eye contact. She was loath to admit anything of Vaughan's sin, and even less inclined to discuss her own worries, but Henry's presence comforted her. 'Do you think everything will go well tonight?'

'Tonight?' The surprise rang clear in Henry's voice. He didn't believe she was worried about the party. 'Of course. Everything has been carefully planned.'

'And after that?' she said, looking at her toes.

He stopped and swung his cane up into his hand. 'I'm not sure what you're asking me. And I don't like to predict your brother. He's a conniving sod, but he's ruled by his emotions.'

'Henry, does everybody know?' she blurted.

'About?' Henry cocked an eyebrow but his expression was sober.

'Him and Lord Marlinscar. Is it common knowledge? You know what I'm asking you, don't you?'

His tongue wetted his rouged lips, which he then rubbed thoughtfully together. 'There's no sense in worrying about it,' he said, avoiding the question but answering it well enough all the same. He took her hand and patted it, then laid it on his sleeve and began walking again. 'What was, is done. Save your thoughts for your friend Bella. She's hurting.'

'Has it ended between them too?'

Henry took a breath and held it. 'I'm not certain.'

Flustered, Niamh paced forward, shaking her head. 'It won't have. He doesn't know how to let go, not properly. It's why he keeps everyone at a distance, so he doesn't get too attached. He'll just run away from everything again.' Maybe even back to the Continent, she added to herself.

'Hush, now. I have an idea but I need your help. We'll help Vaughan to see things the way we see them.'

She gazed up at him in puzzlement.

'Later, m'dear.' He wrapped a comforting arm about her shoulders. 'For now, worry about yourself and your man.' His voice sounded strained as he spoke, as if he had to force himself to sound reasonable. 'You should do whatever it takes to make you happy.'

That was a problem. She didn't know what would make her happy any more. The issue with Alicia aside, she no longer felt so sure that marrying Edward would do so. His touch excited her, but the glow faded quickly when they were apart, and the touch of another might elicit much the same.

'Henry, would you do something for me?' she asked. 'You might think it a strange request.'

He forced a laugh but the oppressive mist seemed to steal his humour. 'You certainly know how to make a man curious.'

'I wondered if you'd kiss me.'

'What?' He swung abruptly, so that he stepped in front of her and stared at her. 'God's blood, woman! Do you know what you're asking? I've no death wish.'

She pressed a hand to his enormous lapel. 'You needn't worry about Vaughan. No one need ever know.'

His unease remained etched in the powdered lines of his face. 'I swear if we were in London and you made that request, you'd get more than you bargained for, but here, on this day,' he glanced warily at the shadowy castle, 'he's likely to skin me.'

She looked down in disappointment.

Henry sighed. 'I never said I wouldn't do it.' He placed his hands firmly upon her shoulders, then ran his thumb up her neck to her chin. 'I just don't think it's a good idea.'

'Why not?'

It was his turn to look uncomfortable. 'Because, sweet Niamh, one kiss won't be nearly enough.'

17

Henry's kiss tingled on her lips long after they parted. Niamh had walked past her brother and into the castle with a smirk on her face she couldn't repress. Poor Henry, he'd looked positively terrified, as if Vaughan would read what they'd done in their expressions.

Henry tasted of sugar and rouge. He wasn't demanding like Edward, whose kisses had been all probing heat and lazy gratification of his own desires. Henry explored her mouth gently, his touch whispery light and coaxing. He didn't claim or conquer. Henry never demanded more than she was prepared to give.

She'd meant the kiss as an experiment to help define her own feelings, not expecting the slow melding of their mouths to bring such a rush of joy. When they'd parted, she'd had to untangle herself from his oversized clothes, and sticky heat had bathed her body. She hadn't really wanted to let go.

There was an entire ensemble of rakehells in the great hall, all stretched out across sofas and perched within the window bays. There were no women about. They'd all retired to their rooms to prepare for the evening. Feeling decidedly like a lamb set free among a pack of slavering wolves, she headed for the safety of her bed-chamber.

'Milady.' Her maid was there laying out her clothes. She

thrust a note into Niamh's hand. 'The butcher's boy brought it from the village about an hour gone.'

'Thank you.' Niamh cracked the wax seal, then settled upon the striped chaise longue to read. 'Would you find Alicia for me?'

The hand was Edward's.

Beloved Niamh,

Be assured that I am well despite your brother's best efforts. Fear not for your safety. I will deliver you from his tyranny. I'll come tonight and we can be wed. The special licence is already arranged. Be ready to fly.

Your devoted servant,

Edward

'No!' She clasped the paper to her lips, then ran to the fire and cast it into the flames. He musn't come for her tonight or any night. Had she not told him a thousand times that she wouldn't elope with him, even before Vaughan had sown the seeds of doubt in her mind?

A treacherous memory reared in her mind. Edward's hand across her lips. Had he wanted to stifle her cries?

There was a knock at the door. 'Come,' she said, as she rubbed at her hands as if to remove invisible ink from her fingers.

'Niamh, what is it?' Alicia Allenthorpe scampered to her side and peered curiously at Niamh's hands. 'I was half out of my frock ready to start to dress for this evening. Aunt Beatrice has an entire beauty regime worked out that she swears is effective at capturing husbands. I think she intended it just for Fortuna, but she's horribly out of sorts today and just keeps saying that lotions won't help.'

Niamh bit her lip and almost rescinded on her intention.

Her friend was so excited about the party, it seemed horrid to inflict such a vile question on her, but she had to know the truth. 'Do you know a man named Edward Holt?'

The truth was plain in Alicia's eyes. Storm clouds swept through their dancing blue depths. The colour drained from her face. 'I do.' She clasped her hands before her and squeezed tight. 'I do. Though I'd prefer not to speak of him. He seemed so gallant.' She turned away from Niamh's stare and raised her clasped hands to her lips. 'Everyone expected him to propose at the ball we held for Mae's coming out. He'd been courting me so diligently and he made everybody laugh. When he failed to appear, I thought he'd taken ill. I expected a letter would arrive explaining.' She shook her head solemnly. 'Nothing. Then we heard he was wooing some other girl in the country.'

'Me,' said Niamh.

Alicia stared at her in disbelief. 'You?'

Niamh inclined her head. 'I'm afraid it's true, though I swear I had no idea until last night. You never mentioned him in your letters.'

'Nor you in yours.' Alicia's eyes narrowed suspiciously. 'Edward is your mysterious gentleman? I never explained what happened because you sounded so happy and I didn't want to spoil it with my woes. I felt such a fool too. Everyone thought the worst of me, as if it were my fault he'd cast me off.'

She reached out behind her and sought the comfort of the chaise, into which she sank. Niamh dropped to her knees beside her friend, feeling her pain as if it were her own, and in many ways it was. 'I wish I'd known sooner.'

Alicia embraced herself. 'Did he propose to you?'

'Yes, but Vaughan wouldn't give his approval and I

refuse to elope, but Edward doesn't seem to listen.' She searched a moment for the letter she'd already burned. 'Alicia, you have to help me. He's coming here, tonight, intent on carrying me off.'

'Tonight!' Alicia's stoicism dissolved in to a pool of anguish. 'But you won't go with him?'

'Of course not, but I don't want my brother to shoot him either.'

'Maybe he'd pass unnoticed among so many guests.'

Niamh shook her head and marched to the window, which she cast open. 'They're all Vaughan's friends. Not a good crowd if truth be told. It's bound to turn nasty.'

Still on the chaise longue, Alicia hugged herself a little tighter, so her chin pushed into the V made by her arms. 'I'll help, of course, but I don't see what I can do.'

'Write him a letter. I'll write one too. He won't want to face us both. That should keep him away.'

Alicia's terrified frown only deepened. 'I'll do it, but if the threat of facing your brother isn't enough to keep him away, I doubt a note from me will thwart him. Can't you just tell the footmen not to let him in?'

'Oh, Alicia, if only it was that simple, but I doubt he's going to come to the door.'

'Then what about asking your friend, Miss Rushdale, if she has any ideas, for I have none.'

'Bella. I haven't told her. I'm not really sure where she is,' said Niamh. 'Such an awful lot happened last . . .' She shut her mouth when a spark of interest lit in Alicia's eyes. 'Yes, maybe you're right. I'll ask Bella's advice.'

But Bella proved rather difficult to find. She didn't show for dinner, but neither did Vaughan, Henry or de Maresi, and Fortuna only showed under duress. It was difficult to know what was going on, who was hiding and who was involved in preparations for the evening's entertainment. Niamh sent notes from herself and Alicia to Edward and hoped they would stop him. Her only other recourse was to warn Vaughan of his forthcoming arrival, and that seemed distinctly unwise.

Later, she came across Vaughan in the solar, while the other gentlemen were taking port in the great hall. The ladies were assembled in the lower parlour under the stern eyes of Mrs Alvanley, awaiting an invitation to the entertainments.

'Will it be long?' Niamh asked.

Henry stepped out of the shadows by the library door and greeted her. 'Soon, I think,' he said.

She blushed on seeing him, the memory of his kiss a sweet ache in her chest. He made her feel something Edward never had, both excited and strangely safe.

He'd dressed in his most exquisite ensemble for the evening, a candy-striped pink and blue satin suit, with a frothy cravat that, when unfurled, was probably the length of the room.

With some difficulty, she tore her gaze away from him and focused instead on her brother. 'What are you doing?' She leaned over his arm to get a glimpse of the decanter he was holding.

Vaughan looked slyly at her from beneath his eyelashes and swirled the decanter so that the liquor inside sloshed about. Seemingly satisfied with the results, he poured a glass and offered it to her.

Henry drew a little closer and gave a wary shake of his head.

'I'm fine,' she replied.

Vaughan shrugged and raised the glass to her in a salute. 'Death and decadence,' he said and knocked back the ruby liquid. 'Let's summon the revellers, Tristan.'

From the moment she'd left Raffe in the rain that morning, Bella's thoughts had wandered in a perpetual loop: Vaughan, Raffe, Lucerne, Louisa. There was no beginning and no end, only a spiral of gloom. She'd slept away the afternoon cocooned in a nest of blankets and had woken an hour ago, stiff and hungry, when Niamh's maid had arrived to dress her for the evening's entertainment.

Now she stood just inside the door to her room in a snowy evening gown with her hair dressed in intricate loops, preparing herself to face Vaughan and his guests. She could hear them in the hall below, even recognised some of their voices from engagements in London. They were lecherous rogues to a man.

The women were clearly assembled elsewhere, the solar or the lower parlour she guessed. 'Give me strength,' she said, glancing at the pile of Louisa's letters on the dressing table. Then head held high, she glided onto the balcony and down the stairs into the pack.

There weren't so many of them as she'd anticipated, but still enough to make her uncomfortable, and the only friendly face among them was Raffe, whose eyes she deliberately avoided. Part of her wanted to dismiss his proposal as nonsense spoken in the heat of his own orgasm, but she knew that he'd intended it as genuine.

His gaze, along with those of others who undressed her more blatantly, followed her progress across the room. Never had the great hall seemed so huge. She was almost safe when de Maresi stepped forwards and blocked her way.

'*Morue*,' he drawled, 'what a shame to still find you here. We heard you'd departed.'

Tight-lipped, Bella met his hostile gaze.

'Don't think that the competition thinning changes anything.' His lips stretched into a nasty smirk. Clearly, with Lucerne now categorically out of the way, the overscented tulip had decided to up his claim.

'You're deluding yourself,' she hissed. 'Even the ghost of Lucerne is more than you can compete with.'

His narrow nostrils flared, and his composure dissolved in an abusive snarl: '*Connasse*.'

Bella didn't stay to exchange any more pleasantries. She pushed past the raging silken butterfly, only to find her progress hampered by a second picket.

'Pennerley's sent us an aperitif.'

'Didn't I eat you once before?' they teased. Connelly and Dovecote, she recognised, flanked by the flame-haired Darleston twins; four-fifths of the assemblage Vaughan had served her to on a silver platter.

'Where's Marlinscar tonight? I hear he's abandoned you. Got himself a nice new filly. Not so well used.' The remark came from the elder of the twins, who moved in behind her to roll his loins against her bottom.

'I heard it wasn't a filly,' drawled his brother, whom they called Neddy. She'd never enquired why. His real name was Alberic.

'You must be distraught, either way.' A hand stretched across her shoulder and tugged at the lace fichu covering the upward swell of her breasts. Bella slapped them away, but the four of them had her surrounded.

'Let her be, you wretched meatmongers.' Raffe forced his way into the circle. 'Is that any way to talk to a lady?'

'Depends on the lady,' chirped Connelly.

Bella scowled at him, and then at Raffe. If she didn't manage one last trick with Vaughan tonight then she might well have to accept his offer. But she didn't want him setting himself up as her protector for the night. She was perfectly capable of managing alone.

'Excuse me,' she snapped, and she jammed her fan into Connelly's chest, forcing a yelp of protest from his lips.

The other men laughed, but parted just enough to let her pass between them and out of the circle, although hands closed over her bottom and squeezed as she did so. Bella spun to face them with a snarl, and then backed towards the door, only to find herself bruising her bottom on another hard male body.

His scent washed through her like a balm. Bella spun around to find Vaughan poised before her, his dark eyebrows quizzically raised. 'Still with us,' he said.

'You invited me to a party.'

Vaughan inclined his head. 'Ah, yes, you must stay for that. I see the bucks are quite as enthralled with you as ever.'

Though a deal less enthralled than they'd been the moment before his arrival, she noted. Cowards, she thought. None of you dare risk his wrath, you're all too afraid for your skins.

'My lord,' said Bella. She curtsied politely, prompting another eyebrow raise from Vaughan.

He was all snaky hips and firm thighs this evening, his coat dark and his shirt impossibly snowy. She wanted to grab him, shake him, prove to him with her body that if they didn't have each other, then they had nothing.

Despite the pain his rejection had caused, she still

wanted him. He was just hurting and she was easy target. If they could be left alone together, maybe they could work through this.

She reached out to him, but he raised the two decanters he was holding like a barricade.

'You never offered your condolences,' she said.

Vaughan stared at her but his violet eyes were slightly glazed, as if he were looking at her through an opaque film. 'You never offered yours.' With a strange roll of his hips, he wriggled around her so that they bodies didn't touch and joined the other men.

Heart in her mouth, Bella moved into the dingy safety of the corridor, where she pressed her back to the wall. Why was she torturing herself like this? Did she really need an evening of ghosts and phantasms to scare her? She was already half out of her wits.

The women were along the corridor in the lower parlour. She could hear Alicia singing but she wasn't sure she was ready to face them either, not with her heart racing and a blush upon her cheeks. She was saved the agony when Niamh appeared at her shoulder. 'Are you all right?' she asked. 'I was on my way to find you. I looked in earlier but you were asleep.'

'Do you want the long answer or the short?'

Niamh gently stroked her cheek. 'I know a little already. Vaughan was raving last night. I'm not sure he's entirely lucid now. I'm sorry about your friend and,' she dug her teeth into her upper lip, 'about Lord Marlinscar.'

Burdened with a maelstrom of boiling emotions, Bella paced several steps, then turned on the spot. 'Raffe's asked me to marry him,' she blurted.

'He's what!' Niamh's mouth formed a perfect O. 'When?'

Puzzlement replaced the shock, then hardened into a worried frown. 'You haven't accepted?'

Bella licked her lips that still felt swollen from her earlier tears and Raffe's aggressive kisses. 'No, but Vaughan wants me gone.'

'There's gone and there's . . .' Niamh struggled for words, 'married.' She closed the gap between them and held Bella's hands in hers. 'Don't do it, you'll make yourself utterly miserable. Vaughan doesn't really want you to go, he's just being pig-headed.' She rubbed her thumbs across the back of Bella's knuckles in what Bella assumed was supposed to be a comforting fashion, but merely displayed her own anxiety. 'You musn't marry Raffe, Bella. You'll destroy Vaughan if you do. He needs you. What he had with Lord Marlinscar was . . .' she struggled again, '. . . wrong. You have to help him heal.'

Bella shook her head. 'He made his wishes plain this morning, and again just now.' Maybe he did need her but he'd never admit it. Still, there was one thing she needed to correct. 'It wasn't wrong,' she said quietly of Vaughan and Lucerne's relationship. 'It was beautiful.'

Niamh bit her lips and nodded. Slowly her expression became more purposeful. 'I do have one idea. We'll talk later.' A raucous laugh pealed along the corridor from the great hall, drawing both their attention and silencing Bella's immediate questions.

'Niamh, dear sister,' Vaughan shouted. Niamh and Bella appeared in the doorway. 'Stop lurking in the shadows and come and join us. Foster, if you'll inform the other ladies, we can start making our way down to the cellar.'

'The cellar,' remarked one of the bloods. 'What the devil do we want to freeze our nuts off down there for?'

Vaughan turned slowly to face the dissident. 'Scared already, Dovecote?' He passed him the decanter. 'Drink up. It may fortify your spirits.'

'Yes, boy.' The colonel, one of the Horse Guards' finest, clapped him across the back. 'It might even give you some bottom.'

Dovecote laughed. 'If this is what I think it is, it's more likely to give me something else.'

'I thought Miss Rushdale had already furnished you with that,' said Darleston, and smiled a wolf's smile at her.

Vaughan's eyes narrowed to thin slits, prompting Darleston to raise his hands in surrender. 'Merely an observation.'

Vaughan showed his teeth, then his sneer melted into a smile. 'No, she's too hot in the tail for Dovecote, he only likes them fresh from the academy.'

'Inexperienced but game, actually,' said Dovecote, prompting snorts of mirth.

Bella wanted to slap them all but Niamh's hand tightened on her arm so that her nails dug into the flesh. 'Don't let them bait you,' she hissed.

Luckily their ribaldry ceased with the arrival of Mrs Alvanley and the other ladies, who filed into the hall like a parade of vestal virgins. If the chaperone hadn't been among them, there would surely have been rapturous applause.

'Ladies.' Vaughan dropped into a flamboyant bow, which ended with his lips pressed to Mrs Alvanley's knuckles. 'You look enchanting.' He twirled her around and the silly woman actually blushed. Bella groaned inwardly: didn't she realise she was being played? 'May I present to you the colonel,' Vaughan continued, with a smile as twisted as the performance he was giving.

The colonel bowed equally low but with a considerably stiffer back. 'Enchanted, Mrs Alvanley, doubly enchanted. Would you do me the honour of allowing me to escort you to the cellar?'

'Oh,' she cooed, and clasped her fan to her chest. Bella rolled her eyes in disbelief. Her arm draped along the colonel's sleeve, Mrs Alvanley beamed. 'Now girls,' she said with a fleeting backwards glance, as they were each partnered by one of the gentlemen. 'Remember yourselves.'

Mae raised her fan and leaned in to Bella. 'As if we'd dare forget. But she won't notice a thing once the lights go out.'

18

The cellar was dark and, if not dank, then certainly musty. Bella couldn't believe it normally smelled so ensanguined; the metallic taste seeped into her mouth, causing a thickness in her throat.

A cowled figure beckoned them into the unknown from the bottom of the steps. Niamh clung to her arm, already trembling. Beyond the wine cellar, the rooms were lit with a sickly green glow, giving the illusion that they were at the bottom of some murky pool. Cobwebs and tattered linens shrouded barrels and caskets, and a notched scythe stood propped by the door.

Tremulously, they followed their silent guide into a vaulted chamber where four more robed figures formed an arch around a gaping black hole in the brickwork. The guests huddled together behind them, ladies clinging to their escorts' arms and the gentlemen all standing to rigid attention, the only indication of their fear their consciously slow breathing as they waited, ears straining, in fearful anticipation.

It began with a discordant note, like the wail of a child torn from its mother's chest, followed by the hiss of smoke. A white shape flickered in the darkness, suspended in midair within the black maw, and the hooded figures began a liturgical chant, calling forth a being from the void into the realm of the living.

Slowly, the blurred outline sharpened. Bella rubbed her eyes but the hideous apparition of death remained. Jealousy burned in its hollow eye sockets and a grey cloak swaddled its chill white bones.

A shrill scream ratcheted the tension in the room an octave higher. Mae swooned into the arms of her escort, and a titter of laughter escaped several mouths. It died away rapidly as the skeletal figure opened its jaw with a grisly scrape. 'Hear me now,' it cawed, 'the messenger of my lord, Sebastian Alastair Elisud, Marquis of Pennerley, master of this domain. My lord has arisen hungry from his long sleep. He thirsts for the blood of innocents and the black hearts of ignoble curs.' The voice was deep and menacing, hissing sibilants in the semidarkness. 'Once he was like you, with warm flesh and a beating heart.' The skeletal image flickered. Red hungry flames danced in the pits of its eyes. 'Fleeing madness and suicide, he travelled far, seeking what pleasures the ancient world could offer. In Persia, he found a magus, toothless and vile, who promised a glimpse of heaven and hell.'

The image faded and a new sight superimposed itself – the baleful glare of a wizened sorcerer, cruelty etched into his face.

The first figure returned and heatless flames licked around the form, while a light fell from above and gave a ghastly pallor to the death's head. 'My master followed him to the Towers of Silence, where the living have parted from the dead since the days before Mohammed. There united, they commanded the spirits from rotting corpses to do their bidding. But the magus tricked my master.'

The apparition grew larger until it almost touched the cowled figures. Bella gaped, only dimly aware of those around her and Niamh's hand still clasped within her own. To her left Gabriel stood mesmerised, and she watched as the fine hairs on his neck slowly rose until they stood straight out from his skin.

'The magus' bargain was struck but not with my master. He wanted a soul to take his place and suffer his damnation. A horror came, a spirit of murder and rage from the past. Something *unchristian*.'

There were several gasps. Then a shadow rose in the dark space, a leering demon made of red roiling smoke. 'Pursued by that unclean spirit, my master returned to his homeland, back to this castle. And know this: it does not have him yet. The thing is appeased by sacrifice, and has been fed by his hand since that accursed day. Harken! It hungers. It nears.'

The inhuman shriek that had greeted them rose again. Several answering cries came from the audience.

'As he was tricked, so now are you. The thing must have blood. Tonight, one of you must die that he might live again!'

Mocking laughter drowned out the screams of the guests. The apparition flickered and faded. Something cold brushed the back of Bella's neck, then the tip of her nose and one exposed arm. Beside her, Niamh shrieked.

Before them the skeletal apparition solidified again and expanded to monstrous proportions, seeming to grow nearer and more menacing. It yawned impossibly wide and spat a snake from its gaping mouth, which hit the floor with a very real thwack. At the same time, bodies pressed into her from behind, and something soft and wet with a rubbery pustulant flesh brushed her ankles.

The figure vanished, leaving darkness rent by screams, thumps and curses.

Niamh was roughly pulled to one side and her fingers slipped from Bella's own, leaving her clawing frantically at the empty air. Bella felt panic and horror rising, as she was swept in circles by the now hysterical mob. No one took her hand. She recoiled from the touch of coarse fabric against her fingertips and something hairy scuttling near her feet.

Wet briny puddles reflected the eerie green glow, dotting the way out. While the rest of the group surged up the stairs to the hoped-for-safety of the great hall, Bella followed a little more carefully. If she knew Vaughan, the terrors would not be confined to the cellar.

By the time she caught up, the bloods had recovered some of their bravado and the ladies were swooning for effect. In their absence someone had extinguished all the candles and left the great hall illuminated by nothing more than the dying firelight.

'I say, what the devil's afoot here?' exclaimed Connelly at the front of the group. In answer, a light flickered into being at the far end of the hall, then out of the gloom a shape came floating towards them. A pale, slim hand held a forked candelabrum, which cast a baleful glow over the woman who gazed at them. She was dressed in a full-skirted gown which emphasised her tiny waist, the sort worn over a century ago, only it was all of sheer white. Her face might have been beautiful but for the ghastly leprous shade of her skin and the deep shadowed hollows which held her lifeless eyes.

'O Rose, thou art sick,' whispered a voice very much like Darleston's.

Paralysed by the terrible beauty, they watched as she turned away and glided silently towards the stairs opposite, where she began to ascend towards Bella's room. Or more correctly, she realised, towards the lady's chamber.

The figure reached the top of the stairs and entered the gallery, passing beyond their sight, and the group gave a collective sigh. Someone cleared their throat, ready to exercise their wit, but they were never given the chance as an ululating cacophony broke out in the stairwell behind them: the characteristic screech of Sebastian's demon.

The crowd broke and ran for the door shrieking and giggling, but all equally unwilling to be the evening's sacrifice. Bella likewise had no desire to face the thing alone and fled out into the night with the rest.

Outside, heavy mists still curled around the grounds, although starlight showed the outline of the castle around her. The ladies and their ungallant gallants scattered and were soon lost to her sight, though their screams echoed back through the opaque air. Vaughan could not have picked a more perfect night for his grotesque parade. Nervous without an escort or companion, Bella moved forwards to where a pair of candelabra hung eerily, like will-o'-the-wisps. But deathly lure or not, lights surely meant people, and shocks were best enjoyed with a companion to cling to.

The vapours seemed to peel back, then stretch towards her again like clawed hands as she moved. She reached the entryway and saw that the great gate had been thrown wide, as if all the castle's defences had been stripped away and spirits besieged them.

Around her the tunnel walls glistened, their surface cold and slimy to the touch. Ahead, she thought she saw movement, heard the rustle of long skirts, only to see instead a cowled figure at the farther end of the drawbridge. A lump filling her throat, Bella swallowed it down and move hesitantly forwards but when she blinked the vision was gone, only to reappear a moment later part way across the stable yard. It raised a single bony hand and beckoned her forwards.

In fear and trepidation she followed the summons, her arms clasped tight about herself. She was not by nature timid, but the phantasms raised within the cellar were vivid and terrifying, intangible and yet impossibly real. She wondered how they'd managed to achieve what looked like magic.

The coach-house door creaked as she opened it. The space was lit by a single candle, burning inside a jam jar on a shelf below the mildewed window. Next door she could hear the quiet whinnies of the horses. 'Who is it? Where are you?' she called, seeking her ghostly guide. Her footsteps sounded unnaturally loud on the wooden boards inside the entryway. Further in, the timber gave way to straw-strewn flags and a ladder leading up to the hayloft.

A plume of sawdust trickled down from the underside of the loft and Bella moved towards it. 'Who's up there?' she called, nervous excitement propelling her forwards as far as the ladder. 'Niamh?'

The air smelled of straw and of sickly burned sugar. She had her foot on the first rung when a whistling shriek split the still air and a grey blur shot up through the floor. Bella froze. Her eyes stung but she didn't dare blink. The thing hung in the air, its tattered cloak billowing around its amorphous form. With a grisly creak its head snapped towards her, revealing the half-rotted visage of Sebastian's demon. White bone showed through the desiccated flesh. Ram-like horns showed clearly in place of hair upon its head. She screamed and threw herself out of the coach-house door and into the open space of the stable yard.

Panting and clammy, she staggered to the trough on the opposite side of the yard, where she splashed her face with water. Her heart had taken up residence in her skull and all she could hear was the rushing of her own blood.

'It's just a trick,' she told herself, trying to steady her heartbeat. Her reflection in the water stared back at her, pale and almost as ghastly as that of the white lady. 'Just one of Vaughan's clever phantasms.' Her throat felt raw from her screams. She'd never felt so scared or excited in her life. She wanted more, but she hardly dared uncurl her fingers from the edge of the water trough.

Something tapped her shoulder and she spun, terrified she'd find herself facing the vengeful spirit, only to find herself staring into the cowled visage of Henry Tristan.

'Bella,' he said, and stroked her cheek with a long tendril of seaweed. 'Are you all right?'

'No, I'm terrified.' She recoiled from the bladdery frond and glared at him, then clasped tight hold of his arm. Had it been him earlier? Had he led her to the apparition in the coach house? Gradually, she controlled her breathing and relaxed her hold.

'How?' she demanded.

Henry shook his head, but he was smiling. 'Never mind how, just enjoy the show. Are you ready for more?'

Heart fluttering in expectation, she nodded.

'Come then, let's see what other nightmares we can delight you with, before we find Niamh.'

'Niamh,' Bella gasped, not understanding, as he led her away around the curtain wall.

Henry's pleasant face darkened with his frown. 'Has she not spoken to you?'

'No.'

'Then it's definitely time we arranged a meeting. For there's an opportunity we mustn't miss.'

Vaughan waited until all his guests had flown before he crept out from behind the waxed cotton screen stretched across the hole in the brickwork. He'd had one of the cellar's many cubbyholes partially bricked up for the occasion, so that both he and the magic lantern were completely concealed from the audience. The lantern was an ingenious device, brought over from France by de Maresi, an inspirational product of the bloody revolution.

Strangely numb to the pain that had consumed him earlier, and pleasingly euphoric, Vaughan sent a few stragglers fleeing into the night with a demonic snarl, then sneaked across the drawbridge into the south tower. He paused at the base of the stairs and listened to the shrill cries and moans of terror as his guests darted about in the mists, but not for long. He had his role to play yet, one he was looking forward to: his diabolical great-great-great-grandfather Sebastian Alastair Elisud.

Vaughan started up the stairs, chuckling to himself. Oh, how he'd loved the moment when, plunged into darkness, they'd all huddled together, sweat glittering across their brows as he spun the tale of his ancestor. And their expressions as the phantasms moved before them, projected onto smoke.

He reached his bedchamber, only to find Fortuna perched upon his bed. She swept towards him, all shimmering white silk and eyes like brilliants. 'Miss Allenthorpe.' He caught up the decanter of laudanum he'd mixed earlier and raised it and a glass between them. 'Do my games not excite you?'

'Indeed they do.' She took the glass from his hand as though it were an offering and took a sip. 'But you excite me far more.' She drained the glass, then pushed both hands inside the open front of his coat.

'Ah.' He took a step back. 'Don't fool yourself, Miss Allenthorpe. If it's a husband you seek, or even just a lover, you'll be better served chasing spirits in the courtyard. Our time has already passed.'

She looked up at him, her lips slightly parted. 'Yes, but . . .'

'Did you think I'd change my mind? I thought I made my intentions plain last night.' He turned away from her enormous eyes. Eyes that seemed too large for her face. There was nothing he could do for her that would make it better. There was no part of him that wanted her. 'Go,' he said. 'Follow your dreams elsewhere.'

He heard her sob and the soft patter of her pumps against the floorboards. 'You're a fiend, Pennerley,' he told himself, though in truth, he felt surprisingly little. He poured another glass and savoured the sweet port upon his tongue, letting the opiates numb him.

By the mirror lay his costume. He'd had it made especially for the occasion while he was still in London planning the whole affair. It was an exact replica of the suit Sebastian Alastair Elisud wore in his portrait that hung in the solar. They bore a striking resemblance, once he'd donned the preposterously feathered hat, 'petticoat' breeches and furbelows. He'd definitely cause a stir, assuming he wasn't simply mistaken for Henry Tristan.

Taken with the idea, he chuckled at his own wit. Then, hat set at a jaunty angle, he swallowed another two sips of the poison, then discovered the glass was empty. 'Ah, well.' He'd brewed a decanter of the stuff. There'd be plenty of time for further fortification if he needed it, and at the minute, he really didn't.

The numbness had worn off, and now a low level tingle of arousal crawled beneath his skin. He rubbed his hand across his loins and revelled in the dart of pleasure. He'd try to avoid Bella and Fortuna, and focus his torments elsewhere. Tonight, horror and pleasure would collide in a hellish opera.

Vaughan's rejection stung. She'd known it would, but had still sat on his bed waiting for him. Fortuna cursed herself bitterly as she headed down into the courtyard, intending to find her sisters or maybe even her aunt. A strange lethargy seemed to have gripped her by the time she descended the final flight of steps. Limbs shaky and nausea brewing like a potion in her stomach, she staggered as far as the well and promptly threw up over the grass. Fortuna slumped with her back to the stone. Shadows swam before her eyes, ghostly figures in robes, a cavalier, and finally a man. He raised her hand and pressed a kiss to her knuckles, then another to her palm.

'All alone,' Dovecote drawled. 'How fortuitous.' He grinned at his own joke. Two fingers curled beneath her chin, forcing her to look up into his eyes where he knelt before her. They were the deepest green, like two chips of jade. He tilted his head, then ran his thumb up over her lips. 'Too much wine, my pretty poppy?' He surveyed the ground beside her and wiped his thumb upon his coat. 'Here, take the taste away.' He pressed a hip flask upon her. Fortuna instinctively swallowed. The contents were coarse and streaked fire down her throat, causing her to splutter and wheeze.

Dovecote helped her to rise and, after obligingly patting her back, slipped an arm around her waist. 'What do you say we go and find ourselves some excitement? I'm told the churchyard is altogether charming.' His hold was comforting, but also a fraction too intimate.

'I should probably lie down,' she said. Her head felt as if it was full of water and she wanted to rest, not stagger around in the dark and risk being devoured by phantoms and other less fanciful terrors.

'Nonsense.' He shook his head. 'A little light exercise and you'll be right as my leg.'

With his arm firm about her waist and her body moulded to his side, Fortuna found herself propelled towards the drawbridge. They were almost across its rickety boards when Alicia appeared before her from out of the mist, accompanied a moment later by Lord Devonshire.

'We've seen him,' her sister gasped. 'The first marquis. He chased Darleston and Neddy down towards the lake. You should have seen them run. Devonshire and I stayed in the shadows until he'd gone.' Her eyes shone bright with excitement, only for her smile to collapse into a frown when her gaze fastened upon Fortuna's face. 'Tunie.' Her giddy excitement fell away leaving only sisterly concern. She pressed a delicate touch to Fortuna's arm. 'Are you all right? You don't look so well.'

'Just a mild fright,' said Dovecote. He squeezed Fortuna's shoulder who blinked very slowly. 'She saw the marquis too, didn't you, dear?'

With some effort she nodded her head, then the nod turned into a shake. It wasn't the marquis who had scared her. It was the sudden prospect of a future lived according to the dictates of society. It wasn't what she wanted. She didn't want to sit at home and make samplers or nurture a dozen children. She wanted permission to think, feel and maybe love. She'd seen a glimpse of that in a future with Vaughan, but his heart was clearly elsewhere.

As her thoughts drifted, she was hardly aware of Raffe's gaze roving suspiciously over Dovecote and herself. 'Is there a problem here?' asked Raffe, squaring up to Dovecote. 'If the lady isn't feeling too well, surely the castle would seem a more sensible direction, not the gate.'

'She's fine,' Dovecote replied. He was neither as tall nor broad-shouldered as Raffe, and clearly detected the growl behind his words. 'She just needs to walk it off.'

'Then we'll see she does.'

Dovecote's lips twitched at the corner. He seemed set to object, but then bowed his head stiffly and allowed Alicia and Raffe to lead her back the way she'd just come.

'I just want to lie down,' she said, but nobody seemed to pay her any heed.

19

The squally twilight earlier had turned into a crisp and clear night; Vaughan's favourite type of darkness, with stars spangling in the heavens and a great sliver of moonlight, making it perfect for flushing drunken bloods out of bushes, despite the tendrils of mist that still lingered around the graves and hovered over the still waters of the moat. He'd taken a turn upon the battlements, then scared the hell out of the Darleston twins in the vestry of the church. There was a line of statues and he'd posed himself by the last, lit by the grey moonlight and dappled by the stained glass. He'd come to life suddenly before their eyes, then chased them, bleating and cowering, down to the lake. Now he was ready to do full justice to the memory of his ancestor.

His Restoration costume was quite the most lovely thing: rich red coat, heavily braided front and back, with enormous cuffs you could hide a goose in. The breeches were red too, and curiously loose about his legs compared to his usual pantaloons. They seemed to float around him, brushing his skin in a way that made all his hairs stand on end, while the plethora of ribbon adornments flapped like butterflies' wings every time he moved.

He was obliged to remove his hat before entering the castle again. It was at least three feet wide, and decorated with a red silk scarf the size of a tablecloth, bunched and folded into an imitation rose. He rubbed the silk against his face, luxuriating in the sensation of it against his skin, as pleasing as a lover's touch. He was hopelessly purse-proud. Time he caught himself a mouse to play with.

Three promising wenches scattered before him in the great hall, screaming with fright. He pursued them along the endless bottom corridor into the dead end that was the billiards room. 'Come out, come out, my pretties,' he called as he swaggered over the threshold. It was impossible not to swagger in these breeches; they forced his legs so far apart. 'It's been a hundred and forty years since I tasted the flesh of a woman, and I've a mind to speak of country matters.'

He pounced at them. One slipped away under his arm, the other two he caught about their waists. 'No escape now,' he hissed, and clutched them to his chest.

It didn't matter who they were, only that they were soft and lithe and wriggling against him, almost paralysing him with the sensation of their warm bodies rubbing against his skin. And their scent. Fear with a dash of innocence, or was it the other way round?

'Let go, Vaughan! Let go!'

The girl on his right looked just like an ancient cameo of his mother, her eyes impossibly blue. Blue like cornflowers, blue like Lucerne's. He forced his mouth down over hers to take away the memory and felt her go rigid.

The other girl gasped and managed to free herself from his hold. She backed away, up against the wall, her fingers curled tight within her palms and her mouth open wide.

Desires wakened with the thrill of the kiss, crude acts most would baulk at asking even a courtesan to perform. Her taste was familiar and precious. She squirmed and he held her tighter. Somehow she got a hand around his throat and forced him off, almost choking him in the process.

'Yuck!' Niamh rubbed her hands across her face, attempting to scrub his taste from her lips. She stared at him, completely horrified. 'You're crazy.'

'I'm Sebastian Alastair Elisud, Marquis of Pennerley, and I take what I desire.'

She smacked him hard across the jaw, leaving him cross-eyed and momentarily speechless. 'And I'm your sister, and you'll damn well keep your hands off me.' She tried to push past him but he caught her wrist. 'No, not Vaughan, Sebastian. And well past time I claimed a victim to appease the *Angra Mainyu*.' He let Niamh's wrist slip through his fingers, his gaze now fixed upon the youngest Miss Allenthorpe, who was still trying to meld with the wall. Slowly he dragged his teeth over his lower lip.

Mae gave a startled squeak as he closed in on her, glancing briefly down at her plump and lovely curves before meeting her gaze with a wicked smile. He saw himself reflected in her eyes, a malevolent spirit with dark eyes and an even darker heart, a single ringlet down the centre of his forehead.

'Grant me a kiss, and maybe I'll spare your life.'

'A kiss?'

'Just that.'

She trembled but nodded her accord.

'You might want to leave, sister, dear.'

Niamh gave a loud snort and left, and he kicked the door closed behind her. No doubt she'd stay pacing the corridor.

'Why did she need to go outside?' Mae asked tremulously.

'Because I never specified where I was going to kiss you. And I was never one to use my tongue fairly.'

Vaughan sank gracefully onto his knees, then, to her shock, he lifted her hem and hoisted it to her waist. He nuzzled against her garter then dabbed his tongue against her labia, releasing a startled gasp that quickly transformed into a moan. She tasted salty and soft against his tongue, curiously familiar but very different to Bella. Vaughan pressed his nose into her dark curls and breathed in her scent. He was quite sure from the way her fingers tightened against his hair and her nails bit into his scalp that this was the first time any man had kissed her in quite such an intimate way. It would take little skill to bring her off, and he was conscious of how his own needs were calling. His prick was now painfully hard but he didn't want to ravish her. He had another victim in mind. Still, it seemed a shame to deny her. Rather, he wanted to give her a memory to do his reputation proud.

'My lord,' she whimpered. He clasped her bottom and tilted her hips towards him. Mae's legs trembled and she made a choking sound in the back of her throat. It softened into a long contented mewl as he focused his attention on her clitoris, flicking his tongue over the surface of the hard little bead with rapid repetitive strokes. It was tempting to deepen his kisses, but he knew that a woman's pleasure was really a very simple thing to coax. If she liked what you were doing, unless you deliberately intended to prolong the discourse, you kept doing it in exactly the same fashion you'd begun. Still, there were limits to even his endurance, and the taste of her was thick upon his tongue, so when she started to sag against him, he urged her forwards, and let her cover his face with her quim. Then when she squirmed he pushed his tongue into her, to lick and jab with its velvety caress.

Mae's breaths came sharper; she writhed against him, enjoying his touch with the whole of her body. She was far curvier then her sisters, impish and merry, and he suspected far more willing to give in return. She was a pleasure-seeker to her very core.

Vaughan returned to rapidly flicking his tongue against her clit, which now stood proudly from beneath its hood. He heard the change in her breathing immediately as she began to soar, and her hips jerked in sharp little waves. She panted as she came, as though she couldn't quite catch her breath, rocking against him so that his face was smeared with her juices.

Vaughan leaned back and wiped them away with the back of his hand. Her pupils were dilated when she looked down at him. He rose and took her hand, pressed a chaste kiss to her knuckles while he held her gaze.

'My lord,' she croaked. Her gaze fastened over the throbbing length of his erection that not even his indulgent Restoration breeches could now disguise. The temptation was there, to coax her to her knees and offer his cock to her mouth and let her learn by her tongue and her imagination how to persuade him to spend.

'My lady.' He bowed with a flourish, then left. He nearly walked into Niamh, pacing on the other side of the door.

'Mae. Are you all right? What did he do?' he heard her ask.

Mae sighed dreamily in response. 'He kissed me. That's all.'

* * *

Outside, Raffe morosely accompanied Alicia and Fortuna Allenthorpe around Pennerley's garden of earthly delights. Despite having been rescued from Dovecote, whose intentions were clearly far from honourable, Fortuna seemed strangely ungrateful. She shared none of her sister's enthusiasm for the events and seemed rather distant behind her huge, sensitive eyes. He wondered if he'd been too late to save her from all Dovecote's charms or whether someone else had upset her. His best guess was their host. Damn the man! Did he have to have every woman in his power?

For her part, Alicia had been both shocked and thrilled by every new nightmare, and seemed to be enjoying herself immensely.

Raffe sighed in frustration. He had hoped to find Bella in the crowd and enjoy the evening with her. He had no illusions that she would swoon conveniently to help his suit along, but he felt more engaged by her company than any woman he could think of. Sadly, she'd been swept away from him. He hadn't spied her since and could hardly abandon his role of guardian and protector of the two sisters, while predatory rakehells prowled the grounds in search of easy meat. His only hope of escape was if they somehow wandered into Mrs Alvanley.

They spied Gabriel and Connelly clinging to one another in terror, Connelly's swagger returning the moment he knew he was observed. Raffe didn't stop to exchange tales, but swung instead towards the north curtain wall in search of new pleasures and hopefully the girls' chaperone.

They had not gone far when a spear of light spilled from an open window high up in the north tower. 'Isn't that Bella's room?' Alicia asked.

Sure enough, behind the leaded pane he thought he

spied her figure. Surely she hadn't retired already? But the image was wrong, the woman deathly pale, slim and otherworldly, not curvaceous and fine. In disconcerting fascination the three of them watched as the apparition they'd first seen in the great hall gazed mournfully down at them, then with an anguished wail toppled from the window.

The ladies' screams rang out clear and sharp. Raffe gasped as her slim white body fell. There came a sickening thump and a splash as the waters of the moat opened to receive her.

'The marchioness,' hissed Alicia. She caught tight hold of his sleeve. 'Niamh told me of her earlier. She was driven mad by her husband's wickedness and perversions, and threw herself to her death.'

He was aware of the story too, but God's teeth! this had gone too far, if Pennerley had expected some poor servant girl to pitch herself into the filthy moat for their entertainment. In point of fact, the craziness was all beginning to wear rather thin.

Raffe sprinted to the wall, aware of the two girls following, and stretched over the wall to seek her body in the black water but he could make out nothing besides reeds and brambles.

'See.' Alicia appeared at his side and he followed the line of her outstretched arm to where she was pointing. Halfway up the castle wall, an oversized marionette dangled upon its strings as it was dragged back up to the tower. Relief washed through him, leaving him feeling rather foolish for being so gullible.

'Just a scarecrow in a frock.' Fortuna laughed. She seemed

to have roused herself a little, and she propelled herself closer to the wall. Raffe stopped her slithering too far over and scowled into the darkness. Across the water, coloured flames bobbed among the tombs.

'Look, there's Mae and Niamh.' Alicia continued to tug on his arm until he left the wall. 'Let's catch them. I want to know what they've seen and maybe we ought to find Aunt Bea for Fortuna. I bet she's over there too.'

Raffe nodded his assent. Fortuna still looked rather pale, and maybe he'd find Bella among the dancing light in the graveyard too.

After their abortive conversation in the lower corridor, and before Vaughan had loosed his demons upon the castle, it had been Niamh's intention to stick with Bella throughout the evening and take the opportunity to expand upon the plan Henry had presented and she herself had developed. She didn't feel her friend needed to be mothered, but she understood that she felt both cornered and constrained by circumstances. In some ways, the phantasmagoria could not have fallen at a worse time. There was too much going on and too many other guests trying to trap Vaughan with their insecurities. Niamh knew only that her brother and her friend were hurting, but she didn't understand why they found it so hard to take comfort in one another. Surely Lucerne's loss should bind them together . . .

There were other advantages to be had from sticking with Bella though, like the worldly experience which Niamh lacked, and Bella's ability to ward off the rogues who where roving the castle grounds. Vaughan could not have collected a more rakish ensemble if he had scoured the whole of

England and, while Niamh was sure none of them would lay a finger upon her for fear of Vaughan's retribution, there was one spectre she was not so certain of.

Edward had said he would come, and she did not believe her note would stop him. Leaving the castle grounds might even seem like an invitation for him to steal her away, so it was with reluctance that she let Mae tug her along behind Mrs Alvanley and the colonel to the graveyard.

The church. So recently a place of happiness, now a bitter reminder of the confusion she still felt over Edward, clouded even further by the kiss she had demanded of Henry. Regardless of whether Edward came tonight, she had to break it off. There could be no happy ever after between them, despite Vaughan's reluctant blessing. She was sure now that Edward's enthusiasm had been more than a little forceful and too much to endure for a lifetime. She much preferred Henry's subtle intensity. She felt sure that he wouldn't demand anything she wasn't prepared to give. He had even baulked a little at revealing his plan for making her pig-headed brother see sense. He'd feared that she might be shocked or outraged by the suggestion.

The thought raised a smile. For years her brother had misguidedly tried to protect her from rogues such as himself, and all he'd succeeded in doing was making her more vulnerable. She would be far more careful with her heart from now on. Meanwhile, she would repay him in a manner he would not expect, and hopefully make something right about this whole sorry mess.

'Niamh, Niamh. Hurry, please,' Mae squeaked excitedly, tugging her forwards at a faster pace. The young woman was completely thrilled by every new revelation and fever dream that arrived to assail them. She might have liked nothing better than to learn that there really was an ancient demon stalking them in order to feast upon their virgin blood, and not just Vaughan and a parade of household staff.

'Stay close, now,' Aunt Beatrice warned as the gravestones grew more thickly around them.

'Worry not,' said the colonel, and was rewarded by the grotesque sight of Mrs Alvanley's fluttering eyelashes. Still, her coquetry aside, she would turn from simpering old maid to vengeful harridan if there was so much as a hint of a threat to her charges. Edward would be a fool indeed to strike while she was about.

'Look, what are those figures about?' Mae skipped forward, her shawl looped about her arms and her fair shoulders bared to the night breeze.

Niamh squinted into the darkness. The mist had almost cleared, but the night itself was thick and the moon behind a cloud.

'Don't you worry, m'dears. I'm sure it's part of the entertainment.' The colonel protectively stepped to the fore, blocking Mae's view. Not to be stopped, she stepped around him and clutched a nearby stone cross.

The church bell tolled mournfully above them. Fearfully, mouths full of their beating hearts, they watched as four pall-bearers wound their way along the path from the lychgate, each stooped beneath their burden, with their figures completely obscured by billowing amorphous robes. Niamh's imagination filled in the details of the cadaverous features that lay beneath.

They grew closer and set the coffin down by the side of a freshly dug grave, then slowly the lid began to rise.

Niamh knew well enough that this was another of

Vaughan's gruesome twists, another staple of the gothic romances she and Bella so enjoyed, but still she watched the tableau unfold, her limbs frozen and a hiss of fearful anticipation upon her lips. It seemed quite blasphemous to present such images on hallowed ground, but her brother wouldn't give a damn about that.

She expected another white lady or perhaps a capering skeleton to leap from the box. Instead, an ear-splitting scream rent the silence apart as the lid fell aside to reveal Sebastian's demon, come all the way from Persia to drag one of them down to hell. Clearly what offerings Sebastian had so far fed it were not enough.

It did indeed leap from the casket to pound the earth before them and brandish its blood-drenched claws.

Mae's scream rang out, while Mrs Alvanley fainted dead away into the colonel's arms. He struggled a little to support her and had to beg the assistance of one of the pall-bearers, actually the boot boy, in order to lower her gently to the ground.

The demon, meanwhile, chased the still squealing Mae around the tombstones for a few delicious moments before dancing away in search of more tainted souls to consume. There were plenty of those about, Niamh was sure. Maybe it would encounter Edward and send him running.

As if on cue, the Darleston twins emerged from the trees where they had observed the scene. 'Bravo,' exclaimed the elder while they both enthusiastically applauded Mae's part of the melodrama.

While the colonel fanned Mrs Alvanley, Niamh sought her smelling salts and waved them under her nose. Perhaps it was time they went inside and spared themselves any more frights.

'But I don't want to go in,' protested Mae, as Neddy Darleston waltzed her between a row of crosses.

'Well, you're coming,' said Niamh. With a violent sneeze, Mrs Alvanley revived. 'We ought to make your aunt comfortable, and I need to find Bella.'

'Stick-in-the-mud,' Mae complained. She'd always been the most bubbly of the sisters, but after her encounter with Sebastian earlier she seemed borderline mutinous. That, and Niamh distinctly saw her wriggle her bottom against Neddy's loins. The little minx's eyes widened. Clearly, she'd found more than she'd bargained for.

'Mae!' Mrs Alvanley was on her feet again. 'You'll behave yourself this instant.' She gave Neddy a particularly vengeful look. 'Colonel, if you'd escort my niece, I'm sure Mr Darleston and Lady Niamh will help me back.'

20

Vaughan strode through the castle, his focus completely intent upon his next target. He had forced himself to play his role a while longer before he succumbed to his own pleasures, but now he had some vague idea of losing himself in the moment, and of letting Sebastian subsume him and take away the residual pain in his heart.

De Maresi was in the north tower, in the sitting room of the suite he was sharing with Raffe. He had his back to Vaughan as he concentrated on working the strings of the marchioness' grisly puppet, which was suspended halfway down the outside wall.

Vaughan clasped a hand over his mouth. 'Sh-shh!' he hissed. 'Quiet now.'

For once this was going to be entirely on his terms, which is why he bypassed the preamble. Having made quick work of de Maresi's breeches, Vaughan parted his cheeks and slid home. The penetration met with only the faintest resistance and a groan from de Maresi, as his body yielded to the intrusion.

'This is what you wanted, isn't it?' Vaughan whispered.

'Yes . . . God, yes . . .' De Maresi tried to turn his head.

'I said no sound.' Vaughan pushed his gloved fingers into the Vicomte's mouth. He knew their taste. It was oddly powdery, and curiously underscored with a hint of musk. A bitter, cloying taste, although he wasn't sure if it was the smell and not the texture he found so enticing. Either way, there was something about the white kid gloves that he found entrancing, a pleasure only heightened by the sensation of de Maresi's mouth around them.

'This is it,' he said. 'There's no more after this.' Vaughan ploughed him with long steady strokes that forced him face first against the wall. It felt good to dispense with the subtleties and just fuck for a change. The bliss centred on his cock grew more intense with each stroke until he was almost distraught with the sensation of it.

'Are you hard, François?' Are you desperate for a touch?'

De Maresi squirmed in his arms. 'Vaughan, I'm desperate.' He tried to speak around the fingers in his mouth.

'Shhh! I warned you.' He caught the man's earlobe between his teeth. 'You'll have to tug it yourself.'

He clutched de Maresi to his chest, his mouth still hot about his fingers and lost himself in their motion. Time stretched on into infinity. It felt as though a thousand thorns were digging into his skin, and that each pinpoint of pain brought the agony of a little death. He felt certain that de Maresi felt it too. His gasps were deep and raw as he worked his cock in time with Vaughan's rhythm. None of this was about lasting. It was all about coming.

Their breath steamed up the arched glass window. The puppet strings hung limp across the sill. 'How is it with sweet Gabriel?' Vaughan asked. 'What would he think if he saw you like this, your little protégé? Does he know what you are?' Vaughan pushed his fingers deeper into de Maresi's mouth and felt the other man bite down hard. He snatched his bitten fingers away. 'Have you tried to have him yet?'

The groan that erupted from de Maresi's throat expressed

everything clearly. 'I can't, he's skittish. He's young, he doesn't understand.'

'I've never found age to be a great determining factor in such matters. Either he's interested or he's not.'

'I still can't. I gave my word to a lady.'

'You never did,' Vaughan snorted, temporarily losing his rhythm. De Maresi whimpered.

'Not like that. I didn't mean like that.'

Understanding slowly trickled through Vaughan's thoughts, followed immediately by peals of laughter. 'Oh, now I understand! You promised his mother! That's pitiful, François, truly pitiful. Imagine it. "You must understand, Gabriel dear, that I would bugger you senseless, but I promised your mama that my intentions were strictly honourable."'

'That's enough, Vaughan!' De Maresi brought his palm behind him, hard into Vaughan's ribs. He threw him off and turned around. 'I don't need to play your contemptible games.'

'Oh, don't you?' Vaughan grasped de Maresi's cock, which was still hard and weeping tears of precome. 'You'll play this final one to the end with me.'

'Cur,' de Maresi snarled as their mouths met. 'You've only ever used me.'

'As you have me.'

Vaughan's body trembled with a foretaste of orgasm. He rolled his hips in a figure of eight, jerking himself against de Maresi's thigh as he masturbated the other man's cock. The thorns were piercing his skin again, and somewhere in his dream world he wasn't with de Maresi but a blond-haired angel.

'What would sweet Gabriel think if he saw you like this?' he said again, hardly conscious of the repetition.

'Shut up, Vaughan. Shut up!' de Maresi screamed, and his cry of annoyance turned into one of blissful anguish. His come stained Vaughan's hose, but that was a mere irritation, as his own cock bucked and he started the blind climb towards orgasm.

Vaughan let the physical effects roll over him, his emotions so complex and contorted he barely recognised them as his own. His knees buckled and he clung to de Maresi, not letting go until every last drop had been milked from his cock.

'Vaughan,' de Maresi whispered. They stood pressed together, sticky with sweat and semen, until their cocks grew soft. Only then did Vaughan peel himself away and clean himself up.

De Maresi turned to him for a kiss, but Vaughan raised a hand between them. 'Save it for Gabriel.' He patted de Maresi on the shoulder. 'We're done.'

Bella was exhausted, though strangely at peace. After Lucerne had made first one fateful announcement and then a second her world had fallen to ruins. Every moment since had felt like the real horror here was simply a welcome diversion. Why that had changed she wasn't sure but Henry's company had helped a lot. It felt good to laugh and scream. They'd stood on the roof and had howled at the moon until their throats were sore and her ribs ached from laughing. They'd even seen the demented Sebastian striding across the courtyard in his enormous hat, bellowing his threats and desires. Round the battlements they'd followed his progress, up onto the narrow stair that housed the flagpole where a bloody, severed head had fallen at her feet.

Henry had laughed so much at her almighty screech that once she'd calmed herself, she'd thrown the waxwork at him and left a bloody splodge on his cassock.

'You knew,' she said.

'You're damn right I knew. I had to winch the bloody thing up there.' Henry dabbed at the tomato paste in disgust. 'It wasn't easy either, since you and Lady Niamh crop up like mushrooms. One of you always appears at the most inopportune moment.'

'The thing in the coach house. That's what the fishing line was about, wasn't it? I knew he was just trying to distract me by taking me down to the lake.'

'Maybe.' Henry mopped the goop on his torso some more, then held up his soiled handkerchief in disgust. 'I think I'd better get changed.' He tugged the unflattering robe over his head, leaving him in his shirtsleeves and breeches. Bella saucily tapped him across the backside with her fan.

'Hey. You'll get us both into trouble doing things like that.'

'I won't tell Niamh and Vaughan won't care.' The thought instantly sobered her. Apart from that one awkward encounter in the great hall at the start of the evening, she hadn't seen him all night. It was almost as if he were deliberately avoiding her.

'About that plan,' said Henry. He didn't finish the sentence; just let her reflect on the possibility.

Bella bit her thumb. She wasn't sure. Wasn't sure if it would work or if she could play her part with enough conviction, but she supposed anything was worth a try. Assuming Niamh really was game.

Niamh emerged onto the roof a few minutes later while Bella was still cogitating the plan. Henry gasped at the sight of her. Bella turned, and the effect of the costume blew her doubts away. Sable ringlets across Florentine silk and a lithe, slim figure encased in tight pantaloons and black boots, with the soft, purposeful tread of a cat. Save the eyes and a few inches' height, they were identical.

He'd severed another tie. Soon he'd sever them all. Vaughan left de Maresi shocked and soiled by the window in the north tower and headed back towards the great hall. He'd assuaged his lust a little too, although his skin still felt tight and exquisitely sensitised, but he was far from satisfied. His demons demanded more willing victims, perhaps every soul in the castle, before he'd finally rest at peace again.

There was nobody in the great hall. Presumably they were all still running like frightened mice about the gardens, set upon by his phantasms and ghosts. Vaughan crossed to the window and threw open the shutters on the central window. Moonlight spilled onto the stone floor, bathing the darkened hall with its silvery-blue glow. The mist was gone and lights twinkled in the upper storeys of the gatehouse, where he assumed Mrs Alvanley had taken herself to bed. The great gate still stood open, welcoming all into the arms of wickedness.

A lone figure appeared upon the bridge, her long white gown billowing around her. Long brown curls tumbled down her back. Bella. Pain stabbed his chest like a lancet.

He could hardly face looking at her. When he'd first planned this night of phantasms, he'd intended to end it in her arms and Lucerne's. The three of them pressed naked together in his bed, hot skin moving against hot skin, their limbs entwined. But there was no possibility of that ending now. There never would be. Lucerne was gone, and Bella was going.

Vaughan gritted his teeth as images of his two lovers crashed through his brain, wearing away the icy sanctuary he'd constructed around his heart.

Outside, Bella came to an unsteady halt just inside the gateway. She hadn't seen him at the window for her gaze was cast back the way she'd just come, fixed upon her pursuer. Devonshire, he wondered, or one of the other rakehells out to seduce her. He didn't think she'd run from a ghoul. After a breath, she sprang forwards again but not fast enough; the hunter already had her. He spun her into his arms and thrust her back against the stone archway. Their bodies pressed so close it seemed they'd almost melded into one. Bella's arms entwined the man's back to rake at his coat. His dark hair fell in a cascade of ringlets down his back as their mouths locked together, their kiss deep, frenetic and passionate. So intense he was almost embarrassed to watch it.

Heat washed through his groin. Hatred surged like a forest fire in his chest. But it made no sense. How could he be jealous of himself? For the vision before him was of himself with Bella. His mouth crushed hers. His hands moulded her breasts, cupped her bottom and pulled her firmly against his hungry loins.

Yet he was here, and Bella had no right to entwine herself around him so tightly. None of it made any earthly sense. He pressed his fingertips to his face, then looked down at his hands, terrified that he would find them insubstantial, himself no more than the ghost of his long dead ancestor whom he'd raised for the night.

His palms seemed solid enough and a cold sweat broke out across his brow, and shivers trembled down his spine.

Beneath the gateway, their passion burned. The taste of her kisses shivered down his throat. A tightness clenched his chest while her fingers traced lightly over the sensitive skin of his stomach. His gaze was locked upon them. He couldn't blink. He couldn't turn away.

Bella's hand slid lower, skimmed over the surface of his cock, then kneaded him harder. Her teeth troubled his earlobe. His mouth closed upon her throat. He no longer knew where the dream began or ended. Which version of himself was real? He felt every caress as if it were against his own skin until he was hopelessly aroused, his head pounding with the insanity of it all.

Vaughan slammed the shutters closed and put his back to them. No more. He couldn't take any more. The vision stirred all the emotions he'd been working so diligently to bury. He swept through the great hall and upstairs into the solar. Connelly cowered in a corner when he swept in but Vaughan ignored him and reached for a drink.

He didn't know what to do. He didn't even know who he was any more.

It was done. Vaughan had seen them. Niamh didn't know if their plan had worked or what the effect would be. Only time would tell. She rested her back against the curved wall of the tunnel and let out a long expressive sigh. She'd experienced few kisses in her life: Edward's, Henry's, her brother's ... None of them kissed like Bella did. None of them melded their mouths to hers softly but as if a fire raged inside her. Her instincts had told her to pull away. The kiss had shaken her just as thoroughly as Vaughan's but she'd had to continue. The performance had to be convincing. And that meant passion.

She knew how Vaughan kissed – with his entire body, almost his entire soul. How he could walk straight afterwards, she didn't know. She could barely breathe.

'Are you all right?' Bella asked. She turned her head and gave her a quick smile.

'I'm not sure. Do you think it worked?'

Bella bowed her head. 'Did he even watch us?'

'Oh, he watched all right.' Henry had a peculiar look on his face, as he emerged from the shadows at the far end of the tunnel. 'Stood in the window and gawped at you. If that hasn't shocked some sense into him, nothing on earth will.' He squeezed Bella's shoulder and gave her a reassuring smile. 'Give it a chance to filter through the laudanum haze.'

'How much has he taken, Henry?' Niamh asked, concern stiffening her back.

Henry turned towards her and she self-consciously tugged Vaughan's waistcoat down at the front, aware that his breeches left little to the imagination. They clung to her curves a little too well, a fact Henry could hardly ignore. 'More than enough,' he said, moistening his lips. 'But I doubt it'll leave any lasting damage unless he makes a habit of it. His pupils were like pinpricks the last time I saw him up close and he's certainly gone a little crackbrained tonight, but your brother's demons have always ridden him hard.' He took her hand and pulled her a fraction closer. 'We'd best not linger here too long. You ought to get changed out of his clothes.' Niamh nodded and felt a blush heat her cheeks. 'If he realises he's been tricked, his vengeance is likely to be swift and brutal, and the plan will absolutely fail.'

Bella nodded her agreement and all three of them walked back to the south tower. They paused outside the door. 'I think I'm going to go in and see where he's got to,' said Henry. He bowed to them and went indoors.

Niamh and Bella looked at one another. 'Thank you,' said Bella. 'Though Lord knows if it'll work. He might not even remember it come morning.'

'Niamh, Bella,' called Mae as she slipped out of the gatehouse, followed by Alicia a moment later. The pair joined them by the door. 'Aunt Bea's tucking in Fortuna. They've both had enough frights for one night and the colonel's promised to sleep outside their door, just in case. What have you been up to?'

'Oh, nothing much,' said Bella, allowing Niamh to slip away. 'There's a decapitated head at the top of the tower.'

'Really!' Mae squealed. 'Alicia, let's go and look.' She took her sister's hand and they scampered off, leaving Bella alone with her thoughts. Feeling slightly chilled, she went up to her room in search of a wrap.

Niamh's room was dark, apart from the smouldering glow of coals in the grate. She stepped out of Vaughan's coat and breeches and shivered at the cold. It was nearly as chilly as outside since she'd stupidly left the window unlatched.

Dressed in Vaughan's oversized white shirt, she padded across the darkened room to close it.

'Niamh.' The sound of his voice chilled her further. Edward. No. Not in her room. Not now, while she was alone. She'd almost forgotten him in the excitement of the night.

'Niamh,' he said again, this time emerging from the shadows behind her. They turned in unison to face one another.

'I told you not to come. I sent a message.' The welt across his cheekbone from Raffe's blow had now darkened to a livid shade of maroon.

'I couldn't desert you.' He slid her wrap from her fingers and arranged it around her shoulders. 'Come now.' With a singular purpose, he guided her towards the open window. There was a long drop on the other side, easily thirty feet until you hit the murky depths of the moat. She saw now that there was a grapple hooked over the stone sill. Its steel prongs glinted with the same ill intent visible in Edward's eyes.

'I'm not coming with you, Edward. I told you that even before I found out about Alicia.' She backed away from the window even as he ushered her closer.

'Hush,' he said. Every muscle in his body pulled tight against hers. 'Why should that affect us? It was a mistake and I never made her any promises.' He clasped both of her shoulders, then sought her lips.

'No.' Niamh fought against his grasp by stamping on his toes. She pushed him off but there was no way past him. She was backed against the open window. 'You deceived me. You lied to me. All you want is my money.'

Edward shook his head in a twitchy nervous sort of way. His scowl, combined with the bruises around his eye, made him look sinister. 'Do you think I'd take such a risk if I didn't care for you? Your brother shot at me last time we met.'

'I think you'd risk anything for gain. Did you think I wouldn't find out about you? Alicia is my friend.'

Edward drew himself up to his full height so that he towered over her. Niamh clung to the windowsill. The wind caught her hair and fanned it around her face. 'You'll come with me,' he said, and he caught her wrist in an iron pinch. 'I've a special licence. Everything is arranged for dawn.'

'Let go of me.' She struggled, but fear of falling limited her movement.

With a sadistic chuckle Edward lifted her onto the sill and covered her mouth while he pushed a hand up her bare thigh under the shirt. 'I don't know which I'll enjoy most, hearing you say, "I do" or feeling you tight about my cock.' His gloved fingers dipped into the lips of her quim. Niamh bit his fingers where they covered her mouth and screamed, 'Vaughan!'

'Bad move.' He pulled his fingers from her sex and sniffed at her musk upon the leather. Niamh froze as he pulled a leather belt from around his waist, thinking he would strike her, but instead he tightened it around her waist. She felt the buckle cold against her back, then the snap of metal. She lifted her knee and caught him between the leg, but not hard enough. He doubled but recovered quickly and, despite her kicking, shoved her backwards out of the window.

For a horrid moment, she was precariously balanced; her upper body suspended over the moat and her legs still curled over the ledge. The door burst open, and Mae and Alicia Allenthorpe rushed in. 'Let her go!' Their breasts heaved from the effort of the sprint down from the roof. They'd found weapons. Alicia brandished an iron poker that she'd obviously snatched from Vaughan's room and struck him hard across the arse. 'Bastard!' With a yowl of pain, he jerked forwards straight into Niamh.

Niamh screamed as she fell. She anticipated the impact of freezing water, but she stopped a few feet above the moat with an abrupt jerk, and found herself dangling like a spider on a silken thread.

Above her in the tower there were screams of panic, drowned out by a loud clear shot.

Vaughan lurched out of his opiate haze and up out of the chair into which he'd sunk. The crack reverberated in his skull like a tin drum in his ear. 'What in the name of God was that?'

'Another of your phantasms, no doubt,' drawled Connelly from the other fireside chair. Once he'd realised Vaughan was no longer a threat, he'd made himself comfortable with the brandy.

'Sounds like fireworks,' said Henry Tristan, rushing to the window.

Vaughan shook his head. 'The hell it was. It was a gunshot.' His flintlock, if he wasn't mistaken.

He hurtled out of the room and across the drawbridge into the south tower with his beribboned breeches flapping about him like extra appendages. The door to Niamh's room stood open. Vaughan charged in to find two pert bottoms facing him, their owners leaning out over the window ledge and his flintlock pistol spinning like a top upon the wooden floor.

Vaughan stilled it with his foot. 'What the devil is going on?'

21

Bella didn't hear the noise, up in her room on the other side of the castle, and even if she had, it probably wouldn't have stirred her from her thoughts. She had no idea if their performance would have any effect on Vaughan, but anything was worth a try. She'd linger until tomorrow and try to talk to him again then. If his feelings hadn't improved since earlier, she'd consider Raffe's offer. Hell, she'd already given it serious thought. She could do far worse than be with him, regardless of the fact that she loved another man. Raffe, she was sure, would do his best to see her happy.

'Bella?'

Speak of the devil and he appears. Raffe strode into the room and sat down on the bed beside her. 'I've been looking for you all night, where have you been?'

'With Henry,' she said, not meeting his eyes. No need to admit that she'd been deliberately avoiding him. Not out of any lingering contempt but because until she could give him a firm answer, there would be an unavoidable awkwardness between them.

'Have you given my offer any thought?' he asked.

'Don't press me, Raffe. I can't give you an answer yet.'

Lips pursed and brow furrowed, Raffe sank back into the mattress, an action that reminded her far too sharply of Lucerne, and a wave of loss threatened to destroy her composure. Bella stared at Raffe, focusing on his muscular build and earthy manliness, the contrast between him and Lucerne, until her scrutiny caused him to reach up and touch her.

'If you're planning on turning me down, I'd rather you just told me.'

'I don't know what I'm going to do.' She lay back beside him so that their heads pressed together, and they lay in silence for several minutes just staring at the dark wood ceiling beams. She felt weary, but she didn't think that she'd sleep, not without something to take her mind off things. She guessed the phantasmagoria had done that for a while, up until the point when she'd kissed Niamh. She'd had to convince herself that it was Vaughan and not his sister, just to make the performance more real, and then she'd let her passion burn for him as if it was the very last kiss they'd ever share. Perhaps it was.

Beside her, Raffe rolled onto his stomach and propped himself up on his elbows. 'You do know he doesn't give a rat's arse about you, don't you?'

'Maybe,' she said vaguely. Henry, Niamh and her gut instincts told her otherwise.

Raffe sat up. His frown had forced his handsome face into wrinkles, and she caught a flash of what he might look like twenty years down the line. Still ruggedly handsome, but slightly more weathered. Age, she decided, would improve him.

'Bella, he's bored with you. Everyone says he's been trying to steal you from Viscount Marlinscar for years, but since you broke it off yesterday you're not a challenge to him any more.'

'That's not what happened.'

'Isn't it?' He cocked his head to one side.

Bella got off the bed and turned to face him, her hands on her hips. Raffe rolled onto his side, a frown troubling his brow. 'No.'

He took hold of her hands and pulled her before him, so he sat staring up beseechingly into her eyes. 'I'm offering you a good life. You know it yourself, and face it: your reputation is in tatters. If we marry, none of that will matter. Society will have to accept you.'

She'd churned the same argument over in her thoughts, but the risk of social ostracism wasn't enough. 'Do you honestly think I care what people think? I've been sharing my bed with two men for the last three years. I think if I was worried about my reputation, I'd have been more concerned about it then.'

His eyes widened and his mouth fell open in a gasp of disbelief. 'Both of them?' he blurted. Clearly the truth of her relationship with Vaughan and Lucerne wasn't quite such common knowledge as she'd thought. 'You don't mean separately either, do you?'

Bella let his hands slip from hers and quietly shook her head.

Raffe's broad shoulders slumped. 'I guess there's no way to compete with that. God, you must think me a right flaming fool.'

'Raffe.' She touched his forehead, not really sure how to comfort him, but he didn't look up. Bella frowned. What had happened to simplicity? When had everything in her life become so serious and tangled? In Yorkshire ... at Lauwine ... nothing had been this complex. She'd slept with three men once in one day and felt no guilt at it. She'd wanted Lucerne but taken her pleasures elsewhere too, and she'd been happy except for a few minor hiccups. Bella stared at his bowed head and tried to remember what she'd thought of him when they'd first met. It was only a few days ago. She thought she'd admired him; he'd been dashing and tall, if a little too forward. His smile, she remembered, had been wicked.

She wasn't quite sure when she made the decision but she was conscious of the change it made her feel inside herself. London had changed too many things. It had altered her in ways she hadn't expected and in ways she wasn't sure she liked. It was time for the old Bella again. She'd take Raffe to her bed tonight; there was no earthly reason why she shouldn't. Besides, in some ways he was just like a tidier version of Mark, her former groom, who'd liked to stud for her. Then tomorrow she'd have it out with Vaughan, and if he couldn't manage to be polite, then she'd have done with him and make the best of things with Raffe.

She touched his brow again and drew her fingertips down to his lips. 'Stay with me tonight.'

There was a curious glint in his eyes when he looked up at her. 'I don't understand.'

Bella leaned in and kissed him slowly, luxuriating in the feel of his mouth against hers. He tasted of spiced oranges and cinnamon, and he groaned nicely as she straddled his lap.

Edward was gone and it was unlikely he'd ever be back. After he'd pushed Niamh out of the window, Mae had shot at him. It seemed she'd missed, something attested to by the chunk missing from the window frame, but Edward hadn't stuck around to chance his luck again. He'd jumped, dropping into the moat with an explosive splash, which had left Niamh soaked to the skin and blowing like wet washing in a gale.

It was lucky, Niamh supposed, that he had jumped because Vaughan had rushed in just a moment later and, despite the hampering of his senses, she was certain that he wouldn't have missed. As it was, Mae and Alicia practically had to sit on him just to stop him tearing off in pursuit. Henry had organised the rescue with the aid of the other men. They'd hauled her back in through the first-floor window, for that had seemed less arduous and somewhat safer than driving a punt around the moat and lowering her onto its moored surface. She'd finally slithered back over the window frame, dripping wet and feverish with cold, still attached to the rope with something that looked like a cross between a wrist iron and a piece of riding tack.

Now she was huddled in her bed in her thickest flannel nightgown, just about warmed through, and feeling exceedingly lucky to not be wallowing at the bottom of the moat with whatever other corpses lay at its murky depths.

Nobody seemed to have noticed she was wearing one of Vaughan's shirts and not her gown and shift when they pulled her back in through the window.

Vaughan slipped into the room carrying a tray on which rested two steaming mugs. He perched on the bed beside her and offered her a drink – chocolate laced with his best Jamaican rum by the taste of it. Niamh gave him a purse-lipped smile. He seemed more himself than he'd been just twenty minutes earlier when he'd been forced out of the room by the combined efforts of Mae, Alicia and Henry, but his pupils were still tightly contracted so that his eyes were all deep violet.

'What was he doing here?' he asked.

Niamh cradled the mug, allowing the hot liquid to warm her hands through the pottery. 'I didn't invite him, if that's what you think. I told him not to come.'

'Hmm.' Vaughan stared thoughtfully into his own drink, which he showed no signs of touching.

'You should have told me about Alicia earlier.'

'I assumed she'd mentioned him herself. You do claim to be close friends.'

Niamh dipped her head. He had a point. They'd all been keeping far too many secrets this past year, and no good had come of any of it. She supposed that's what made her want to speak now. Her brother was hurting. He was not self-destructive by nature, leastways not in any ordinary sense, but he wasn't coping at all well with Lord Marlinscar's departure. Normally graceful and still, he was twitchy and distracted. She watched him pick up the poker and stab the coals, causing several sparks to fly up the chimney.

'Vaughan.' Niamh returned her drink to the tray that lay upon the coverlet and swung her legs out of the bed. Almost immediately, he was by her side again.

'Stay warm,' he snapped, although he tucked the blankets around her gently. 'I'll leave you to sleep. We can discuss things when you're rested.' He pressed a burning kiss to her forehead.

'Wait.' Niamh curled her fingers into the thick lapel of his coat. 'Bella.'

Vaughan shook his head before she had a chance to explain. Regardless of his black look, she began again.

'You're hurting her. And I like her.' He tried to pull away but she held on tight to the cloth. 'Hear me out, Vaughan. You ought at least to know. Raffe's asked her to marry him.'

'He's what!' Vaughan was off the bed and halfway to the door before his brain caught up with his gut reaction. 'Confound the bastard! I didn't invite him here so he could make doe eyes at my ...' He clamped his mouth closed tight. Niamh stared expectantly at him.

'Your what?'

'My whore.' He held her gaze, daring her to refute him but shaken by the revelation of what was unspoken.

'You're going to lose her,' she hissed, holding his intense gaze. 'And then where will you be, brother?'

Vaughan's rage contorted his beauty into something every bit as horrific as the parade of phantoms he'd set before them that evening. 'I never had Bella,' he snapped.

'Fiddlesticks!'

Vaughan's eyes glittered. For a moment he looked as if he was going to swear at her; instead he swirled away from her so his coat fanned out behind him and he threw himself onto the chaise longue. 'I can't expect you to understand. You thought Edward was heaven-sent just because he flattered you.' He pulled his knees up to his chin. 'It was plain there was no passion between you.'

'There's plenty between you and Bella.'

Vaughan blinked slowly, his expression growing suddenly guarded. 'Some, perhaps.'

'Then do something.' She wasn't sure in the flickering firelight, but she thought she saw a tear run down his cheek and across his parted lips.

Raffe could barely credit where he was. It seemed as unreal as Pennerley's phantasms. Bella straddled his hips, her head thrown back, as she rode him towards climax. He thought she was the most sensual creature he'd ever met. Her whole body responded to each and every touch. He groaned as her quaint sucked him deeper, hardly able to credit that the moment was real and not just some nocturnal fantasy.

Would she still be his tomorrow? He could only pray.

Bella trembled. Raffe's cock filled her, satisfying a burning need, but there was still something missing. No matter how deep he sank himself into her and no matter how hard she rode him, his thrusts alone just didn't seem to be enough. She wanted more, much more, things she knew only Vaughan could provide. He understood her. He didn't even need words to turn her on, just the touch of him and the smell of him. She only had to see him and her mind turned to sex. Vaughan had a way of rubbing against her that made her heart turn over and her insides knot with desire, and as for what he was capable of doing to her with his tongue . . . well, there was simply no comparison.

'Oh, Bella!' Raffe groaned. 'You're so fine, so fine. Come, please come.'

He jerked his hips up into her, knocking her off balance so that she fell forwards against his chest. Bella grabbed his hands and held him down against the mattress. She slid herself back and forth along his pole until his eyes started to glaze. The angle was good but she needed something else. Bella closed her eyes and let it slide mercilessly into her thoughts.

In the dark of her mind, their positions were reversed. Vaughan knelt above her, with her hands pinned above her head by one of his. He didn't speak, just gazed at her while driving himself into her.

He sucked greedily at her breasts while his loins slapped mercilessly against hers. Bella cried out each time he filled her until her gasps became one glorious keen as she reached her peak.

Raffe rolled them over and pulled out. His grey eyes were as wide as saucers as he took his cock in hand and finished himself off with several rapid strokes so that his come spilled across her stomach in pearly jets.

Bella smiled as he mopped the sticky mess from her skin with a lacy kerchief. What was it with 'fine gentlemen' these days? They'd never been so reluctant to come inside her in the past.

22

After he left Niamh to rest, Vaughan shunned his own room and paced through the long dreary corridors of the castle. The portraits mocked him. The wind keened her name. Bella. He wanted her but couldn't bear the thought of her. He wanted to be able to blame her, to lay the tatters of his relationship with Lucerne at her door, but the truth was that it was not anyone's fault. They had all hidden aspects of themselves from each other. They had never spoken of the future; they'd simply existed, as if in a fairytale realm from which they'd never wake. Nobody could live like that for ever, him least of all.

He'd walked the length of the great hall perhaps six or seven times before he finally halted at the base of the stair and raised his head towards the balcony. Long shadows made the platform nestled among the wooden rafters almost invisible. He'd taken her at both ends of these worn stairs, right there on the balcony, his body pressed to hers and his fingers in her cunt, and here, his vision shifted, at the base, with her bottom rudely displayed. He wanted her now, his desire a still persistent ache. But he still felt angry with her. She'd chased him here, and then let her feelings rise too close to the surface. He hadn't wanted that from her. He'd wanted it from Lucerne.

Vaughan put a foot on the bottom step. There was no reason to race up there. Lord knows what he'd find. Bile rose up his throat at the thought of finding her in the midst of passion with Devonshire. His body's response confused him further. He'd seen her with Lucerne often enough, why should the thought of her with another man bother him so much? Unless he really did care.

He prodded his own feelings a bit but he knew the answer.

Vaughan glided up the stairs, a deeper shadow in the gloom, then paused in the inky darkness outside her door. Relying on the laudanum to get him through the spectacle of the phantasmagoria had been foolish, its embrace a seductive, compelling and lunatic world of shades and illusion. He knew he couldn't continue like that, trying to blot out the pain. He had to face some of it. He'd made a mess of things.

Facing Bella's love was the first step. It wasn't as if he hadn't realised there was a bond between them that went beyond a shared desire for Lucerne. Hell, hadn't they admitted as much just before they left Lauwine? Vaughan shook his head. Life had seemed a whole lot simpler then. They should have stayed there. Even if it had been hellish cold.

The door opened with barely a creak. He hesitated momentarily on the threshold before he remembered he was master of his own house.

Raffe was naked, his broad hairy chest on display and his solid limbs sprawled across the bed, taking up virtually its entire surface. He felt no envy for his rival. He felt very little of anything other than disgust for his unbearable maleness. Thankfully, the sheets covered his genitals. The man was a beast with his layers of finery peeled away, all vulgar hair and muscle.

Bella, in contrast, was curled in a small protective ball in the bottom corner of the bed. No blissful curling like spoons closeness for them. A stray curl lay against her cheek, which he gently tucked behind her ear. What are you doing here, he wondered, though he was at a loss as to whom he was asking, her or himself.

Her breathing was ragged, her chemise damp beneath his fingertips as he traced the swell of her breast. The urge to take her, to possess her completely and leave marks upon her slender throat hit him like a wave. It sent him reeling onto his heels.

Vaughan straightened, his jaw clenched tight. He knew what he had to do. What he wanted to do. A smile trembled upon his lips. Then he bent and scooped her from the bed up into his arms.

His second moonlit walk through the sleeping castle was more purposeful. Bella's head lay cradled against his chest, her breathing more even. Her long hair spilled over his arm in an auburn wave. She smelled curiously clean, not of sex but of lavender soap, and of something else, something he couldn't quite place, sharp and vaguely metallic.

The narrow winding stairs up to his room represented something of a challenge, but he managed, though she was stirring by the time he reached his bed. 'Bella,' he whispered, as he smoothed out her hair and her nightdress. He kissed her nose, then trailed his lips down her body. 'Ah,' he said, realisation dawning as he reached her quim. Well, that certainly made things more interesting. 'Bella,' he whispered again, and covered her face and breasts in kisses.

Bella languished in a half-wakeful realm of nonsensical images. She knew she'd lain down to sleep beside Raffe after washing his essence from her skin, but she didn't seem to be in her room any more. She turned her head upon the pillow. The shadows didn't make sense. The bed ... Her bed didn't have curtains. Nor was it made of blackened oak. For a moment she imagined herself back in London, waking from a horrid dream, but the bed was more lavishly detailed than the one the three of them had shared, and it smelled not of their combined scent but of Vaughan ...

'Are you awake?' His lips troubled her earlobe and she sensed his presence above her.

'Where am I?'

'My bed.'

Bella raised herself up a fraction, but she could make little out beyond his vague silhouette, upon which her memory painted a likeness. He must have carried her here. Taken her from the bed beside Raffe. Her heart beat a little faster at the thought of what Vaughan might have done, and what he had planned for her. He'd been a swine to her. She had to expect something else unkind. 'Can we not have some light?'

'If it pleases.' His voice was soft. Not tense and hard as it had been earlier or as she expected. He reached out a hand and peeled away the blackness. With the drape drawn back against the bedpost, the light from the fireplace spilled over them in a warm orange glow. Vaughan's hair shone like spun black silk, his pale skin glowing with a fragile luminescence.

Her breath hitched in her throat. He was completely naked, not even the locket adorning his throat. She reached out and touched the scar across his abdomen. 'What did you bring me here for?'

He stretched himself over her and looked down into her

eyes. His were twin black pools. 'Is it not obvious? I'm going to give you what you asked for.'

The muscles twitched across the back of her shoulders. 'Bastard,' she hissed between her teeth. 'What game are you playing with me?'

'No game, not tonight.' His breath whispered warm and sweet over her lips. 'Will you let me kiss you, Bella?'

She had to laugh at that. 'You've never needed permission before.'

Vaughan tilted his head to one side and smiled unguardedly at her, inviting her pity and forgiveness. She didn't really feel anger towards him, her feelings were too muddled for any single emotion to dominate, but his smile was stripping that away, making her want to take him in her arms and hold him tight.

'Very well, kiss me.'

She parted her lips, but he didn't seek her mouth but her throat. His tongue tickled over the pulse-point, sending shivers of expectation through her limbs. Then he sucked, hard, and she flopped like a rag doll in his arms, unable to move or resist, hardly able to breathe. It hurt. He was marking her. The feel of his teeth sent a ripple of fear and excitement shooting through her body. Her breasts tingled, her nipples rasped against his chest and, lower, she grew moist.

Finally he released her and she sucked down a great shuddering gasp of air. Now she wanted his lips. His mouth on hers, but Vaughan's kiss moved down her body. He threw her chemise up over her face, while he teased her nipples then licked the undersides of her breasts. Bella panted into the cotton covering her face as his tongue dipped into her navel, then moved lower to where she was desperate to feel him.

His tongue flicked mercilessly until she opened like a flower and her clitoris peeped from its hood, eager and attentive. He kissed her cunt with the same intensity he'd lavished upon her throat, so that she writhed upon the bed, hot and wanting, her hands tangled in his hair.

Every single part of her craved penetration.

'Vaughan, make love to me, please!' She bit her lip, afraid he would deny her yet again.

Vaughan raised his head. 'I am, with my tongue.' And he was, God damn him. She dug her fingers into his scalp, but that only made him work harder. It was evil what he could do with his tongue, bringing her to the boil with a few simple strokes.

She came, shaking and clawing at him. Still aching for his cock.

Vaughan slithered up her body like an exotic snake until he covered her from shoulders to toes and his erection lay like lance against her thigh. She wriggled, trying to manoeuvre him closer, but he pressed his weight upon her.

'Delicious.'

Bella looked at him, a strangled cry forcing its way from her throat. There was blood in his mouth and smeared across his lips. What was he? What sort of creature had he become? The tale of the blood curse ran through her head. Was there truth in the legend after all?

Frightened, she touched her fingers to the bruise he'd left upon her throat.

Vaughan rubbed at his mouth, leaving a bloody streak across the back of his hand.

'My menses,' she groaned in sudden realisation. Why now?

'Shhh,' Vaughan soothed, and he pressed a silencing finger to her lips. 'What's a little blood between us?'

'It's messy,' she gasped.

'I like messy.'

Of course he did. Everything he did was complicated and disordered. Besides, she didn't just want him. She craved him. 'It'll ruin the sheets,' she said as a last pretence of civility.

Vaughan threw his head back and laughed. 'I have more sheets. And even if I didn't . . .' All in a rush, he entered her, filling her up in one divine thrust. 'You're mine, little bird,' he said, and he rolled his hips. Bella twined her calves around his thighs and rose to meet his thrusts. Deeper. She wanted him deeper. The bed groaned beneath them. Vaughan wrestled her nightgown over her head and twisted the fabric so that it bound her wrists, stopping her from clawing at his back. 'You know this is how it will be,' he said, 'if you're mine. Obsessive, cruel . . . demanding. You don't know the half of what I expected of Lucerne.'

Didn't she. She'd spied on them often enough when they'd tried to lock her out of their relationship, and she'd seen them fighting, tearing at each other. Hadn't she always craved what they shared? Hadn't she begged for the same treatment?

Vaughan thrust into her, taking her mercilessly. Possessing her. Filling her.

'Harder,' she panted. She was climbing again. Any minute she was going to come and she wanted him to come too.

His teeth grazed her throat, causing the bite mark to

ache. Every nerve seemed to connect, then explode. Black heat consumed her. The muscles in her quaint clenched around him, drawing him deeper, his body taut as a bow-string against hers. She watched him arch away from her; his head tossed wildly, while his cock bucked and he spilt his seed inside her in great shuddering jerks.

Finally he collapsed against her and she nuzzled against his cheek. 'I love you, Vaughan,' she whispered.

He stiffened very slightly, then the muscles across his back unknotted and he kissed her deeply and slowly. 'I know. I may even love you too.'

Bella wrinkled her nose at him, but he merely licked it in return.

For that, she poked him in the ribs and then smeared kisses across his face.

23

In the half-light before dawn, Bella stirred, her vivid imagination having painted a wonderful and preposterous image of her embraced within Vaughan's arms. Sleepily, she squinted into the darkness. Vaughan lay next to her on the pillow, his dark ringlets spilled around him like a tarnished halo. She reached out and touched his soft skin, amazed to find the image didn't fracture. A smile crept across her lips and she snuggled into his shoulder.

When she next woke, she was alone in the bed.

Bella sat up and rubbed the sleep from her eyes. The heavy curtains were drawn around the bed, completely obscuring the room. She fished around for her shift but failed to find it. Cautiously, she stuck an arm out from the curtains to feel for it on the floor.

'You're awake.'

Bella stuck her head out between the gap. There were no servants in the room, just Vaughan, reclining before the fire in a bathtub. Curls of steam rose and swirled in the air above him, while rose petals formed tiny boats across the surface of the water. His arm lay along the edge of the tub and he beckoned her with the curl of his fingers.

'My shift?' she enquired.

'Needs a wash.' Bella frowned and eyed the distance between the bed and the bathtub dubiously. She gave the door a wary glance, then scuttled across the floor and stepped into the tub, causing water to splash over the sides in choppy waves. She curled her legs up before her and stared at the rose petals bobbing on the surface. She felt awkward. It had been easy to imagine the future while he was embracing her, but with all the phantasms dissolved by daylight, the way forward suddenly seemed wrought with peril.

Vaughan's reflection shimmered before her once the water stilled. His expression was guarded and he'd put the locket back on.

'You made love to me,' she said.

'I did.' There was no question in his voice, just agreement.

'Will you do it again?'

'That depends.'

'On what?'

'On whether you're going to marry Lord Devonshire.'

'Ah . . .' So he'd heard. Had she given Raffe an official answer? Not in words, she'd merely said she hadn't made a decision, but he could be forgiven for having some expectations after what they'd shared before Vaughan had stolen her away.

Vaughan's expression remained guarded. He bowed his head so his hair fell forward over his face in a cascade of damp ringlets. Bella reached out and touched his curls where they lay against his shoulders.

'I haven't given him an answer.'

'But when you do.' He looked up at her, his eyes clear and bright, the pupils back to their normal size.

'What do you want?' she asked.

'A great many things, some of which I can't have.'

'I know.' She bowed her head again, trying to find the correct words to express herself. 'From me, I mean.' She encompassed the room, the bed with a gesture. 'Is there a future for us, Vaughan?'

'That rather depends on what sort of future you want.'

Bella bit her lip. He'd always said he wouldn't marry. There was no reason to suppose that would change just because he no longer had Lucerne. Still, it felt like a rejection on some deep level. But was marriage really what she wanted from him?

'No false promises,' he said, and his sensual red lips widened into a smile. He tugged her up the length of the bathtub into his arms and kissed her.

'Do you promise you won't run away again?'

He grinned and shook his head. 'Nor can I promise absolute fidelity. There are some urges you simply cannot satisfy. Though you are exceedingly accommodating.' His fingers curled around the gold pendant that rested against his chest. 'I understand if you can't live with that.'

Bella sucked her tongue. Could she live with it? Not on a regular basis, but Vaughan she thought would be discreet, at least. Most other men would tup the kitchen maids and damn who knew.

'Can I watch sometimes?'

He spluttered.

Vaughan splashed her then got out of the bath. Bella watched mesmerised as he stalked across the room, his skin alive with a thousand glittering jewels. He was her jewel.

'You understand that I won't be going back to town for a while,' he said as he pulled on a dressing-gown. 'I'm not disposed to entertain the gossips.'

She already knew Lucerne's absence from the party had

been noted. No doubt before the day was out rumours would be spreading about a fall-out, along with plenty of speculation as to the cause. Troubled by the thought, she sank below the surface, and let the warm water soothe away the worries.

The bloods departed one after another. Darleston pinched her bottom but she let it go when she realised he'd pinched everybody else's too. Then Connelly went and the colonel. Dovecote lingered until mid-afternoon talking to the Allenthorpes, who also said their goodbyes and headed off with de Maresi.

Finally, Bella found herself standing on the drawbridge with Raffe. 'I'm sorry,' she said. 'It would probably never have worked out.'

Raffe remained silent for far too long, just staring at her. 'I think it would have been perfect, but I guess the better man won.' He sucked his lip slowly, then leaned in and kissed her once upon the lips. 'Goodbye, Bella, I hope we see each other again, and that when we do, you are happy.'

Bella threw her arms around his back and squeezed him tight. 'You're a good man. Someone out there deserves you. It's just not me.' She walked with him to the carriage steps and waved as his carriage trundled away down the drive.

The castle was almost oppressively quiet after they'd all gone. The four of them, she, Vaughan, Niamh and Henry, ate huddled at one end of the enormous dining table. Henry had announced his intention to stay a while longer and, while Vaughan had raised an eyebrow, he didn't object. He also agreed that Niamh could go up to London when Henry returned, in the company of her maid. She was to stay with their mother's sister, Mrs Lily Cadoux, an arrangement that pleased Niamh very well, although Vaughan held that the woman was a fury and a prude.

At twilight, they went up to the battlements, just the two of them. The waxwork head still lay against the base of the flagpole tower steps where it had rolled after hitting Henry the previous night. Vaughan picked it up and looked at it, then threw it over the wall to land in the garden among the roses.

Bella watched his hair billow in the breeze. Despite the wind he was wearing only a silk shirt left open at the neck and his thigh-hugging pantaloons. The locket lay clasped within his palm, a constant reminder of what separated them. Bella touched his shoulder and he gave her a wan smile.

'You still love him, don't you?' she said.

Vaughan didn't reply. The sheen in his dark eyes was answer enough as he worked his thumb back and forth over the polished surface. Making a wish, she thought.

'What about you?'

Bella shook her head. 'I'll miss his company. There were good times. Lots of good times but I'm not sure it was ever really love.' In contemplation she stared at her feet. She was too pleased to have come this far to dwell too deeply on her feelings for Lucerne. 'It might have been at one point. I think that's what I hoped for initially, but then you came along and changed everything.'

'Don't rewrite history, Bella. You hated me.'

'Is that why I've never been able to keep my hands off you?' She slid her hand across his back and pulled herself against his loins. Vaughan kissed the tip of her nose. They stood pressed together, breathing each other's scent while several clouds scudded across darkening hilltop. Eventually,

Vaughan turned away and leaned his chin against the top of one of the crenellations.

'It's cold, we should go inside,' Bella said. She stroked a finger down the side of his cheek but Vaughan's gaze remained fastened upon the horizon. 'Please, Vaughan.'

For a moment he resisted. Then she saw it, a bright flash of gold against the darkness as the locket spun in the air and fell like a teardrop into the moat to lie, guarded by the pike, with what other treasures the centuries had seen fit to entrust.

Vaughan clasped her hand tight. 'Come on. I've had enough of old ghosts.'

LOOK OUT FOR THE ALL-NEW BLACK LACE BOOKS – AVAILABLE NOW!

All books priced £7.99 in the UK. Please note publication dates apply to the UK only. For other territories, please contact your retailer.

CASSANDRA'S CONFLICT
Fredrica Alleyn
ISBN 978 0 352 34186 0

A house in Hampstead. Present-day. Behind a façade of cultured respectability lies a world of decadent indulgence and dark eroticism. Cassandra's sheltered life is transformed when she gets employed as governess to the Baron's children. He draws her into games where lust can feed on the erotic charge of submission. Games where only he knows the rules and where unusual pleasures can flourish.

To be published in April 2008

GOTHIC HEAT
Portia Da Costa
ISBN 978 0 352 34170 9

Paula Beckett has a problem. The spirit of the wicked and voluptuous sorceress Isidora Katori is trying to possess her body and Paula finds herself driven by dark desires and a delicious wanton recklessness. Rafe Hathaway is irresistibly drawn to both women. But who will he finally choose – feisty and sexy Paula, who is fighting impossible odds to hang on to her very existence, or sultry and ruthless Isidora, who offers him the key to immortality?

GEMINI HEAT
Portia Da Costa
ISBN 978 0 352 34187 7

As the metropolis sizzles in the freak early summer temperatures, identical twin sisters Deana and Delia Ferraro are cooking up a heat wave of their own. Surrounded by an atmosphere of relentless humidity, Deanna and Delia find themselves rivals for the attentions of Jackson de Guile, an exotic, wealthy entrepreneur and master of power dynamics who draws them both into a web of luxurious debauchery. The erotic encounters become increasingly bizarre as the twins vie for the rewards that pleasuring him brings them – tainted rewards which only serve to confuse their perceptions of the limits of sexual experience.

THE NEW BLACK LACE BOOK OF WOMEN'S SEXUAL FANTASIES
Edited and compiled by Mitzi Szereto
ISBN 978 0 352 34172 3

The second anthology of detailed sexual fantasies contributed by women from all over the world. The book is a result of a year's research by an expert on erotic writing and gives a fascinating insight into the rich diversity of the female sexual imagination.

To be published in May 2008

BLACK ORCHID
Roxanne Carr
ISBN 978 0 352 34188 4

At the Black Orchid Club, adventurous women who yearn for the pleasures of exotic, even kinky sex can quench their desires in discreet and luxurious surroundings. Having tasted the fulfilment of unique and powerful lusts, one such adventurous woman learns what happens when the need for limitless indulgence becomes an addiction.

MAGIC AND DESIRE
Portia Da Costa, Janine Ashbless, Olivia Knight
ISBN 978 0 352 34183 9

The third BL paranormal novella collection. Three top authors writing three otherwordly short novels of fantasy and sorcery.

Ill Met By Moonlight: Can it be possible that a handsome stranger met by moonlight is a mischievous fairy set out to sample a taste of human love and passion? But what will happen when the magic witching month of May is over? When he loses his human form will he lose his memories of her as well?

The House Of Dust: The king is dead. But the queen cannot grieve until she's had vengeance. Ishara must descend into the Underworld and brave its challenges in order to bring her lover back from the dead.

The Dragon Lord: In the misty marshlands of Navarone, the princess is being married. Her parents desperately hope this will cure her 'problem', which they have fought to keep secret for years. Her 'problem' has always been her tendency to play with fire – she lights fires in the grate with her eyes when no-one is looking and she is lustful in a land of rigid morality.

CHILLI HEAT
Carrie Williams
ISBN 978 0 352 34178 5

Let down by her travelling companion at short notice, Nadia Kapur reluctantly agrees to take her recently divorced mother, Valerie, on her gap-year trip to India. However, her mother turns out to be anything but the conservative presence she had feared. As the two women explore India's most exotic locations, it is Valerie who experiences a sexual reawakening with a succession of lovers and Nadia who is forced to wrestle with her own inhibitions and repressed desires. The landscape and the people ultimately work their transforming magic on both mother and daughter, causing Valerie to think again about her ex-husband and tempting Nadia with the possibility of true love.

Black Lace Booklist

Information is correct at time of printing. To avoid disappointment, check availability before ordering. Go to www.black-lace-books.com.
All books are priced £7.99 unless another price is given.

BLACK LACE BOOKS WITH A CONTEMPORARY SETTING

- ❑ THE ANGELS' SHARE Maya Hess ISBN 978 0 352 34043 6
- ❑ ASKING FOR TROUBLE Kristina Lloyd ISBN 978 0 352 33362 9
- ❑ BLACK LIPSTICK KISSES Monica Belle ISBN 978 0 352 33885 3 £6.99
- ❑ THE BLUE GUIDE Carrie Williams ISBN 978 0 352 34132 7
- ❑ THE BOSS Monica Belle ISBN 978 0 352 34088 7
- ❑ BOUND IN BLUE Monica Belle ISBN 978 0 352 34012 2
- ❑ CAMPAIGN HEAT Gabrielle Marcola ISBN 978 0 352 33941 6
- ❑ CAT SCRATCH FEVER Sophie Mouette ISBN 978 0 352 34021 4
- ❑ CIRCUS EXCITE Nikki Magennis ISBN 978 0 352 34033 7
- ❑ CLUB CRÈME Primula Bond ISBN 978 0 352 33907 2 £6.99
- ❑ CONFESSIONAL Judith Roycroft ISBN 978 0 352 33421 3
- ❑ CONTINUUM Portia Da Costa ISBN 978 0 352 33120 5
- ❑ DANGEROUS CONSEQUENCES Pamela Rochford ISBN 978 0 352 33185 4
- ❑ DARK DESIGNS Madelynne Ellis ISBN 978 0 352 34075 7
- ❑ THE DEVIL INSIDE Portia Da Costa ISBN 978 0 352 32993 6
- ❑ EQUAL OPPORTUNITIES Mathilde Madden ISBN 978 0 352 34070 2
- ❑ FIRE AND ICE Laura Hamilton ISBN 978 0 352 33486 2
- ❑ GONE WILD Maria Eppie ISBN 978 0 352 33670 5
- ❑ HOTBED Portia Da Costa ISBN 978 0 352 33614 9
- ❑ IN PURSUIT OF ANNA Natasha Rostova ISBN 978 0 352 34060 3
- ❑ IN THE FLESH Emma Holly ISBN 978 0 352 34117 4
- ❑ LEARNING TO LOVE IT Alison Tyler ISBN 978 0 352 33535 7
- ❑ MAD ABOUT THE BOY Mathilde Madden ISBN 978 0 352 34001 6
- ❑ MAKE YOU A MAN Anna Clare ISBN 978 0 352 34006 1
- ❑ MAN HUNT Cathleen Ross ISBN 978 0 352 33583 8
- ❑ THE MASTER OF SHILDEN Lucinda Carrington ISBN 978 0 352 33140 3
- ❑ MIXED DOUBLES Zoe le Verdier ISBN 978 0 352 33312 4 £6.99
- ❑ MIXED SIGNALS Anna Clare ISBN 978 0 352 33889 1 £6.99

❑ MS BEHAVIOUR Mini Lee ISBN 978 0 352 33962 1

❑ PACKING HEAT Karina Moore ISBN 978 0 352 33356 8 £6.99

❑ PAGAN HEAT Monica Belle ISBN 978 0 352 33974 4

❑ PEEP SHOW Mathilde Madden ISBN 978 0 352 33924 9

❑ THE POWER GAME Carrera Devonshire ISBN 978 0 352 33990 4

❑ THE PRIVATE UNDOING OF A PUBLIC SERVANT Leonie Martel ISBN 978 0 352 34066 5

❑ RUDE AWAKENING Pamela Kyle ISBN 978 0 352 33036 9

❑ SAUCE FOR THE GOOSE Mary Rose Maxwell ISBN 978 0 352 33492 3

❑ SPLIT Kristina Lloyd ISBN 978 0 352 34154 9

❑ STELLA DOES HOLLYWOOD Stella Black ISBN 978 0 352 33588 3

❑ THE STRANGER Portia Da Costa ISBN 978 0 352 33211 0

❑ SUITE SEVENTEEN Portia Da Costa ISBN 978 0 352 34109 9

❑ TONGUE IN CHEEK Tabitha Flyte ISBN 978 0 352 33484 8

❑ THE TOP OF HER GAME Emma Holly ISBN 978 0 352 34116 7

❑ UNNATURAL SELECTION Alaine Hood ISBN 978 0 352 33963 8

❑ VELVET GLOVE Emma Holly ISBN 978 0 352 34115 0

❑ VILLAGE OF SECRETS Mercedes Kelly ISBN 978 0 352 33344 5

❑ WILD BY NATURE Monica Belle ISBN 978 0 352 33915 7 £6.99

❑ WILD CARD Madeline Moore ISBN 978 0 352 34038 2

❑ WING OF MADNESS Mae Nixon ISBN 978 0 352 34099 3

BLACK LACE BOOKS WITH AN HISTORICAL SETTING

❑ THE BARBARIAN GEISHA Charlotte Royal ISBN 978 0 352 33267 7

❑ BARBARIAN PRIZE Deanna Ashford ISBN 978 0 352 34017 7

❑ THE CAPTIVATION Natasha Rostova ISBN 978 0 352 33234 9

❑ DARKER THAN LOVE Kristina Lloyd ISBN 978 0 352 33279 0

❑ WILD KINGDOM Deanna Ashford ISBN 978 0 352 33549 4

❑ DIVINE TORMENT Janine Ashbless ISBN 978 0 352 33719 1

❑ FRENCH MANNERS Olivia Christie ISBN 978 0 352 33214 1

❑ LORD WRAXALL'S FANCY Anna Lieff Saxby ISBN 978 0 352 33080 2

❑ NICOLE'S REVENGE Lisette Allen ISBN 978 0 352 32984 4

❑ THE SENSES BEJEWELLED Cleo Cordell ISBN 978 0 352 32904 2 £6.99

❑ THE SOCIETY OF SIN Sian Lacey Taylder ISBN 978 0 352 34080 1

❑ TEMPLAR PRIZE Deanna Ashford ISBN 978 0 352 34137 2

❑ UNDRESSING THE DEVIL Angel Strand ISBN 978 0 352 33938 6

BLACK LACE BOOKS WITH A PARANORMAL THEME

- ❑ BRIGHT FIRE Maya Hess ISBN 978 0 352 34104 4
- ❑ BURNING BRIGHT Janine Ashbless ISBN 978 0 352 34085 6
- ❑ CRUEL ENCHANTMENT Janine Ashbless ISBN 978 0 352 33483 1
- ❑ FLOOD Anna Clare ISBN 978 0 352 34094 8
- ❑ GOTHIC BLUE Portia Da Costa ISBN 978 0 352 33075 8
- ❑ THE PRIDE Edie Bingham ISBN 978 0 352 33997 3
- ❑ THE SILVER COLLAR Mathilde Madden ISBN 978 0 352 34141 9
- ❑ THE TEN VISIONS Olivia Knight ISBN 978 0 352 34119 8

BLACK LACE ANTHOLOGIES

- ❑ BLACK LACE QUICKIES 1 Various ISBN 978 0 352 34126 6 £2.99
- ❑ BLACK LACE QUICKIES 2 Various ISBN 978 0 352 34127 3 £2.99
- ❑ BLACK LACE QUICKIES 3 Various ISBN 978 0 352 34128 0 £2.99
- ❑ BLACK LACE QUICKIES 4 Various ISBN 978 0 352 34129 7 £2.99
- ❑ BLACK LACE QUICKIES 5 Various ISBN 978 0 352 34130 3 £2.99
- ❑ BLACK LACE QUICKIES 6 Various ISBN 978 0 352 34133 4 £2.99
- ❑ BLACK LACE QUICKIES 7 Various ISBN 978 0 352 34146 4 £2.99
- ❑ BLACK LACE QUICKIES 8 Various ISBN 978 0 352 34147 1 £2.99
- ❑ BLACK LACE QUICKIES 9 Various ISBN 978 0 352 34155 6 £2.99
- ❑ MORE WICKED WORDS Various ISBN 978 0 352 33487 9 £6.99
- ❑ WICKED WORDS 3 Various ISBN 978 0 352 33522 7 £6.99
- ❑ WICKED WORDS 4 Various ISBN 978 0 352 33603 3 £6.99
- ❑ WICKED WORDS 5 Various ISBN 978 0 352 33642 2 £6.99
- ❑ WICKED WORDS 6 Various ISBN 978 0 352 33690 3 £6.99
- ❑ WICKED WORDS 7 Various ISBN 978 0 352 33743 6 £6.99
- ❑ WICKED WORDS 8 Various ISBN 978 0 352 33787 0 £6.99
- ❑ WICKED WORDS 9 Various ISBN 978 0 352 33860 0
- ❑ WICKED WORDS 10 Various ISBN 978 0 352 33893 8
- ❑ THE BEST OF BLACK LACE 2 Various ISBN 978 0 352 33718 4
- ❑ WICKED WORDS: SEX IN THE OFFICE Various ISBN 978 0 352 33944 7
- ❑ WICKED WORDS: SEX AT THE SPORTS CLUB Various ISBN 978 0 352 33991 1
- ❑ WICKED WORDS: SEX ON HOLIDAY Various ISBN 978 0 352 33961 4
- ❑ WICKED WORDS: SEX IN UNIFORM Various ISBN 978 0 352 34002 3
- ❑ WICKED WORDS: SEX IN THE KITCHEN Various ISBN 978 0 352 34018 4

❑ WICKED WORDS: SEX ON THE MOVE Various — ISBN 978 0 352 34034 4

❑ WICKED WORDS: SEX AND MUSIC Various — ISBN 978 0 352 34061 0

❑ WICKED WORDS: SEX AND SHOPPING Various — ISBN 978 0 352 34076 4

❑ SEX IN PUBLIC Various — ISBN 978 0 352 34089 4

❑ SEX WITH STRANGERS Various — ISBN 978 0 352 34105 1

❑ LOVE ON THE DARK SIDE Various — ISBN 978 0 352 34132 7

❑ LUST BITES Various — ISBN 978 0 352 34153 2

BLACK LACE NON-FICTION

❑ THE BLACK LACE BOOK OF WOMEN'S SEXUAL FANTASIES Edited by Kerri Sharp — ISBN 978 0 352 33793 1 £6.99

To find out the latest information about Black Lace titles, check out the website: www.black-lace-books.com or send for a booklist with complete synopses by writing to:

Black Lace Booklist, Virgin Books Ltd
Thames Wharf Studios
Rainville Road
London W6 9HA

Please include an SAE of decent size. Please note only British stamps are valid.

Our privacy policy
We will not disclose information you supply us to any other parties. We will not disclose any information which identifies you personally to any person without your express consent.

From time to time we may send out information about Black Lace books and special offers. Please tick here if you do not wish to receive Black Lace information. ❑

Please send me the books I have ticked above.

Name ....

Address ....

....

....

....

Post Code ....

Send to: Virgin Books Cash Sales, Thames Wharf Studios, Rainville Road, London W6 9HA.

US customers: for prices and details of how to order books for delivery by mail, call 888-330-8477.

Please enclose a cheque or postal order, made payable to Virgin Books Ltd, to the value of the books you have ordered plus postage and packing costs as follows:

UK and BFPO – £1.00 for the first book, 50p for each subsequent book.

Overseas (including Republic of Ireland) – £2.00 for the first book, £1.00 for each subsequent book.

If you would prefer to pay by VISA, ACCESS/MASTERCARD, DINERS CLUB, AMEX or SWITCH, please write your card number and expiry date here:

....

Signature ....

Please allow up to 28 days for delivery.